DARK
PERSUASION

By

Susan M Cowley

Edited by John Parker

DARK PERSUASION

This book is dedicated to my brother Stuart Oakes for his encouragement, and belief in me and of course, his red lines

Left alone in the room the elderly woman stood by the window and gazed out across the river to the far bank. She had never seen the Thames from this elevation. Everything about the building she had been so mysteriously summoned to surprised her, in one way or another. What other surprises were in store she wondered.

She remembered the old War Department office - the creaking filing cabinets and clunky telephones, the clatter of typewriters and the rich aroma of tobacco drifting calmly from her boss Colonel Heath's pipe.

God, after sixty years she could almost smell it! She looked around at the spotless carpet, the bare chrome and glass desk and blank computer screen. Traffic streamed past outside, but not a sound penetrated the plate glass; the whole place was still, and utterly silent. The Colonel would never have believed this faceless hygienic space was the nerve centre of British Intelligence.

And now, in a new century, that secret, clandestine world had called her back. What for? : A reunion, handshakes and flowers, fond reminiscences? She shivered. Presumably she was about to find out.

Catching her reflection in a glass partition she instinctively attended to her expensive matching attire and straightened a wisp of an unruly white curl. She couldn't help smiling at the image; the years had been kind to her; she had grown old gracefully and retained even now her fresh, innocent 'county-girl' air.

As the door opened she stiffened. A young man in a stylish understated suit smiled perfunctorily and gestured to the desk. They sat opposite one another. He turned a dog-eared cardboard file towards her. How young he was she thought, studying his fresh, ridiculously unlined complexion, a schoolboy sent to do a man's job. The file bore the words 'Top Secret' in large red letters. She opened it. On the first page, held in place with a large paper clip was a curling sepia photograph of a young girl.
She closed her eyes.

"Why?" she said almost in a whisper. "Why can't you leave us alone? We're finished with all this - we finished with it a lifetime ago."

4

"Nothing's finished – not yet." The young man's smile was cold, superior. "The file's still open," he said quietly. "We need the name. She can get it."

The old woman gave an ironic smile,

"We've been trying for sixty years, why would she make a difference?"

"You know the rules."

"But she knows nothing, she never did."

The young man slowly leaned towards her, his eyes boring into hers. Suddenly she felt afraid.

"Get the name my dear." There was menace in his voice now, an unmistakable threat. "Whatever it takes - however you do it – just get me the name."

CHAPTER ONE

The Visitor

Joyce's early morning telephone call yesterday had unsettled me. Not so much what she said, but rather what she didn't. There seemed to be sadness in her voice, a sense of inevitability of something yet to happen.

She wished me a happy birthday in advance and apologised that she wasn't going to come and see me on the day itself. I had hoped this year would be different as it's my eightieth, but since I've been living in an old people's home Joyce is no longer a frequent visitor; probably frightened she might end up somewhere like this herself. I don't think her son would do that to her though, not like my two charming offspring. They couldn't wait, and had chosen Hartlands for me even before I came out of hospital after the heart attack. How considerate. And when I sold my lovely house they'd wanted their share straight away, only to relieve me of money worries in my old age, or course. How nice of them.

Anyway I had begun chattering to Joyce as usual about our families, but it seemed she couldn't wait to get off the phone. We've been friends for so many years and I could always tell when something was on her mind, and this was definitely one of those occasions. When I asked her if anything was the matter she laughed, rather nervously I felt, told me not to worry and said cheerio. Then, just as I had decided there was probably nothing to worry about, it happened, something that turned my whole world upside down.

Maria had taken me on our morning stroll down by the river an hour earlier than usual, as she had an appointment with the doctor later about her back. She was not one for complaining but I could tell she was finding it difficult to push the wheelchair. She said something about pulling a muscle turning a mattress.

Anyway we did the usual round trip and headed back to Hartlands just after 11am. Just as we passed the main gate a sleek, black and very expensive looking car turned in and headed slowly towards the house. It impressed dear Maria.

"Wow!" she exclaimed, "don't get many cars like that coming here, eh Annabelle? Perhaps it's a celebrity!"
I didn't answer. I too was intrigued, not by the car but by the figure I had glimpsed fleetingly in the back.

6

On reaching the house we saw the car parked by the steps. Both the driver, formally suited and the passenger, an elderly man, had already got out. Maria stopped pushing the wheelchair for a moment - perhaps to ease her back, perhaps like me to scrutinise the figure of the passenger, now standing a few yards away. He wore brown corduroy trousers, a crinkled linen jacket of soft cream and a straw Panama hat; not unfamiliar attire for an English country gentleman of more mature years.

Yet there was something else about him. Memories and emotions of a past I had long thought dead and buried, a closed door, raced into my mind like a flash flood.

Maria had started to push me up the ramp towards the door of the home. I raised my hand.

"Maria, can you wait a moment?" I realised I was breathless for some reason. "Let the gentleman go in first."

Maria shrugged "OK," she said with some degree of nonchalance, belied by her searching eyes.

It was no act of courtesy on my part. I was afraid of the face beneath the Panama, and afraid too he might look at me.

The driver nodded courteously to us and ushered the gentleman up the steps and into the building. I asked Maria to wait a little longer.

A minute or two later, he returned alone and got back in the car. As it moved off I beckoned to Maria to wheel me into the house. Inside I dared not look around but kept my eyes lowered to the floor.

"Are you feeling OK Annabelle?" Maria asked solicitously.

"Yes," I replied, "a little tired that's all."

There was no one in the lobby, not even Amy the receptionist. Maria pushed me past the desk and headed for the lift. My nerves were subsiding now; what a fool I was, thinking it could have been him! Then I heard Amy.

"Oh Annabelle," she called cheerfully, emerging from the library, "you have a visitor. Says he's an old acquaintance..."

I felt myself shudder; my pulse was racing

"A very nice gentleman," she continued babbling and held the library door open. "He's waiting in here now. He'd like to see you."

I made no reply, too dumbstruck to utter the simplest of words.

"Are you all right Annabelle? You're very pale."

"She's a little tired," Maria answered for me.

I was feeling distinctly uneasy. "Maria, my room - please."

"But what about your visitor?" Amy's voice was annoyingly chirpy.

"Maria, my room – now!" I hissed.

"She's a bit done in." Maria whispered loudly to Amy. "All that fresh air, bless her."

In the seclusion of my room, the door firmly closed, I breathed out again. Maria left to go to her therapy and I was alone. Whoever this man was I knew I could not, must not see him.
Some ten minutes later there was a gentle knock on my door.

"Annabelle its Amy, can I come in?"
I said nothing. The door slowly opened.

"I've brought the gentleman along, I hope you don't mind?"
I looked up, my heart pounding like the devil's hooves in my chest. Amy turned and beckoned to someone in the hallway.

"She's very tired," she said in an aside, "don't keep her too long."

In he came, the man from the limousine. He smiled at Amy as she departed then turned slowly to face me. Even before he had removed his straw hat I knew at once. Even through my dimmed eyes, and the passage of the years I knew. Could a body shape, stooped and thinned by time, a face wizened by the sun, be such an unmistakable signature? To one who has known them, it seemed so.

My sense of wonder, not to say shock was immense, but I registered nothing. I felt struck dumb, could only stare. He looked remarkably solid for someone who had died over half a century ago.

I was transported back to the time we met, in all the white-hot passion of youth. I remembered his smooth handsome face, tinted by the sunlit fields of France that summer of '38. Now the skin was lined, the cheeks pale and sunken. Yet when he smiled, the eyes, those ice blue, hypnotic eyes were the same, just as I had always remembered them. My mind was numb - with confusion, and a renewed wave of sheer disbelief. I was mistaken surely – either that or I was dreaming. Then he spoke, in a voice cracked with age but whose cadences I recognised, whose particular phrasing I recalled so well now. He began by apologising for his unannounced arrival and saying he couldn't stay long.

"I know it's your birthday tomorrow." he said, then took my trembling hand in his. "But I'll come back, the day after, around three. Then I'll tell you everything, I promise."

8

Everything. What was 'everything', what did that mean?

He continued with small talk, pleasantries. I could only murmur and nod in fearful avoidance of all the questions my mind was screaming to utter.

When the anniversary clock on my mantelpiece chimed the hour he leaned over to say goodbye, and lightly kissed my cheek. My face felt on fire. He asked if I was sure I wanted him to return. Like an automaton I nodded, "Yes, yes..." And then he was gone.

My peaceful uncomplicated humdrum world had been turned upside down, shattered by an earthquake.

I had made myself a promise many years ago to keep that part of my life, the part concerning him, a closed book. Yet perhaps I had always known deep down, that one day I would have to open it.

There was no one in the home I could talk to, no one who took any notice of my ramblings normally – and this? No one would believe this! Only Joyce would listen – and how! How I wished she were with me.

After wrestling with my emotions for several minutes I called her. Thomas, her son answered: she was out shopping but he would ask her to call me back. When she did she seemed more normal, the tension I had heard in her voice the last time we spoke now gone.

"I'm on my mobile telephone Annie," she laughed. "I can chat as long as I like on it, my son doesn't pay the bill."

I let her rattle on for a while then dropped the bombshell. There was silence on the other end. It was as if the earth had opened up beneath us and we were both teetering on the edge, staring down, afraid of plummeting over and into some bottomless abyss.

The seconds ticked by. Joyce said quietly. "Have you told anyone else?"

"No." I answered, "Who would understand?"

"Listen, I'm coming up. I'll cancel my appointments. You'll want to spend your birthday with the family so I'll come the day after."

"That's when he's coming again - Thursday - in the afternoon."

"Oh my god – he's coming back? But what...what did he say, I mean...?"

"He didn't. He's going to tell me everything on Thursday."

"Everything, what do you mean everything?"

"I've no idea Joyce– probably what he's been doing for the last sixty years – about his family if he has one, his house in Torquay or wherever – god knows."

"Why didn't he say more straightaway?"

"I was tired, he could see that, I normally have a nap mid morning, and he must have known, seen, what a shock it was for me, felt it tactful to leave – who knows?"

I could hear Joyce breathing hard. She said, "Look I'll book a hotel in the town. I'll be there first thing - You do want me to be there?"

"Oh Joyce," I said, "Of course I do."

"I'll see you on Thursday morning, about ten-ish. Oh Annie – what does it mean?"

"I don't know any more than you. Joyce," I replied

She was silent again for a moment then said, "Annie - be careful."

"Of what?'

"Well, I mean, he may be gaga or deranged or something."

"That'll make two of us!"

"I'm serious – suppose he blames you, for what happened, and spins you all sorts of yarns, perhaps to try and get money out of you or something…"

"Some hope, I don't have any. Besides he seemed pretty well off already, big fancy car, a chauffeur. But oh, Joyce, what does it mean – him turning up after all these years? What does he want?"

"I – I don't know Annie – I'll see you on Thursday. And Annie, are you sure – sure it was him I mean?"

"Unless I'm going crazy, or it was a ghost, yes, I'm sure."

"Well *do* take care." She said kindly, "Bye now, bye."

Good old Joyce. It was some relief to have told her at least. I wondered again if I was mistaken. Perhaps the man in the straw hat was someone else after all, an eccentric who liked visiting old ladies, or a con man.

I sat in silence and let my thoughts wander. Could one ever really know a person? The question was as old as time. Had I ever known him? 'An enigma wrapped in an enigma' someone had once called him. That was what Churchill said about Russia. God, it felt a lifetime ago and yet at the same time like yesterday, and here he was, back it seemed from the dead. How?

What had actually happened? Life seemed so *fast* in those days, we lived on the adrenalin of youth, and of danger.

Perhaps, given this development, it was after all, time now to open the door to the past and let everyone see in, time to open the box and all of its dark secrets.

CHAPTER TWO

It has arrived, my big day – eighty years of age. I feel a bit tearful, the sense of the occasion maybe or is it the melancholy creeping over me, that deep and gloomy pool of sadness that's been with me since I arrived here?

Maria came early this morning, breezing in at 7 o'clock singing a cheery 'Happy Birthday' ditty and placing some envelopes on the table next to me. She seemed much better, not in as much pain as yesterday.

"Is there one from him?' she asked impishly watching me opening each one. "I don't know - you're a real woman of mystery; what with that box in the wardrobe and now this handsome stranger turning up out of the blue. How do you know him?"
I didn't want to let her in on anything. She, like the rest of them would now know soon enough.

"He used to like to paint trees." I said, reading Joyce's card. I knew the handwriting, it had barely changed in over half a century; it was as ever, thoughtfully and humorously worded. She had never let our friendship drift. The clock chimed the quarter.

Maria looked at me. "Is he coming back tomorrow, yes? Well it's not every week you're eighty."

The constant reminder of my age and of him was beginning to irritate me and I wished she would be quiet. Already I was fighting the tears, but it was better to get them out of the way now perhaps, rather than in a few hours time, given what I had decided to do.

"Maria, would you be an angel and bring me the box?"

"Ah, the magic box – perhaps he's in there eh, your artist? Some love letters perhaps?"

She went eagerly to my wardrobe and took out the plain wooden box and placed it on the table beside me, and remained close by, expectant.

"Thank you Maria," I said politely.
With a mumble and a slight curtsey Maria reluctantly took her leave.

Unfastening the chain from around my neck I removed the tiny key and unlocked the box. I searched for his picture, always beneath the bulky brown envelope.

"They have to know about you," I whispered, gazing at the handsome face, frozen in time that stared back at me.

And here they are now, my family. From the window, through the net curtains I've just seen them arrive. Laura, my beautiful selfish daughter has a new car I see, sporty job; wonder how long that will make her happy; I give it a week. And there's Nicholas my gentle son, so like his father - and my favourite of all, my darling granddaughter Sally.

My eyes follow their progress along the path and up the steps to the door. I know what I've got to tell them will leave them wringing their hands, and their hearts in disbelief. When that is done with, they will perhaps, understand.

Closing my eyes I wondered where I should begin my story. At the beginning, where else? And where was that? I saw the prow of a boat, the rugged French coast, and felt the fresh sea breeze running through my young, auburn hair. How clearly the pictures flowed now…

CHAPTER THREE

"August 1938 was a beautiful summer in more ways than one. I was just eighteen and, not that I would ever have guessed it, about to fall in love for the very first time.

Dieppe harbour looked pretty as a scene in a picture book, the sun was shining and the soaring gulls were crying out their joyful welcome. Standing on the top deck of the boat I leaned as far as I dared over the white, rust speckled railing to drink in every sight and sound as we docked.

"He's here Mother," I shouted, waving to the old man, who was waving frantically back to me from the quayside. "Gramps is here."

Daddy puffed gently up the metal steps to join me.

"Get away from the rails, you'll slip."

Ignoring my father and not taking my eyes from the harbour I carried on waving.

"I'm not a child anymore Daddy, I'm 18, or have you forgotten?"

Laughing heartily Daddy, suitably reprimanded, didn't reply but slipped a securing hand around my waist and joined me in waving.

As the chains clanked against the harbour wall and the heavy ropes were wrapped around the thick capstans I couldn't contain my excitement. At the sound of the gangplank lowering I brushed off my father's arm, clattered down the steps and onto the dockside. I ran to Gramps and kissed him. Now my holiday could begin.

"I'm sitting here," I said hoisting myself into the back of my grandfather's lorry. Squeezing between the small wire cages of clucking, squawking hens I settled on the rough cloth sacks of corn ready for the journey to Maison Vert.

"Don't let them out or there will be no eggs for breakfast." He started the engine and the smoking noisy wreck of a vehicle fired into life. "Now are we all ready?"

"Papa, why don't you sell this contraption; buy a new one." said my mother settling herself next to Daddy in the driver's cab.

Grandfather tutted, "Just like your mother. I keep telling her, there is not a thing wrong with it, and now you start. George what do you think? You agree with me?"

The smoke from Daddy's pipe billowed slightly at the question. Ever the diplomat he said, "Do whatever is best. For all concerned, that is."

"It is best for me." Gramps thrust the gear stick with some force and the vehicle lurched forward.

"Be careful Papa!" I heard Mother cry as he threw his vehicle with careless panache around the twisting Normandy lanes. "You'll get us all killed."

"I know every pothole in the road," he replied, ignoring her protestations, "Most of which I have created, and don't mar the moment with talk of death. From my point of view, it is a long way off."

Sitting among the hens, I laughed out loud as my mother and grandfather played out their annual performance. Soon, all animosity would be forgotten as the French countryside cast its spell. Like a bright green patchwork cloth, it swiftly unravelled, trimmed at the seams with an endless ragged lace of old stonewalls and embroidered with the white fluff of sheep.

"But I want to live a while longer," Mother continued emphatically as the old man veered across the road into the long farm drive.

"How you worry," he tutted, "The Germans tried to kill me for four years in the last war without success, so driving to my own farm in peacetime is hardly likely to bother me."

He brought the vehicle to a sudden jerking halt and amid fond greetings and hugs from Gran, and much barking and jumping up from Gaston the farm dog, we all alighted.

Maison Vert never changed; it was the same from each year to the next. The small farm nestled on the outskirts of the village of St Jacques. I stood in the yard, breathed in the fresh untainted air and looked about me.

To one side stood a large barn, its huge doors always wide open with enough hay to feed the animals right through the year, and next to it a couple of stables, containing some obsolete farming implements and a very rusty old bicycle. The few chickens ran wherever they wanted and mainly scraped and scratched in the rough gravel along the hedgerows either side the road.

In a small field at the side of the house were the customary two pigs, with the same hole in the hedge they regularly escaped through, finding their way into Grandpa's pride and joy, the huge vegetable plot running adjacent to the field. How he would shout, chase them back and threaten they would be going to the very next market! I sighed happily. Everything was its charming, ramshackle self. Maison Vert was a very special place.

Mother loved the old farm just as much, and as soon as she arrived would open out, relax. It was the same with all of us. However this year something was different; mother was on edge. She had been talking lately about the trouble in Europe, hinting at dark days to come, fearful of everything.

It was eight o'clock when we gathered round the kitchen table, anticipating the evening meal. Gran had lovingly prepared the dish she knew would delight us all, rabbit stew; the tender meat slowly cooked with the farm's own potatoes, vegetables and herbs till a thick, rich, wholesome sauce lay around the flesh, enticing it from the bone. Gran lifted the crock-pot from the kitchen range, set it down on the table and proudly ladled out the first generous helping to me.

After serving the rest of the family she took her own place between Mother and Gramps.

"Now Annabelle," she said in her accented English "Have you found yourself a young man yet? Your mother tells me that Michael Oakes is sweet on you."

I shot my mother an icy glare then directed my answer to Gran.

"He's my employer, and my friend, nothing more. I'm definitely not interested in him or anyone else for that matter. Anyway, I want to concentrate on my job."

"What is it you do again?"

"I'm a secretary, I prepare legal documents and letters for Michael, he's a solicitor, the junior partner in his father's business."

Gran's eyebrows lifted, "A good catch for a young lady eh?"

"I suppose so," I laughed, "But definitely not for me."

"There's plenty of time for that," Mother said, cutting into the laughter. "She's only eighteen, and what if there is a war?"

Sensing mother's grim mood, I blew noisily on the stew and stirred vigorously. The others paused, and looked at her with a faint air of concern.

"Now, now dear," said Daddy gently. "You know Michel," he said to Gramps, "she's been worrying about Hitler, all the way across the channel. Reasonable enough to be concerned I suppose."

"Eloise my dear, George, there will be no war," Michel Amontelle said quietly. "Hitler is all talk and no action you'll see."

"But what if he isn't?" Mummy asked. "He's already invaded Austria. We don't want any more fighting not like the last time."

"Well if there is a war I'm joining up." I said assuredly. "I could see myself in a uniform. Maybe I could be a French translator."

"Neither my girl," Mummy said vehemently. "War is not fun, or an adventure."

"Well it didn't do you two any harm," I said. "The handsome young doctor and the French nurse."

Mummy glared. "Do not be disrespectful." Her voice wavered, "It was awful in the field hospitals, the things we saw…"

Daddy covered her hand and gave it a gentle squeeze. "Let's have no more of this unhappy talk. After all we are on holiday."

"Mama, Papa, you know I want you to come to England with us."

Mother had long been imploring her parents to pack up the farm and stay with them in Kingsford, in view of what she called 'the international situation' "Have you thought about what we said?"

Gran shook her head. "We couldn't leave the farm Cherie," she said pouring out more wine for everyone.

"Well of course" said Daddy, "we do understand, but Eloise has a point. Hitler's doing anything but disarming."

"I know," said Gramps "But I tell you, if any German were to step through that door I have a present for him"

So saying, he reached under the table and pulled out a heavy, double-barrelled shotgun.

"Good lord," laughed Daddy, "that's a fearsome thing. Is it an antique?"

"I mostly use it for the rabbits now – and the foxes. It is certainly old. But don't be fooled, I keep it primed and ready. This gun can stop an elephant." Michel said proudly, "It's been in my family for generations."

Gran chuckled. "And so, my dear Michel, has rheumatism." How we all laughed.

We had been at the farmhouse a couple of days when Gran asked me to go to the village for some provisions. I was glad of a diversion from Mum's brooding talk of war. The old rusty bicycle was in the stables where I had left it the previous year. I pumped up the tyres, dusted the seat and set off along the lane for the village.

Mademoiselle Barr's shop was an Aladdin's Cave of all kinds of goodies - the shelves piled high with provisions. As I propped the cycle against the wall I could smell the tobacco, the chocolate and wine – a delight to the nostrils.

After warm greetings from the proprietor, my purchases complete, I returned to the bicycle, placed the shopping in the basket and knelt down to check the tyres. I was about to straighten up when some unseen force from behind sent me swaying towards the wall.

I gripped the bicycle to save myself from falling but it was too late, I toppled backwards, dragging the bicycle with me and braced myself for a hard landing on the cobbles. I didn't however fall directly upon the ground. Something, or rather someone, was underneath me.

While endeavouring to get up I saw a brown corduroy trouser leg sticking out from beneath my own, an elbow pressed into my back. Then I saw him, the man onto whom I had fallen, lying on his front, motionless in the dusty road.

"Oh Monsieur, are you all right?" I cried out. He didn't move. "Monsieur, Monsieur" I called again, but still no movement.

As I leaned over him, he groaned and turned, then looked up and smiled. It was one of the most remarkable smiles I had ever seen, an expanse of even, brilliant teeth illuminating a most handsome face. More stunning still were the eyes. What captivating eyes they were, ice blue, they didn't twinkle so much as flash. I couldn't quite believe such an extraordinarily good-looking man should be there, sprawled on the road in a little village in France. And the more I stared at him, the more I felt a strange, almost alarming excitement.

"What on earth do you mean?" the young man then said.
I was brought back to reality. "I…. I'm sorry." I stammered reverting to English, "I don't know really…"

"I mean, why are you apologising to me?" he asked, "I should be the one apologising. I was walking backwards when we collided"

"Whatever for?"

The young man dusted himself off.

"I was studying those trees to the left of that church." He pointed to a small clump of bushes in the distance. "Wasn't watching where I was going. Are you hurt? That bicycle looks heavy."

"No - maybe a grazed shin…"

He bent down and looked at my wound. "Make sure to clean it," he said, "the bicycle may be rusty. No offence."

"No, no, it is rusty. It's my grandfather's. It's as old as him probably."

"Then maybe he should buy a new one. This looks as if its about to fall apart."

"I don't believe he's ever bought anything new. He showed us an old gun yesterday. Said he'd shoot any stranger that walked in."

"Would he shoot me if I paid a visit?"

"Only if you were a German."

"Thank goodness," he laughed, "Where did you say you're staying?"

"I didn't." I replied, feeling myself start to blush.

"Well wherever it is, what are the trees like?"

"I've never really noticed. Why?"

"I might paint them. But seeing as you haven't told me where you are staying, I'll have to look elsewhere…"

"Maison Vert," I said. "My grandparents' farm"

"Well," he said dusting off the brown cloth cap that had fallen in the road, "if you're sure you're in one piece I'll bid you good day Miss…?"

"Frazer. Annabelle Frazer."

"Miss Frazer" He gave a polite bow, replaced the cap on his head and turned towards the shop.

"Perhaps, we'll meet again," I said hurriedly. "Maybe you'll come to the farm."

"Perhaps," he said absently. "Though I'm going to be rather busy - those trees."

"You didn't tell me your name."

"Peter Barker - I come when I'm called."

"I'm sorry?"

"Woof-woof!"

"Oh – oh yes, that's jolly funny!"

19

"Not really," he smiled, "well, goodbye."

Then a puzzling thought came into my head.

"How did you know I was English?" I said.

The young man paused on the step, his face turned away from me.

"You spoke to me in English," I went on "though I'd addressed you in French. How did you know?"

"So you do notice things." His smile returned, and with an exaggerated low bow, he disappeared into Mademoiselle Barr's shop. I stood there for a moment, in a kind of shock, trying to comprehend what had occurred, trying to make sense of it.

As I pedalled back to Maison Vert, in the small of my back I could still feel a slight discomfort where his elbow had pressed into me.

I found it hard to sleep that night, wondering about the young man, whether I would ever see him again. I kept worrying that he had forgotten the name of Maison Vert, though he seemed so precise about everything. Perhaps he would think it too forward to call on me. I decided that the only way it would happen was to go back to the village and wait.

Next day I told Gran I wanted to buy a postcard to send to my best friend Joyce, and left the farmhouse before mother could ask questions. She had a knack of always making me feel guilty about the silliest things. Today I didn't want to give her the chance. I wheeled the bicycle as quietly as I could out of the barn and headed for the village.

Reaching the shop I leaned the bike against the wall and looked across to the trees beside the church, the place he had pointed out. The church clock was just chiming nine; as yet there was no sign of him. I decided the best place to observe the street would be from inside Mademoiselle Barr's shop.

Casting another look up and down, I set the bicycle in a more prominent position, just in case he should stroll by. It then occurred to me to ask Mademoiselle Barr about him, as she generally knew everything that went on in the village. I decided against this idea however. The Mademoiselle's intelligence was highly efficient but also indiscriminate; if I were known to be seeking information about a young man, my mother would also be alerted to this fact before the day was out.

I entered the shop and began chatting with the Mademoiselle, trying at the same time to keep an eye on the street.

I flipped through some cards on the rack, selected two and asked if I could take them out onto the step, to compare them in daylight. After standing there, holding the postcards up at various angles for as long as seemed plausible, I felt sure he was not coming.

Replacing the postcards, I said goodbye to Mademoiselle Barr, who gave me a most curious look. I felt convinced she had noticed my antics and knew what I'd been up to, and would be telling my mother at the first opportunity. I would have to think up some story. Feeling very foolish and annoyed with myself, I peddled frantically for Maison Vert.

As I rounded a bend I noticed someone sitting on a camping stool at the side of the road. They had their back to me and were bent towards an easel, painting. Could this be him, Peter Barker, the painter of trees?

I stopped and dismounted. The figure seemed lost in concentration, motionless apart from an odd twist of their hair with the end of the brush. I moved a little closer. It was he!

My heart thumped. Should I turn around and go? Or dare I just ride right up to him, at least say hello. By then, my gaze had fixed on the little twist of the hair - there was really no contest.

"Hello again."

"Good morning Miss Frazer, how nice to see you."

I looked steadily at his face. It had not been a daydream yesterday; he really was as extraordinarily handsome as I remembered, more so, and those eyes, looking into mine; no one else had eyes like those.

"What are you painting?" I asked, realising how long I had been staring.

"Can't you tell?" he said. "That says a lot for my work."

I felt my cheeks redden again. "Sorry - of course I can, it's a tree. Quite a talent you have."

"Where are you off to this time of day? Its too hot for cycling."

"I've been to the village" I began to stutter, "to buy a postcard for my friend, I'm on my way back to the farm."

Peter smiled again. "You can stay and watch me paint if you've nothing better to do. I'll be moving shortly towards those elders. Maybe we could have some lunch, I've got some apples and cheese, and wine - you do drink wine?"

"Well, not during the day, not ordinarily...."

"Maybe today will be not be ordinary," he said folding the camping stool and tucking the easel under his arm. "Shall we go?"

As I followed him along the path to the trees heading for the ruined abbey, I knew that the hours, days, months and years of my life ahead were not ever to be ordinary again."

August 1938 - Berlin

"Aren't you forgetting something?" said Frau Gruber in a coy, chiding voice as her son stepped out over the threshold. Kurt obediently turned back and bent his cheek to receive his mother's kiss. It was a brief though sweet kiss she gave, tempering her natural emotion with a mother's good common sense. She knew the need for restraint, especially now.

Kurt stood in the hallway of his parent's apartment. The time had finally come and he was now due to leave. Leave his family; leave Germany, his destination confidential, even his parents were forbidden from knowing. His filial observances were now fulfilled.

Two weeks previously, he had received his orders to rejoin the military and, since it seemed likely he would be away for some time, they had all travelled up from the family home in Wittenberg to see him off.

Like most young men, Kurt disliked his parents fussing over him, but in fact it had been an enjoyable weekend they'd spent together in the city.

Berlin was very much the place to be right now, and there were many foreign tourists visiting. Last night, as a special treat, he'd arranged tickets for the Berlin State Opera to hear "Tristan and Isolde" conducted by a talented up-and-coming composer called Hubert Von Karajan.

Kurt's mother had wept as she always did at Wagner, and his father had slept, waking only during the noisier moments, as he always did at the opera, whoever the composer happened to be. Privately, Herr Gruber would have preferred to visit the exhibition of so-called Degenerate Art at Konigsplatz 4, having seen it advertised in "The Nation Capital".

Even though he found it difficult to stay awake at the opera, Herr Gruber was a cultured mind, interested in art of all varieties. But of course, entarte kunst was out of the question with Kurt around.

23

After the opera they'd dined at one of Berlin's finest restaurants where, despite the shortages, the steaks were huge and succulent. They had drunk sparkling Sekt and Herr Gruber had said he was so hungry he could eat a horse, adding jokingly that the steaks probably were horsemeat. Frau Gruber felt this might be only too true, having recently heard some unpalatable rumours about the meat trade in Berlin.

"Have you no idea when you might be back" asked Frau Gruber of her son as they all three lingered in the doorway of the apartment, Kurt eager to be on his way, his parents prolonging, as parents do, the final farewell, the inevitable separation.

"The Fuhrer will decide Mother," said Kurt.

"Well tell him to decide soon"

"Mother" laughed Kurt, "I could no more tell the Fuhrer what to do than I could tell…."

"God?" suggested his father.

Kurt stared coldly at him, "Now, now, father," he said more seriously

"Oh that's right, he is God, isn't he? I was forgetting."

"Don't make mischief Hans, not today" said Frau Gruber

Herr Gruber had certain stubborn, unfashionable reservations about the Fuhrer.

"Don't worry Mother," smiled Kurt "I know you're both good Germans."

He kissed his mother once more and embraced his father in a firm manly way.

"And now I must take my leave of you"

Herr Gruber looked over his spectacles at his son, the fine strong fellow, whom it seemed only yesterday had been at his mother's breast, who had wailed and woken their neighbours at all hours of the night and who, as a sturdy boy, had had such fun camping out in the forest with the Hitler Youth. This same child now stood proudly as a man before his father.

Putting his hand on his son's shoulder, Herr Gruber said, "Remember my boy, there is more than one way to be a good German"

Kurt gave his father a respectful smile. He then clicked his heels, made the Nazi salute with a "Heil Hitler" turned and marched down the hall. He did not look back.

The Berlin streets were busy with trams, cars and buses though Kurt quickly found a taxi and jumped in.

"Where to Mien Herr?" asked the moustachioed driver.

"The train station"

The driver swung his vehicle back into the stream of traffic. Kurt gazed out at the crowds on the pavement.

I'll have to take the side roads," said the driver, "The main road will be filling up for the parade."

There was to be a march that day by the Viennese Battalion to celebrate the reunion of Germany with Austria.

"They've already set off," went on the driver, "and it'll be packed all the way to Unter Den Linden" This was the site of the Berlin War Memorial.

"No. We'll take the main road," said Kurt, "I wish to see the parade"

His train was not leaving until the afternoon and he had calculated enough time to witness the celebrations on the way.

He had tried to persuade his parents to view the event but they both, especially his father, disliked large crowds. Kurt however loved to see marching regiments, flag waving and bands, onlookers cheering.

The spectacle and sense of occasion stirred him. He often wished his father would take more interest in current affairs. But then, his father was a simple man, who did not really understand the new Germany, the new pride in the Fatherland and the necessity for national unity at this time.

There was an absolute need for a single purpose to secure Germany's future prosperity. How else could people's pride be restored and the awful social problems removed. And god knows these things were evident enough when one visited Berlin, in certain parts of the city especially. But whenever Kurt had political discussions with his father Herr Gruber would always insist on complicating the issues with unnecessary detail.

It was a mark of old age, Kurt supposed at last; there was after all, no fool like an old fool.

Cars were now clogging the road as pedestrians overflowed from the pavement, and the taxi had slowed to a crawl. It had been like this in 1935, when, as a teenager, Kurt had taken the tram to the Berlin Dome on the day of Herr Goering's wedding. The bride, Emmy Sonnemann being a beautiful and famous actress, might have been thought to be the reason so many people had gathered in the surrounding streets that day. In fact, far more, the young Kurt included, had come hoping for a glimpse of the groom's best man, a certain Herr Adolf Hitler.

The taxi had now been forced almost to a standstill. The driver turned to Kurt.

"Look, I'll have to turn off, it'll take you an hour this way!" he protested, "The parade's only a lot of prancing soldiers banging drums anyway."

"To hell with it, we'll go the way I say!" said Kurt. Who the devil did this fellow think he was; he was talking just like a communist, perhaps thought Kurt.

"You're the boss" shrugged the driver, and pulled out again into the gathering throng of cars.

"Yes" replied Kurt, sinking back into the taxi's leather upholstery and smiling now." I am the boss."

"Good lord young man" said the driver laughing, "the way you give out orders – you're just like those SS fellows!"
He turned round, grinning at Kurt as he spoke. His passenger however, making no reply, stared impassively back, his handsome, youthful face now a blank, unsmiling mask.

Only the eyes seemed alive, looking steadily, deeply into the driver's own eyes. The older man's laughter evaporated and he returned his gaze quickly to the stationary traffic.

From somewhere up ahead a young girl shouted "Heil Hitler!"

CHAPTER FOUR

The next two weeks were certainly extraordinary, and the change in my behaviour did not go unnoticed. My mother in particular became very curious about my comings and goings.

I didn't take Peter to the farm to meet the family; he wanted to go, but I wasn't quite ready for the third degree and Mother's knowing looks. I wanted, for a while, to keep him under wraps, my little secret. And everyone knew holiday romances never really amounted to much, just flirtations usually.

Countless couples say their goodbyes, kiss and promise to write, and then never find the time or the inclination once the heady days of summer are gone. Peter too had promised to write; but something in the way he looked at me, the way his lips kissed mine, the way he held me, told me this was going to be a promise kept.

Peter left for England two days before us. He was in the army and had to return to his H.Q. in London. Thank goodness it was only two days, I felt so miserable.

I couldn't wait to get back to tell Vera Dove about my holiday. Vera and I were secretaries at Oakes & Son, the solicitors in Kingsford. Vera did most of Mr. Oakes senior's work and I assisted his son Michael. I had been with them since leaving school, and though Michael was my boss we had become great friends. He was a kind soul, very good looking with dark hair and green eyes. He had always appealed to me as someone who might one day become more than a friend. That is until Peter came along of course.

Strange how I was already regarding that part of my life before the holiday – the time before Peter – as ancient history, an irrelevance. Peter had arrived and that was that.

Once home I thought more carefully about whether to tell Vera Dove what had happened in France. She was a worse gossip even than Mademoiselle Barr, and any "confidences" about my little adventure would reach the ears of my mother sooner rather than later.

Maybe that was a good thing, for at least by then Peter would have written to me and we could put the relationship on a proper footing.

And so on the first day back in the office I regaled her with the whole story, of how I had chanced to meet the most wonderfully handsome man, and how blissfully happy we both were.

On hearing my description of Peter, she remarked on how similar he sounded to a friend of Michael's who had recently visited him at the office, on the day before we left for France.

This I imagined was Vera trying to trump me in her usual way, giving the impression that perhaps this other young man had been interested in her. I could understand it; I after all, had been unable to contain myself about Peter.

It was as we were speaking that a loud buzz emitted from the desk. It was the newly installed intercom. Michael's voice crackled through: Can you spare a minute please Annabelle?"

Entering Michael's office, he asked me to sit down. It seemed unusually formal. I almost wondered if I were about to get the sack. He began asking me questions. Did I have a good holiday? Did I meet anyone? It was very odd all round and he seemed uncomfortable, not at all himself, but cross with me. Then I realised; he had heard me on the intercom, my conversation with Miss Dove about Peter. When I asked him outright if that were so, he became quite angry.

Feeling very aggrieved myself now I confirmed what he had, either deliberately or by chance overheard, and went further, to say that Peter and I would probably be getting married very soon. I was jumping the gun here of course, if Peter did not write to me the embarrassment would be terrible to suffer. But there it was, I had said it.

A week went by and the promised letter had not yet arrived. Peter hadn't given me his address so I had no way of contacting him. With each passing day I wished more fervently that I had kept my wonderful man to myself instead of boasting to Vera and Michael. I felt consumed with shame, and with the painful sense that I had 'lost' Michael, lost his respect, lost some intangible but precious thing that I now realised had always been balanced delicately between us. What a fool I had been. I could almost hear them now: "What else did she expect from a holiday romance!"

September 1938

It was late evening when Gruber arrived at his destination. He stepped from the train and looked up and down the platform. The little station seemed quite deserted. Once through the gate he crossed the lane and moved swiftly into the undergrowth, making for the far end of the wood. On reaching the river he stopped. A beam of light flashed out.

"Who's there?" a voice hissed, "Gruber is that you?" Gruber drew a small pistol from his coat and stepped into the torchlight. "Be careful, you do not know who may be listening."

"Put the gun away Gruber, these woods are quite safe, my men have searched them for unwanted guests."

"I trust no one, nor should you."
The other man took hold of Gruber's arm.

"Let's get you to the house," he said, "there are some people I'd like you to meet."

CHAPTER FIVE

As the second week wore on I had almost given up hope when the letter arrived half way through. I knew it was from Peter even before I had torn it open, hurrying upstairs with my prize before Mother or Father should notice.

I had made no mention of Peter to my parents, and nothing on their part indicated their knowledge of what I had told Vera Dove. I assumed she had quickly dismissed my story as fantasy. Now at last the proof was in my hands, proof that Peter existed, that we existed. I was not disappointed; his words were full of all the eagerness and affection I had so longed to hear. What was more, he was on his way to see me the very next evening!

Unable to contain my happiness, I took the letter with me into work that day, waving the envelope over my head in a state of sheer euphoria as I entered the office.

"He's written!" I cried, "Peter has written to me."
The mood that greeted me was not congratulatory. In fact there was absolute silence. Miss Dove gave me a vacant stare, while Michael looked distinctly hostile. Naïve as I was, I had thought they would both be happy for me.

"So he is real?" ventured Vera at last, "Thank goodness for that, I don't think I could stand another week of your moping about." I laughed at this. "Yes Vera, very real and he's coming here tonight, arriving on the 11 o'clock train."

At this point Michael turned and disappeared into his office, slamming the door behind him. There was a reason for this anger, jealousy yes, but of a more complicated nature than I could possibly have realised, and I had a shock in store.

In his letter Peter, offering his profuse apologies for not being able to catch an earlier train had asked me because of the late hour, to meet him in our local pub the Horse and Groom the following lunchtime. But I couldn't wait that long and deciding to ignore his request formed the perfect plan.

Of course Mother would not have to know about it, 11 o'clock in her opinion was far too late for a young lady to be out alone and should I be caught that would be the end of it. But my mind was made up, I would meet him from the train and nothing and no one would stop me.

The morning went very slowly, the afternoon even slower and the evening at home seemed endless. Michael had spent most of the day avoiding me.

When I tried to make conversation with him he was either too busy to talk or in deep conversation on the telephone and left the office in the middle of the after noon saying he was going home. Even Miss Dove was surprised at this gesture remarking that something or someone had upset him and giving me a very strange and awkward stare.

After dinner Mother and Father and I had as usual listened to the radio, the time dragged with every minute seeming like an hour. Finally the clock chimed nine thirty, this was my cue, so feigning tiredness, I bid them goodnight and climbed the stairs.

Closing the bedroom door I began to put my plan into action. I wanted to wear something appropriate yet attractive to meet my beau but the September nights had a slight chill to them now and I chose a simple green cotton dress and cardigan.

Quickly I dressed and then got into bed so far my plan was working, but I had an anxiously long wait for the next part of it. The clock in the hall struck ten times, my parents would soon be coming up the stairs. Mother would take the supper tray into the kitchen and I could hear Father bolting the front door. Then they came up the stairs, said goodnight to me as they always did whether I was asleep or awake and go into their room closing the door.

It seemed as if I noticed the clock every few minutes, waiting for that long half hour to pass was endless, then finally the clock strike a single note, 10.30 had arrived. I pushed back the covers straightened my clothes and remade my bed. Then, as quietly as I could I carefully opened the bedroom door and crept down the stairs.

Once into the kitchen I felt safer and remembering to take the key with me I locked the back door and went to the shed for the bicycle. Now I peddle as fast as I could for the High street. It should only take me five minutes but time was pressing. I had to get there before the train arrived. In the distance I could hear the train then the whistle blew, I knew it was rounding the bend and would soon be in the station.

I peddled harder and turning into the station yard looked over the white fence; I could just see the top of the train shunting noisily alongside amid a thickening cloud of steam, billowing up into the night. There was a long deafening squeal of brakes as metal chaffed against metal, and then a series of sharp thuds as the mighty engine was brought to a halt.

I parked my bicycle and was just about to step onto the platform when I saw Michael coming out of the waiting room. Immediately I hid behind a brick pillar and peering round the corner of the bridge I could see him on the platform, turning rapidly this way and that to scrutinise the line of carriages.

Several doors on the train opened, disgorging some dozen or so passengers; old ladies with dogs, some businessmen with bowler hats and briefcases and a couple of men in uniform. There was no sign of Peter. Michael began moving up and down the platform, waiting to see if another door would open. Henry the stationmaster moved forward with flag and whistle at the ready.

"Hurry up sir" he called out to some unseen person, "here, let me"

The stationmaster approached the goods van and took hold of a bicycle wheel, which was now protruding. He gave the wheel a tug and the rest of the bicycle followed, together with its owner. I narrowed my eyes in an attempt to penetrate the steam wafting along the platform, blanketing my vision.

The whistle blew, the engine shunted back into life and the train slowly moved along the platform. Soon it was out of the station and on its way - all was quiet again.

Slowly, the clouds of steam dispersed to reveal the troublesome bicycle and its owner. It *was* Peter. Michael walked towards him and shook his hand.

A wave of mixed emotions surfaced in me. I slunk deeper into the shadows as the pair walked passed me laughing and joking and carried on along the station yard into the street. It was definitely Peter and why was Michael meeting him, and more to the point, how did they know each other.

When I thought the coast was clear, I emerged from behind the pillar onto the Station platform, grabbed my bicycle and began the journey home. Tomorrow I would confront Michael and sort out this mystery once and for all.

CHAPTER SIX

From my bedroom I heard the loud knocking on the front door and Mother shouting "Alright, Alright" equally as loud as she marched down the hallway. I opened my bedroom door to see who it was making such an urgent racket

"Michael," My mother greeted him "What on earth is going on? Annabelle has come home from work in such a dreadful state and is sobbing in her bedroom; she refuses to come out. Now you're here looking very perplexed."

"Please, Mrs Frazer, I have to see her," he said with some urgency. "I've only tried to explain to her but..."
I opened my door wider and shouted, "I don't want to see you, or that creep of a friend." then I slammed it firmly shut.

"It's not like it seems, Annie," Michael pleaded, "It's my fault, not Peter's"
I could hear Mother's soothing tones, trying to appease the situation.

"I think you'd better come in," she said "Go through to the sitting room, she'll be down in a minute."
That I wouldn't! I was not going down to see him ever again, as far as I was concerned I never wanted to speak to him or Peter again.
Suddenly all went quiet, then I heard Mother making her way up the stairs.

"I don't know what's gone on dear but he does seem very sorry," she whispered through the closed door. "I think you should hear what he's got to say."

"He should be." I snivelled opening the door, "I don't want to talk to him, or his friend."

"So it's about his friend is it?"
I'd said too much, Mother didn't know anything about Peter and I wanted to keep it that way until I was ready to tell her. But it looked like now that would never happen.

"Well – yes, but it really doesn't matter, I don't want to see either of them now." Then I began to cry again.
Mother put her arms about me and held me tight.

"Dry your eyes" she whispered, "See what Michael has to say, he looks terribly worried."

"As I said, he should be."
Mother offered me a handkerchief; I blew into it with a resounding snort,

"If you don't go and find out what it is he has got to say," she said softly "you'll only wonder. After all, it may not be as bad as you think. Now, get it over and done with, then you need not have anything more to do with him or this friend of his."

As I flung the sitting room door open. Michael perched on the edge of the settee turned towards me

"I'm sorry Annie," he apologised," It's all my fault, don't blame Peter."

"I'm blaming the both of you, and you can keep your job. I won't be coming back."

"Annie, please. Let me explain."

I sat down heavily on the settee, I felt wretched, and seeing Michael I knew that I didn't want our friendship to end.

"Very well Michael, but my mind's made up. I don't want to see him or you again."

Michael drew in a long deep breath.

"It was the Friday before you were going on holiday. I didn't know Peter was coming up to see me; he just turned up out of the blue. He saw you running with the post and asked whom you were.

I met him at a cricket match at the Oval last year when I was visiting my Aunty Gladys and Uncle Bob. We had a few drinks in Piccadilly and exchanged addresses. I thought it just a friendly gesture and never expected to see him again, after all him living in Surrey and me up here, but a week later I got a letter from him saying he was due some leave from the army and was planning a cycling tour and would I like to meet up.

The next week he arrived on the train, and I booked him in at the Groom."

I frowned, "So what did he do while he was here and why come all the way to Cheshire. I'm sure the countryside is just a s nice in Surrey."

Michael nodded "That did make me curious I must admit, he didn't do much cycling and I couldn't understand why he wanted my friendship. But we seemed to get on well with each other and to be honest, I like him, he's good fun. He is very different though…. quite a character, an enigma. …"

"I'll say. Where does he live? He didn't give me his address, although I did ask him for it."

"Guilford, with his aunt and uncle; he was orphaned as a child, mother and father killed in some boating accident when he was about 3 years old."

"I didn't know that…"

"It took him a while to tell me. He's a very good artist," Michael continued changing the subject ever so slightly "I've seen some of his work."

"He was going to paint the day we met… Why did he follow me to France?"

"Why do you think? He fancies you."

"So I wasn't a bet then."

"Annie. You've got to believe me," Michael said earnestly. "I'd no idea he would do that, when you said he was coming up that night I couldn't believe that he hadn't told me. So I went to meet him at the station, he's staying at the Groom, I've been to see him after you left the office this morning, he's very upset about it all. Look Annie, we were going to tell you today, surprise you. We thought you'd be pleased.

"Pleased…Why couldn't you both tell me before now, Oh no you would rather lie to me, instead of being honest, No Michael I can't forgive that."

Michael took my hand but I snatched it away.

"Because," he swallowed hard, "because I want you to be sure he's the right one for you."

"Michael what are you saying, he's your friend."

"Yes he is," Michael, answered "But I don't know him that well; plays his cards close to his chest."

"You're just trying to put me off him. You're jealous. Vera said you would be."

Michael sighed again. "Annie don't be taken in by him, you know him even less than I do. I never meant to hurt you. You mean so very much to me and…."

At that moment I stared at Michael. Like Peter, Michael had the classic good looks, a defined, regular profile, a pleasing symmetry of face and a lean, athletic physique. The men's colouring was different though, Peter's blonde hair, blue eyes and bronze skin making him a sort of reverse image to Michael's dark-haired, green-eyed, slightly grey look.

35

I'd never really noticed before how handsome he really was. If I hadn't fallen for Peter, well, maybe we would have started walking out.

"But I'm in love with him Michael" I said. "I can't help it. I love him."

"Then you'd better come to the pub at lunchtime" He said rising from the settee, "He'll be waiting for you. 12 noon on the dot. He told me to tell you, if you didn't come, he's going, and you'll never see him again. Your choice Annie."

"Michael, what's wrong?" But Michael didn't answer; he'd already closed the door.

"Joyce – Joyce wait for me!"

Joyce Robinson paused on the steps of the bank where she worked and looked around to see me hurrying across the High Street towards her.

"Every thing alright Annie, you looked worried."

"Please, come with me!" I said slightly breathlessly, "I don't want to go to the Groom on my own!"

"Why would you want to?"

"Because I - have to."

"Are you meeting someone?"

I blushed

"You are!" Joyce exclaimed, "Is it the chap you met in France that I've heard the rumours, but you seem to have forgotten to tell me about."

I slightly winced at Joyce's vitriolic words.

"Sorry Joyce. I didn't want to tell any one just in case, well, just in case it was all too good to be true, and he was just a holiday romance, but he's written to me and now he's here."

Her eyes widened.

"Here! As in, here in Kingsford?" she exclaimed. This was news indeed.

"He came up last night, on the 11oclock train I wasn't supposed to meet him till today but I went anyway, but when I got there Michael was waiting for him. It turns out he and Peter were friends but neither of them told me. I went into work this morning and confronted Michael and before he could explain I ran home………….Oh Joyce, what a fool I've been."

Joyce nodded in agreement

"I bet they've had a good laugh at my expense"

"Why would they?"

"Oh, I don't know," I said rather glumly "I thought they'd had a bet or something, but Michael's been to see me and said that Peter wants me to go to the pub to meet him at lunchtime and… Oh Joyce please come with me. I'm sorry, am I making you late?"

No it's alright," said Joyce eagerly wanting to know more. "I've just taken the post, the bank's going to have to wait, tell me more about this Peter."

"That's just it, I don't know a lot about him. He's in the military, and he paints landscapes; and he followed me to St Jacques this summer. Oh Joyce, it feels so right."

"He must really fancy you. But I thought you and Michael were…after the village fete…"

"It was just a kiss." I frowned dismissively, "I'm not interested in him, we're just friends, nothing more."

Someone had better tell him that."

"Oh Joyce you're impossible," I laughed, "So, will you come with me?"

"Your try and stop me." Joyce smiled "Meet me here at ten to twelve."

"Thank you," I smiled as my very best friend ran up the remaining steps and disappeared into the bank. "What would I do without her?"

It was after midday when Joyce and I entered the saloon of the Horse and Groom. The pub appeared empty save for Cornelius Farrer, the gravedigger and Joshua Bracegirdle the blacksmith, perched in their usual places on the opposite side of the bar. The two men had been fixtures in the village for as long as I could remember, their ancient yet somehow ageless faces always full of gentle mischief.

By day Joshua kept the smithy in the High Street, and after dark was known to pursue another occupation. Nothing had ever been proven, but ask him for a fresh rabbit or pheasant and he'd have one for you by the morning.

No connection of course with the proliferation of wildlife to be found on the nearby estate of our neighbour the Colonel. Cornelius was known to be Joshua's occasional right hand man in these nocturnal activities. Fortunately for all concerned the Colonel was good-natured, and turned a blind eye.

Cornelius and Joshua exchanged a cordial nod to us as we hesitated by the door and looked around. It was then that I saw Michael and Peter, stood at the bar with their backs to us. For a moment my heart sank. I wanted to turn and run, but before I had the chance Joyce pushed me forward.

"Come on," she whispered, "it's now or never."

Hearing Michael order some drinks, I said, "two orange juices please." Where my courage had come from I don't know. Both Michael and Peter turned around. Joyce made straight for Peter and introduced herself then settled next to Michael. I hadn't realised till then how much Joyce liked him. Now it was suddenly so obvious. Michael however didn't seem to see it at all. Peter took my hand and held me close. "I'm glad you came." He whispered.

It was such a wonderful moment that I did not dare to ask about his friendship with Michael, his having deceived me when we met. Perhaps he would tell me now.

It was at this precise moment that Joshua mentioned the lights. His voice had risen so loud it was impossible to ignore.

"Down at Hunters Bridge, I tells you Cornie, it was them same lights again, fair frittened me 'death." Hunters Bridge bordered the Colonel's estate. Joshua was known for 'seeing' things in the dead of night. Cornelius was often laughing at him and his ghosts. This evening though, his account seemed more earnest than usual.

"Summat's going on, I tell yea! Them lights are real, real torches, that's what they are, and there's real people holdin' 'em."

Cornelius laughed loudly at this. "Real people, not ghosts, well now ain't that strange!"

As the men's banter continued, Peter looked serious.

"What's he talking about?" he asked Michael. Michael smiled and told him Cornelius was the village storyteller, a spinner of intrigue and improbable yarns.

It was only the appearance of Colonel Travers that altered Peter's thoughtful countenance. Now he looked distinctly ill at ease. The Colonel hadn't noticed Peter, who was now half turned away from the group. The Colonel was in jovial mood and asked us if we were going to the New Year's Eve dance in the village hall.

"It's months off," Michael answered nervously.

Joyce replied immediately that she would be going, and that if Michael should be in need of a partner, she was available. We all laughed.

Then something peculiar happened. Colonel Travers had suddenly noticed Peter, and, for a second he looked, well, startled is the only way I can describe it. It was the briefest flicker, so quick that I wasn't sure exactly what I had seen. Maybe nothing.

Half an hour later we finished our drinks, Joyce and Michael went back to their work and Peter and I sauntered across towards the office. When I asked him if we could meet up later he seemed preoccupied.

"I'm having an early night." he said, "the beer's made me tired. I hope you don't mind."

Of course I minded. But perhaps my pensive mood had affected him. I still hadn't mentioned him following me to France, or of Michael and he being friends. He must have assumed Michael had already told me, that I loved him and would accept it all.

"So when will I see you?" I asked. He then kissed me tenderly, and put his arms around me in a warm embrace.

"Tomorrow," he whispered, "I promise. I'll see you then. Goodbye Annie."

As I watched him return to the Horse and Groom, I wondered why, having come all the way from Surrey to see me, he suddenly felt too tired to spend the evening together. Peter had lied to me already, now he was lying again, and I wanted to know why.

That afternoon I spoke to Michael. I appealed to him, saying I had to know what Peter was about, what if anything he was up to as regards me or anybody else. I asked Michael to come and see me that same evening. He agreed, and turned up at my house around 7.30 in his father's little black Austin.

Unconvinced by my suspicions, he nevertheless drove me back into the village, to see what I could observe of Peter's movements.

"I say you're wrong about him Annie," Michael said turning into the High street "I know he's vague about himself, and hasn't come clean about following you to France, which is admittedly dishonest, but in Peter's case not dishonourable, there's a difference."

As we approached the Horse and Groom I saw Peter, dressed in a dinner suit, standing out under the front porch. I shrank down in the seat as we drove past. Michael stopped a short distance away.

My eyes remained fixed on Peter as he looked up and down the now quiet street, glancing at his watch.

"What did I tell you? He's meeting a woman, I knew he was lying," I hissed. "How could he do this to me?" I suddenly felt so wretched.

"Perhaps he is waiting for someone," said Michael, "what of it?"

Suddenly, from behind us a car sped down the street, then stopped outside the pub. Peter got into the passenger seat and the vehicle sped away.

"That's the Colonel," said Michael, and without a further word started the engine.

The light was beginning to fade as we watched the Colonel's car disappear down the long drive that led from Hunter's Bridge to the manor house.

After arguing for a moment about whether to follow or not, we decided the only safe way was on foot. Leaving the car we made our way along the mossy wall and into the wide avenue, staying in the cover of the trees.

Rounding a bend the house suddenly rose up before us. Lights blazed out from the undraped downstairs windows, illuminating a collection of expensive looking motorcars parked on the gravel.

Several figures could be made out through the main window, though not their faces. The Colonel it seemed was throwing a party. But where was Peter? I nudged Michael and nodded towards the house. I had to get a closer look.

Skirting the gravel we crept across the grass and up to the window. Now I could see the faces, but none that I recognised, apart from the Colonel's. Hung above the mantle, gleaming majestically in the bright lights was the Colonel's family coat of arms, the rearing horses with the two crossed swords. Then I saw Peter, standing by the fireplace, glass in hand and seemingly enjoying the company.

"He must know them all," I whispered, "Did he tell you he knew the Colonel?"

"No," Michael said, interested now. At that moment the front door to the house opened, and from the hallway sounds of laughter pierced the silence of the cold night air as a young man and woman staggered drunkenly down the steps. Michael suddenly grabbed me and began kissing me.

"You see Hilda," the young man burbled, "We're not the only ones taking the night air." The couple laughed hysterically and headed for one of the cars.

For a while I lingered in Michael's arms, the kiss had been brief yet passionate, wonderful.

"This is no place for us," he whispered taking my hand. "We'll…"

He was interrupted by the sound of barking from the back of the house, a frantic commotion, growing louder by the second. Michael yanked my arm. "Run!" he said loudly "For God's sake run."

We sat in the car outside my home; I pondered what to do next. I felt desperate to confront Peter, to hear his explanation, to be reassured. Had he simply forgotten about having to attend a party? That was impossible. Then it came to me; the Colonel must have bumped into Peter late yesterday afternoon, got talking and asked him up to the manor house. Peter being a newcomer to the village it was just the sort of thing the Colonel would do.

But this didn't explain how he happened to have an evening suit with him. And there was still the business in the pub, the odd look on the Colonel's face when he first saw Peter.

"Michael, there's something going on."

"He is in the army. They're a secretive lot. If there is anything "going on" it's not for us to know."

"I'm going to find out"

"Be careful Annie, we don't know what we might be getting into."

"Tomorrow, 11 o'clock in the Groom," I said. "Peter's going to tell us both the truth whether he likes it or not."

The mood in the pub the next day was quite sombre. Neither Tom the landlord nor Cornelius seemed at all their usual jovial selves. I had just sat at the table by the window when Michael joined me.

"What's up with them?" I said. "They look as if the world's about to end."

Tom came over I asked if he had seen Peter yet that morning.

"Yes Miss, he got a telephone call early. No sooner had he put the phone down, he went to pack, paid his bill and left. Seemed in a fair hurry."

My heart sank; I couldn't believe what I had heard. Peter gone, disappeared out of my life again, perhaps forever. Tom reached into his white apron pocket and took out a cream-coloured envelope.

"I nearly forgot, your boyfriend left this for you."
I tore open the envelope and read the note inside:

> *My Dear Annabelle,*
>
> *Sorry, but I have to leave. Duty calls. Will see you soon and try to make it up to you. Hope you like the flowers.*
>
> *Peter.*

I was elated. He hadn't walked out on me; he loved me and would come back. Nothing else mattered now.

Tom nodded towards a vase of red roses on the far end of the bar. I could count twelve, there might have been more.

"I was supposed to bring them to your house," he said, "but what with the trouble and all…. well, there wasn't time."
"What trouble?" Michael asked.
"Joshua," said Tom. "Cornelius found him, this morning."
Michael looked concerned. "What do you mean, found him?"
"I told him to be careful, now the old fool's dead." Tom answered.
"Dead - but how, where…?
"In the river, up by Hunter's Bridge."

CHAPTER SEVEN

It was five days since Peter's sudden departure, and there had been no word from him. I was beginning to reconcile myself to the fact that I would never see him again. On the sixth morning I set out as usual for work, meeting Vera Dove on the way.

On reaching the offices we found the door already unlocked. Normally Vera opened up. On my desk was a huge vase of red roses. With them was a message:

Arriving on 2 o'clock train.
Meet me in the pub tonight 7 o'clock.
Peter.

Ignoring Vera I ran into Michael's office.

"Did you know he was coming back?" Michael assured me he was as much in the dark as I was. He had found the flowers outside on the step that morning, and read the message.

"Arriving on the 2 o'clock train eh! Well that's Peter," Michael said, with a wave of his hands. "They seek him here they seek him there."

"What?"

"Is he in heaven, is he in hell..." he laughed "That darned elusive Pimpernel!"

That evening I decided to go the Horse and Groom alone. After all I was meeting my boyfriend, or so I hoped. Nervous, I garbled something to my parents about meeting Joyce and left the house.

Closing the front gate I stepped into the lane; the autumn air had a chill in it and I turned the collar of my coat up. It was about half a mile into Kingsford and after crossing the open countryside it normally took me ten minutes to walk into the village.

But tonight was different; there was a spring in my step, and a sense of excitement. I was soon passing the smithy, now closed up and the row of terraced houses adjacent to the bank.

Across the road the church clock was striking seven as I reached the Horse and Groom. For a moment I paused, drew in a deep breath then pushed on the heavy oak door. The aroma of tobacco and ale gave me heart.

"He's through there," said Tom discreetly, indicating a small room at the far end. "On his own."

Peter was sitting by the window staring out at the street. He hadn't seen me and for a moment I paused. I was nervous of his reaction, and of my feelings. I so much wanted to trust him now, to believe that he really did want me, to put his erratic behaviour down to something else, that didn't matter, so long as it could not touch us.

Suddenly, without turning round he grabbed the papers and stuffed them hurriedly into a rucksack. As he did so, a loose sheet fluttered away and fell to the floor at my feet. Stooping to retrieve it for him I noticed it was a map of Kingsford.

"Give that to me please!" snapped Peter.
Taken aback I thrust the paper at his outstretched hand and stepped back.

"I'm so sorry" I hastily apologised, quite taken aback for the moment at this unwarranted display of anger.

"No, no," he said his mood now subsiding, "I'm sorry. I didn't mean to shout. Its just, you know, work matters." He got up and took my hand in his. I felt suddenly powerless. His other hand brushed against my cheek, and a thrill of passion surged through my body. I was once again under his spell.

After we had kissed we sat together in silence for a minute. It was a bliss that I did not want to shatter, but eventually I spoke.

"Peter?" I said.

"Yes what is it?"

"You know, I was afraid I wouldn't see you again after last time."

"What about the roses?"

"They were beautiful."

"So are you."
I felt dizzy, weak beyond happiness, but I had to go on.

"So why did you leave so suddenly?"

"I was afraid you would ask me that."

"Why afraid?"

"An urgent call, they wanted me back in London. You understand."

"Not really Peter" I said. "I don't understand at all"

"What is the matter?"

"Peter, we saw you, Michael and I, with the Colonel at the manor. The night you said you couldn't meet me, said you had reports to write. Why did you lie?"

Peter tensed for a moment, then got up and closed the door.

"You should not have followed me, that was foolish. There are things going on that I can't explain, you know what my job entails."

"I know you're in the military."

"I'm in British intelligence," he said, "I shouldn't even be telling you this. If anyone finds out I'll be court marshalled. You read the newspapers, hear on the radio about what's going on in Europe, with Herr Hitler. The Colonel is retired but...look I can't say more. Annie you have to trust me. The important thing to know is that I would never hurt you. How could I when... Oh to hell with it - Annabelle Frazer, I love you."

In an instant all my questions were swept aside. All my confusion, all my doubt had vanished. It was as if they had never existed.

Suddenly there was no need to worry. Peter was here in my life forever and it was the only thing that mattered. Now at last, I could tell my parents about us.

CHAPTER EIGHT

The village hall was already quite full by the time I arrived. Apparently Tom had insisted on closing up early at the Horse and Groom and came over to help organise the kegs of ale. The New Year, he had told his protesting regulars, after calling time a half hour earlier than usual, only came once a year, and it should be seen in properly.

Furthermore, he had pointed out, a lot of people who never frequented the pub would be in the hall for the party, and it was only fair to see they got a drink just like everyone else. The regulars had then grumbled that their loyalty to Tom should ensure the 'Groom' stayed open for them till midnight. Then, as if to prove that loyalty, to a man they had trooped up to the hall to be first at the trough here. This gossip was gleefully relayed to me as I entered the hall, by a dear old man from the 'Groom' whose name I had never known.

I looked around. It was now about eleven-thirty and the band had just taken a break. From a hatch to the kitchen, Mother and Mrs Robinson were serving tea and orange juice to those who'd taken the pledge and to the children, some of whom had just been chased off the stage by Henry the station master, who also acted as caretaker for the hall.

While the band took their refreshment, the revellers stood or sat around eating, drinking and holding forth in lively conversation. To the side of the stage, propping up the makeshift bar of trestle tables was Daddy, talking animatedly to Mr. Oakes senior and Cornelius the gravedigger, the subject, from what I could gather, being the average time it took for a corpse to decompose under differing conditions. In the opposite corner, Vera Dove, looking very elegant in a long blue dress was regaling Joyce with some story.

Then I saw Michael, sitting alone a few yards away from them. Every now and then Miss Dove gave him a reassuring flutter of her hand and a smile.

Joyce would smile too, and then the two women's heads would lower again in intense conversation. Seeing me, Michael lifted his beer glass. I smiled at him. I assumed Peter hadn't yet arrived.

It had now been some weeks since I had seen him. The day after his declaration of love for me, I had invited him to tea with my parents on the following Saturday. The occasion brought an unexpected reaction. Mummy, thrilled at the prospect of finally meeting Peter, had been at pains to reassure my father beforehand that his intentions were almost certainly honourable. She need not have worried on that score.

From the moment Peter arrived, he and Daddy got on like a house on fire. They discussed - and agreed on - politics, music and the arts and much more besides. Taking me aside at one point, Daddy said he thought Peter extremely well informed, and an eminently sensible young man. He also thought he was handsome and charming, and clearly much in love with me. What more could I have asked for?

The unsettling part however was yet to come, and it concerned my mother. From the excited woman of a few hours earlier, already hinting at wedding plans and living arrangements, she had fallen strangely quiet after meeting Peter. I didn't really notice it over tea, as the rest of us had all been talking nineteen to the dozen. It was only when Peter left, the table had been cleared and Daddy was twiddling with the radio to catch the seven o'clock news, that we both became aware of Mother's silence.

I had been expecting annoying questions, but when none came, I pressed her for some comment about Peter. All she would say was: "Yes dear, he's very nice, very nice indeed." Her expression, her tone, her absent eyes however, all belied her words.

Since that day she had made no further mention of weddings, or of Peter whatsoever. She had though suggested that Michael Oakes might come to tea one day. I could only assume Mother had taken an instant dislike to Peter.

Perhaps the idea of him had sounded nice, but then the reality of 'losing' her daughter was too much. As I saw it, she had suffered a sort of shock, unable to contemplate the prospect of me getting married to anyone. Maybe she thought Peter would take me far away from Kingsford, and saw the tame, parochial Michael as the preferable son-in-law after all.

But Peter was my choice and not hers. Daddy, bless him had sensed it all of course, and made discreet enquiries about Peter when Mother wasn't in earshot.

Peter realised something was bothering me the next time we met. Not wanting to hurt his feelings I avoided the issue at first, but eventually I had to tell him. He was very understanding.

We agreed on a softly, softly approach, whereby rather than coming to the house, he would instead find an opportunity of seeing my parents next on neutral ground, ideally at some social gathering. Where better than the village New Year's Eve party? Mother would by then have had a few weeks to think about things. She would also be mellowed by the general exuberance of the party, and hopefully a good few glasses of sherry!

So, the scene had been set and here we were. Mother certainly looked in a good mood, dispensing fond smiles and orange juice to the junior celebrants. All that was needed now was Peter.

"Annie, – we thought you'd never get here!" Daddy's face was flushed with beer and bonhomie. "I said to your mother, if she takes any longer getting ready, she's going to miss the chimes." He squashed a clumsy kiss on my cheek. "And there's young Michael all alone poor boy. I'll send him over for a dance. Peter won't mind will he? Where is he by the way? Thought you said he was coming up for the evening?"

Not wanting to admit that I didn't know where Peter was, I pointed out Colonel Travers waving a piece of paper in our direction.

"Daddy I think the Colonel wants you."

"Oh good lord yes! Nearly time for the speeches."

The band struck up again, and couples began taking the floor once more. Everyone seemed very jolly. I watched as Daddy, having finished his conference with Colonel Travers, and fired by the gaiety of the music, crossed to the kitchen and prised Mother out from behind the tea urn. Hand in hand, laughing like schoolchildren, they moved into the throng and effortlessly took up the rhythm. It was a joyful sight, and made me wish at that moment that Peter and I would be as happy as my parents.

Within a few minutes, almost everyone was on the floor. The only two people not dancing, apart from some elderly villagers were myself, and Michael. Mother, whirling by, caught my eye and jerked her head meaningfully towards him. The band segued into 'I'll Be Seeing You'. I looked at the clock and saw it was nearly midnight. Where was Peter? I felt a surge of panic, giddiness, like when falling in a dream.

Glancing across at Michael our eyes met. He got up and made his way towards me.

"Care for this one?" he said.

"Yes," I replied without hesitation.

With a quiet, formal elegance, Michael escorted me to the edge of the dance floor. After a couple of false starts we were in tandem, the music taking us round as if on a carousel

"I thought Peter might be here tonight," said Michael. His tone was noticeably casual.

"Yes, yes" I answered, "he said he would try to get up but – Michael, have you heard from him?"

Michael pulled me towards him as we turned.

"No" he said, "But that's Peter isn't it."

I didn't answer, I couldn't. Peter had let me down, and tonight of all nights, the biggest, most romantic evening of the year. Everyone would know and feel sorry for me. Some would be pleased. I could already picture Vera Dove's face on hearing about it. What a fool I'd been yet again. I could feel the tears rising behind my eyes. I could feel Michael's eyes on me.

"Look, don't worry Annie," he said kindly now. "I'm sure there's a good reason. With the way things are in Europe, there's probably a lot going on right now, things that ordinary people like us don't see. Peter's work is rather special."

"And what about me – aren't I special? I blurted out loudly enough for two nearby couples to turn and look.

"Yes. Yes, you are Annabelle. You're very special indeed," Michael replied immediately, who seemed to be blushing as he spoke.

"Oh god Michael, why can't Peter be normal? A normal, predictable man, kind and plodding and dull like you! - Oh I'm sorry I didn't mean that...I just meant..."

Michael had dropped his hands from around my waist and stood, looking awkward and uncertain amid the moving figures.

"Come on you two," bellowed Daddy as he and mother sailed past us again, "Don't just stand there, it's a waltz!"

Suddenly I laughed rather hysterically. The whole situation seemed crazy, unreal. The sense of enjoyment all around, seeing everyone else in such a carefree mood, made me almost forget my own disappointment for a moment.

"Thank you Michael," I said taking his hands in mine.

"For what?" he replied.

"For being so nice, for being you - please don't ever change."
I glanced again at the clock. It was now ten to twelve. I saw Daddy
signal to the bandleader, who flicked his baton, bringing the music to
a swift finale. Colonel Travers tapped the microphone.

"Ladies and gentlemen, as we are approaching the big
moment I would like to make a few announcements if I may – now,
now don't worry its not going to be the Gettysburg address...."

"Thank heavens for that!" came a good-natured interruption
from my father, at which everyone laughed.

"So please stay on your feet," continued the Colonel, "the
chimes of midnight are almost upon us, and you all know what
comes after that..."

"Yes, next year," Daddy quipped.
The whole hall went into uproar. I smiled, half-embarrassed, half
proud of my funny dad - how he loved playing to the gallery. Mother
chided him to be quiet.

Colonel Travers thanked those who had helped prepare for
the party, and after a slight pause, followed by a spate of loud
clapping, he made an exaggerated sweep of his arm towards my
father.

Daddy, taking his cue in similarly music hall style, ascended
the stage, bowed and began repeating the Colonel's votes of thanks.

"Now I think that's it," he said, "I do hope I haven't
forgotten anyone – well, yourselves also of course, thank you,
villagers of Kingsford for being here tonight to see in the New Year,
and, and...."
Then came a voice from the back of the hall:

"Dr Frazer, perhaps I can help you out."
All heads turned to see who was speaking. Someone was making
their way through the throng of people. I caught my breath as,
coming up the steps and onto the stage, in a smart blue suit, his
golden hair glistened back, appeared Peter.
Bowing briefly to my father and the Colonel he came and stood at
the microphone. There in the spotlight he looked like a matinee idol.
No one spoke. All eyes were on him.

"I apologise good villagers of Kingsford for interrupting your celebrations." He smiled as he spoke, though his tone was measured, respectful. "Though some of you know me, I am an outsider here. I do not belong." He paused. Colonel Travers coughed and looked up at the clock.

"However, I hope that I soon will belong here in your village, and belong too, most wholeheartedly, to the lovely, the wonderful Annabelle".

There was an intake of breath from the whole hall, followed by some murmuring and turning of heads as all eyes sought out the object of the young man's address.

I was stood against the wall with Mummy and Michael. My mothers face had changed, the smiles and gaiety vanished, she had gripped Michael's arm and was staring towards the stage.

"Some weeks ago," Peter continued, "I took the liberty of asking Dr Frazer for his daughter's hand in marriage. While he kindly gave his assent, he told me that the only person who could give me my answer was Annabelle herself. I am therefore taking the further liberty of arriving here at the eleventh hour, to seek that answer in the company of Annabelle's dear family, friends and neighbours. It's a special night for you all, and I hope it will be special for us too. Annabelle darling – will you ever forgive me for this? And, if so, will you marry me?"

A deathly hush fell upon the hall, all heads turned towards me, all ears waiting for my reply. I looked at Michael but his head was bowed.

Mother too had her face averted. I gazed up at Peter. The man I had fallen in love with was here, proclaiming his love for me, for all to witness. He had not let me down.

"Yes," I said, "yes Peter, I will marry you!"

There was an explosion of cheering, shouts and applause. The band struck up an impromptu rendering of 'Here Comes the Bride', people hugged one another, lifted their partners up and kissed, glasses were raised, hats thrown in the air and tables hammered with cutlery, cups, plates and every other utensil of item of crockery to hand.

The noise seemed to go on and on. Peter ran from the stage and began pushing through the crowd, people slapping him on the back and shaking his hand vigorously as he passed. On reaching me, he scooped me up in his arms and kissed me.

Everyone seemed so excited and happy for us. Even my mother's look of shock seemed to have given way to a smile. There was someone missing though.

"Where's Michael, Mummy?" I asked,

"He's just left." My mother replied, "He said something about it being too late."

I turned to the door just in time to see Michael leaving. Peter noticed it too, and I suggested that perhaps we should go after him, but at that moment someone grabbed Peter's shoulder. It was Colonel Travers.

"These Johnny foreigners Annabelle – they take all our lovely young ladies."

"I'm from Surrey, Colonel," Peter replied smiling.

"Quite!" glowered the Colonel, giving me a wink. He then returned to the stage and addressed the hall again.

"Our warmest congratulations to Annabelle and Peter, I'm sure we wish them all the very best. Now I'm reliably informed the chimes are about to begin, so can I ask you to join hands with your nearest and dearest, as we prepare to see out the old year and welcome in the new!"

Henry, who had rigged a loudspeaker to his wireless set, was already in position and tuned to the Home Service.

As he turned the volume full up, the first strike of Big Ben reverberated out into the hall. The crowd began counting, each time louder, building to a huge crescendo: "One…two…three…"

On the stroke of midnight, the band began Auld Lang Syne. The villagers, their clasped hands rising and falling in time, had formed a huge circle, in the centre of which Peter and I now stood. The scene, shimmering and beautiful as a fairytale, transported me.

When the song finished, my father climbed back onto the stage. Flushed and perspiring, he announced, "Villagers of Kingsford, welcome to 1939. It's going to be a year to remember!"

CHAPTER NINE

"Mother, why didn't you tell us all this before now? Mother are you listening to me?"

For a second I was confused, not knowing where I was. The recollection had been so clear in my mind, the memory of the emotion and the sound of his voice, all so vivid.

I leant back in the chair, picked up the glass of cooled water from the table beside me and took a sip.

"Oh, yes Laura, I am listening, but this is only the beginning," I said, "merely the opening prelude to my story."

"Sounds like we're going to be here all day," replied Laura with a slight sigh

"Forgive me but I thought that was the idea. It is my birthday you know."

"Yes, we could hardly be allowed to…."

"So what happened next Nan?" Sally interrupted, "Please carry on."

I closed my eyes. The feelings, those feelings were all still there. I could see him so clearly.

"It was February 1939. I was eighteen, engaged to the man I loved and blissfully happy. The marriage was set for June. Mother and I were making arrangements"

At this point I took the box and opened it, removed a faded envelope and handed it to my granddaughter.

"A love letter Nan?" said Sally, unfolding the crinkled paper and holding it very carefully, studied the mismatched fragments clipped from old newspapers, which had been stuck on. Where the glue had dried out, two of the words came loose and fluttered to the floor. Laura and Nicholas, their interest now aroused stooped to help Sally retrieve the small pieces of paper. Setting the letter down on the coffee table, Sally repositioned the loose words and read out:

DO NOT MARRY HIM. HE IS NO GOOD FOR YOU.

"More a letter of hate wouldn't you agree?" I said.

"Who sent it Nan?"

"Someone who hadn't the courage to sign it, but I had my suspicions. Whoever it was didn't know me very well. I was headstrong. If they thought for one moment I would change my mind because of a despicable letter they were mistaken. If anything it had the opposite effect. Happiness for me meant being with Peter. I loved him and nothing was going to stand in the way of it.

On the morning of 30th June 1939 I stood outside St Catherine's Church as the summer sun warmed the ancient oak doors. My father had not stopped smiling all morning.

"Well Annie, you look a picture," he said, tucking my arm in his. "You can still change your mind you know…"

"I'm not going to do that Daddy," I laughed clutching the white roses he had grown especially for the day.

"Thank heavens, your mother would never forgive you after all the time she spent making the dress."

Mother had indeed spent many hours lovingly measuring, sewing, altering and transforming the cream silk fabric she had ordered from London into a beautiful, perfect wedding dress. And now here I was resplendent in the finished article, with a diamante tiara, and a cream veil worn the same way as my mother had when she married Daddy. I was ready to walk down the aisle to stand next to my beloved Peter, to take the solemn vows to love, honour and cherish, and become his wife until death should part us.

As the doors opened and the organ began to play, my bridesmaids, Joyce and Jean, my two best friends, moved to their positions behind Daddy and me. Jean I must tell was profoundly deaf, and very conscious of her disability. She couldn't hear the music, but could lip-read extremely well, and with Joyce's help she overcame her nervousness.

Either side of the aisle the pews were filled with our family and our friends. Standing with his back to us near the altar, with Michael his best man at his side, was Peter. My heart beat faster, and for a second I faltered.

"Annie," Daddy asked, "Are you alright?"

I drew in a deep breath and recovered. This was my day and I was going to relish every minute of it.

"Yes. I'm fine." I whispered

He squeezed my hand. "Come on then," he smiled as the organ sounded to announce the bride's arrival. "Better not keep him waiting any longer,"

An hour later with the bells of St Catherine's pealing, we, Mr. and Mrs Peter Barker, stepped out from the church into the warm June sunshine. Everyone seemed so happy, the photographer did his job well, as did Michael, organising the guests and directing them to the Colonels house where the reception was to be held, and reminding me when it was time for me to throw the bouquet. It was Joyce who caught it.

"Well held Joyce!" Michael called out to her above the whooping and cheering of the ladies. Unusually for Joyce, she blushed.

Colonel Travers and his wife Agnes were holding the reception as a wedding present for us. It must have cost them a pretty penny too.

The manor house was decorated beautifully, with gorgeous arrays of ribbons and flowers everywhere you looked, and the most lavish spread had been laid on, with seemingly endless champagne. Daddy swore the Colonel's cellar led directly under the English Channel to the French vineyards.

When the speeches were over, and most of the guests departed I felt I really must say something to Colonel Travers. After such a wonderful day I wanted to thank him and his wife in person, and went in from the garden in search of them.

Approaching the sitting room, I found the door slightly open, and within saw Mother and Lady Travers talking. About to knock, I hesitated; mother seemed quite distressed and had reverted to speaking in both French and English. I heard Peter's name mentioned, then she said a most curious thing:

"L'homme, il est trop parfait."

I could see quite clearly the look on Lady Travers face, which was one of bewilderment.

"Too perfect?" she exclaimed, "What on earth do you mean my dear?"

Mother then blew her nose rather noisily as if she had been crying, and continued.

"I don't know," she said, "maybe I am being silly, but there is something…oh dear…"

Lady Travers made vague soothing noises, obviously unable to fathom my mother's strange utterance, but nevertheless reassure her. Finally I couldn't stand it any longer, and went in.

"Mummy," I said, "why are you crying?"

"My child…!" Startled at my sudden appearance, she rose from her chair, took me in her arms and held me tight.

"Oh Annie," she sobbed, "I'm being silly. I should not be sad when my daughter has just married the man she loves."
Unsettled though I was by her odd behaviour, I put my arm around her.

"No mother," I said, "you should not. Now, who is too perfect?"

"It is I being foolish again. Ignore me."
At this point Lady Travers stepped in.

"You know what the problem is Annabelle?" she said. "No man is ever good enough as far as one's mother is concerned! Why, my son-in-laws are wonderful but…."
Then I smiled to myself at the thought of Mother seeing Peter as some sort of ridiculously ideal man.

"Peter's not perfect," I said, laughing now, "far from it. But he is just perfect for me."
I can still see the sadness in my mother's eyes as she hugged me again then whispered softly,

"Then my darling, that will have to be good enough for me."

CHAPTER TEN

"So I concluded that my mother was simply a little jealous, that's all." I said, taking another sip of water.

"Of course! Because you'd found happiness," said Sally. "Mum's like that with me." She glanced across to her mother. "At least you understand."

"Ah, grandparents and grandchildren," I laughed. "We are natural allies, and should be grateful for that. It was certainly true with my own dear Gran and Gramps – oh they were there too that day. My marrying Peter probably saved their lives, and it almost certainly saved mine."

"How?" Nicholas asked.

"I'll tell you later, one thing at a time! Anyway, nothing could spoil the day for me, not even the hidden tears and secret jealousies of my mother. After the reception we spent our wedding night at the 'Groom' and the next morning left for a honeymoon in Llandudno. It was bliss, sheer bliss. Of course everyone in the hotel there was talking about how there was going to be a war. But it all seemed so very far away. Hitler and the stupid Nazis, and the politicians all arguing - it might have been on another planet, none of it could touch us. I was just so full of happiness - there simply wasn't room in my heart for doubt or anxiety. We thought we were invincible, at least I did."

I closed my eyes for a few seconds; it was such a relief, to reveal him at last. When I opened them again Sally reached out and laid her hand on mine.

"Tell me more about Peter, Nan - did you ever show him the letter?

"I think Mother's talked enough for today." Laura spoke briskly. "I suggest we leave the next episode for another time."

I looked steadily at Laura, who now averted her gaze.

"But I've waited so long to tell you about Peter," I said recalling the happy memories, the good things of the past. "I did show him the letter Sally. Eventually. But you know, families are funny." Time to change the subject, the letter must be shelved, for now.

"There are some things that happen that are just so - comical, especially when it's someone else's dignity that suffers... Cricket!"

"Cricket?" Nicholas echoed, looking up from his teacup as if someone had just suggested getting up a side.

"Yes dear, cricket, the game that only men understand, or so I thought. We'd only been married a few months and Peter had been away during most of that time. Then one Friday, I was in the office when he telephoned. I had been longing for word that he'd be home soon and I wasn't disappointed; he told me he was arriving on the afternoon train.

After I'd finished the call Michael appeared and asked had that been Peter I was talking to? I said yes, but that I wouldn't be allowing him on any fishing trips or boys' adventures over the weekend – we scarcely saw each other as it was.

"I'm sorry Michael," I said, "I know Peter's your friend but he is also my husband now."

"Ah, no longer the gay bachelor," said Michael ruefully, "I understand. Though it was more a favour I was after."

"A favour?" I said.

"Yes. We're a man short on Saturday – the cricket, the 'Groom against the Star. I was going to ask if you could persuade Peter to step in. I've got some spare gear, so he wouldn't have to lug anything up on the train. Anyway not to worry, Henry's always keen to play."

I felt suddenly interested. Two images had flashed before my eyes. The first was Henry the station-master, togged out in cricket flannels puffing up to the crease with considerably less elegance than the engines that rolled alongside his immaculately swept platform each day.

The second picture was of Peter, also in cricket flannels, but loping majestically between the wickets, clocking up a century as the confused opposition scrambled in vain to bowl him out. I turned back to Michael.

"On the other hand," I said, "cricket is cricket. This is for the village, and one mustn't be selfish. I'll tell Peter it's imperative he play on Saturday."

Peter arrived later than expected. Mother, not best pleased at delaying the evening meal, became a little sullen. Daddy pointed out that Peter was only visiting for a short while, and that we should enjoy being together as a family. This was seconded by my grandfather, (he and my grandmother had stayed on after the wedding), which only made Mother sulkier. However when I mentioned that I had volunteered Peter to play for the 'Groom in the cricket match on the morrow, the mood around the table changed. I think it was Peter's reaction that my Mother enjoyed. For Peter himself seemed quite put out, not to say cross. It was alarming too, for none of us had heard him speak sharply before.

"I thought all Englishmen loved cricket Peter," smiled Mummy.

"But if I don't want to play…" he muttered.

Daddy got up from the table.

"Can't get out of it I'm afraid, Peter," he said flopping into his armchair. "Got to do one's duty for the village! On the other hand, look Annie, you shouldn't force a fellow…"

Then Peter's familiar, confident smile reappeared.

"I'm sorry," he said, his tone relaxed again, "it's just that I haven't played cricket for a while. But your father's right. I wouldn't want to let the side down."

"Not much chance of letting our motley crew down old boy," smiled Daddy. "We're all pretty much duffers when it comes to the great game. You'll probably show the lot of us up – 'Groom and Star!"

"As long as you turn up tomorrow Peter," I said, "That's all that really matters."

"So I don't have to play, I just turn up?"

"Of course you have to play," I laughed, "but as Daddy says, you'll probably outshine everyone."

"Do your best old chap," said Daddy, "just do your best."

"Yes Peter," repeated Mother, "just *do* your best." She then looked at him with a curious expression, though what she was thinking about I had no idea."

"So what happened at the match?" asked Sally, her eyes wide with interest. "I'm sure Peter would rather have been thought a show-off than let you down!"

I smiled. My memory was crystal clear.

59

"Well, when it was Peter's turn to go in and bat, he seemed very relaxed. So relaxed that Michael had to nudge him and remind him to go up. As he stepped on the crease the whole green went quiet. The entire village was watching him, waiting. And guess who was bowling for the Star? Henry – they had a man sick and Henry, a Horse and Groom regular of course, had swapped sides. Henry bowled an absolute gift, Peter lifted his bat, and the ball hit him square on the shoulder. Everyone laughed, including myself I'm afraid. It was just so funny we couldn't help it.

It was so obvious from the moment Peter picked up the bat that he couldn't play cricket to save his life. He hadn't been relaxed in the deckchair, it was simply that he barely even knew the order of play, oh dear! No wonder he'd been so distressed the day before. What an ordeal for him, poor boy. Afterwards everyone was very nice, slapping him on the back and thanking him for a good effort, and, perhaps worse 'being a sport'. Peter was most disconsolate, and quietly angry. Even my mother was kind, saying she was pleased to learn not every Englishman played cricket, and that this made him a more interesting person.

He tried to take her remarks with good grace, but said nothing and stomped off to the beer tent to drown his sorrows with Michael. His pride had suffered; he had shown himself to be as human as the next man, both through his sporting incompetence and worse, his anger at the fact.

And poor Colonel Travers got on the wrong side of Peter that day too. The Colonel happened to have brought his nephew I believe it was, a young man of about Peter's age, along to the match. Having introduced him to Peter they had walked off towards the far end of the green.

The three of them seemed deep in conversation when suddenly the Colonel stormed off in a rage. Peter and the other man watched him then carried on talking. I asked my friend Jean, if she knew what they were saying. She had been deaf after contracting mumps when she was two years old and her mother taught her to lip-read. Jean shook her head and laughed.

"Can't make head nor tail of it," she said. "Must be this home made beer, makes everything a blur!"

Anyway I had learned something that day: Peter was not the god-like being he appeared to be. And you know what? I loved him all the more because of it.

That night as Peter lay next to me I watched him, and listened to his slow, rhythmic breathing.

"Peter" I whispered, "There's something I want to tell you."
He turned sleepily towards me. "Can't it wait until morning?" I told him it couldn't. At this he then sat bolt upright.

"You're not pregnant?" he said.

"If I was," I said, "would you be pleased?"
Peter flung back the bedclothes, lit a cigarette and stood by the window looking out into the darkness.

"No I would not,"" he said coolly, "not yet."
Feeling hurt by his answer I replied that in that case, it was a good job I wasn't.

"Then what's so important that it can't wait till morning?" he said closing the curtains and switching on the bedside light.
I went to the dressing table drawer, took out the letter and handed it to him.

"What's this?"

"Read it," I said. "I received it four months before we were married. It refers to you."
He opened the letter and examined it in the lamplight. After a moment he replaced it in the envelope.

"Do you know who sent it?" he said.

"No," I replied.
He then asked if I thought it was true, that he was no good for me, and said if that were the case he would go forever out of my life. This made me cry. I couldn't bear it.
Peter put his arms around me. "I won't go. I promise," he said.

"But what if there is a war like everyone says, and you have to go and fight? Peter, suppose you..."
I didn't finish the awful thing I was about to say, because he kissed me. He kissed me so tenderly, and wiped away my tears.

"Shush my love," he whispered. "I will always return for you."

"Yes but what about the letter Mother?"

Now it was Nicholas wanting to know. I took the letter from Sally and read it out again. Then I said, "I thought it was my mother at first. You see, Mummy never really liked Peter."

Thinking of that moment in the bedroom with Peter, I held the letter out, not to a lamp as he had done, but towards the window and into the sun's rays. "Then I began to suspect Michael," I continued, "but I never …" I stopped suddenly and looked at the letter more closely. The sunlight was showing something on the paper I had not seen before, something *in* the paper.

At first I thought it was a blemish caused by the paper's age, then realised it was a watermark, of a family crest. I felt sure I had seen something similar before, but where? With a shock I remembered. I quickly returned the letter to its envelope, and placed it back in the box.

"Now, where were we?" I begin again "Oh yes Cricket…that was a subject we never mentioned again, especially in Peter's presence."

"Mother - are you alright?" Laura asked.

"Do you want me to tell you about him or not?"

"Not if is upsets you like this." Laura said

"It doesn't."

"Something just did." "That mysterious letter!"

"Yes, the mysterious letter," echoed Nicholas.

My children's concern was admirable but I had to keep going, whatever it was about the letter would have to wait. I took a deep breath. 'Relax Annabelle' I thought '- remember the good things first.'

"Peter and I were very happy all through the summer of '39. We lived with my parents and Gran and Gramps - one big happy family, though I know Peter felt a little left out when Mum, me, and the old-timers all started talking in French. He could speak the language but chose not to. Daddy of course was delighted to have an ally in Peter – whenever the Gallic Gaggle, as he used to call it, started up he'd talk loudly in English to Peter about really English things like Elgar and the Battle of Agincourt, urging Peter to join in."

"And did he?" asked Sally.

"No. He told me he didn't want to take sides. I said it was only in fun. I don't think he knew the Shakespeare speeches – certainly not off by heart like Daddy. But he thought he was expected to, and that made him awkward I suppose.

It was just like the cricket! Oh dear, when I think of poor Peter's face, trying to look so dignified and do the right thing, with my father slapping him on the back. Gramps and Daddy were usually drunk by that time and laughing their heads off, bless them."

"So Peter never joined in these drinking sessions?" said Sally.

"He used to take a drink certainly, but I never saw him drunk. Never. You see he liked to be in control. Failing at cricket, failing to know a speech from Shakespeare, or at anything someone else could do, was a loss of control for Peter."

"But he had his own talents – his painting?" said Sally.

"Certainly – he was a fine artist. But all artists are perfectionists, and maybe the search for perfection is also an urge to control. Though when Peter was painting he was different somehow, more…more free in a way. I think art was a kind of escape for him."

"Escape from what?" said Sally.

"I could never work that out, - himself perhaps. But we were very contented, even with Peter away so much on army business.

When the war started, in September 1939 I knew he would be away, but for how long I didn't know. I did of course miss him but I never worried unduly. I had great faith. People kept saying it would be all over soon, except my mother of course, who forbade Daddy from saying so in the house, lest Gran and Gramps skip back home to Maison Vert.

When the war started, in September 1939 I knew he would be away for a long time. I did of course miss him but I never worried unduly. I had great faith. People kept saying it would be all over soon, except my mother of course, who forbade Daddy from saying so in the house, lest Gran and Gramps skip back home to Maison Vert.

In England the sun carried on shining then autumn passed into winter. Peter wrote me regular letters, beautiful letters…His visits home became less frequent, but as long as he came home I was happy.

To me the war still seemed a million miles away, despite Daddy insisting we listen to the news of it on the wireless every evening. It was only when the Germans went into France that the reality of it hit me.

The thought of Gran and Gramps home being overrun, Nazis stomping through St Jacques, and ordinary French people – their friends and neighbours among them – being brutalised, perhaps murdered, made me cry.

How my Grandmother and my mother wept. Gramps was just very quiet about it all; you could sense a deep sadness in him, and anger too.

After Dunkirk even my father couldn't hide his emotions. There was a sense that France's fate was sealed when all those poor soldiers were cut down on the beaches."

My voice failed me for a moment, my mind held spellbound in a world a lifetime ago.

"Goodness, it's 2 o'clock, how time flies when an old woman talks."

"Goodness is the word Mum," laughed Nicholas, getting up to pour more tea from the pot. "What a fantastic story."

"And all true!"

"No, no, I believe every word," said Nicholas hastily.
Laura looked down at the carpet. I smiled at them both.

"So what happened next?" said Sally, passing me a refilled teacup.

"Peter's visits became very few, but that was the war. I was far from the only woman in that position. But then came September 3rd 1941."
Laura lifted her eyes from the carpet and shot a glance at Nicholas. She had sensed something, the approach of emotion. Laura didn't like emotion.

"You must be tired, Mum, fed up sitting here – maybe we could go into the village, we saw a lovely pub on the way up. Nicholas can drive us all…"
I pretended not to hear. The sadness was coming on. I could feel it filling my heart, like poison.

From here on it would only get worse, unlocking doors that had been sealed for so long. The bad thoughts would soon be spilling, flying out like spectres, wraiths, to haunt and torment me all over again. I began speaking again, with an emphasis suggesting that what I had to say now could not be ignored.

"I was alone in the house that morning. Mother was out at the WRVS centre; Daddy at his surgery and Gran and Gramps had gone into the village.

It was raining, a persistent, dreary downpour, the sky like lead, a grey light everywhere.

I longed for the rain to stop so I could go outside. Meanwhile I sat in the parlour and read a book. The place seemed deathly quiet, nothing but the steady, constant sound of the rain.

At half-past eleven there was a knock on the door. It was a telegram boy. He said

"Mrs Peter Barker?" and looked me straight in the eye for a second before handing me a brown envelope then turning his face away. I remember thanking him and mumbling something as I closed the door.

I took the envelope into the parlour and laid it on the table. I could see it was from the War Department. I thought about not opening it, or putting it on the fire and just returning to my book. Of course, I couldn't.

My hands were already trembling; I got Daddy's paperknife from his desk, slit the envelope open and tore the corner off the message in my haste. I knew the words even as I read them: 'It is with regret that we have to inform you your husband Captain Peter Barker is missing in action, presumed dead.'

I can't recall what I did in those immediate few seconds afterwards. Did I cry, scream, faint? Strangely I don't think I did any of those things. I can recall a kind of rushing of air, like some howling gale had swept past, sucking all the oxygen from me. That's it, I remember feeling unable to breath, and dizziness.

At the same time I saw Peter framed in the doorway, as he had been the day he went away, the last time I saw him.

"Don't look back," he had called out as he walked down the path. But as he reached the gate he had turned and run back to me, taken me in his arms and kissed me once more."

CHAPTER ELEVEN

"In the days following the telegram I was in a catatonic state, barely speaking, hardly moving from my room.

As the grief took effect I succumbed to fearfully intense fits of crying, hour after hour of sobbing, sometimes with my mother, and sometimes, to her greater distress, locked in my bedroom.

Daddy proffered sleeping draughts, which sometimes I took, and sometimes vehemently refused.

Then I became much quieter, sitting either upstairs or in the parlour with a book, my body quite still; my breathing barely perceptible.

For long periods I did not look at the page, but stared into space, my cheeks wet with tears.

I had written to Peter's Aunt and Uncle in Surrey – it was they who were his closet relatives, since his parents were both dead. I hoped perhaps for some comfort in that quarter, but never received a reply, from which I concluded that they had never liked me.

Mother, Father, Gran and Gramps were cosseting me, wrapping me up in cotton wool and avoiding any conversation about Peter. I was feeling smothered, and yearned for some outlet, a proper conversation; some activity other than the well-meaning sympathy my family and their friends specialised in.

On an impulse I telephoned Joyce, who had by this time joined the army and was living in London. Apart from the desire to talk to her, I thought she might be able to find out something of what had happened to Peter, perhaps obtain confirmation of his death.

A fortnight later she took leave and came back to Kingsford. It was the first time I had seen her since the telegram, and being my oldest friend I was looking forward to her visit; little did I anticipate the can of worms it would open in my mind.

I was in the parlour when she arrived. Through the half-open hall door I heard her and my mother talking in hushed tones, as if visiting a sick person. Mother then asked Joyce if there was any news about Peter.

"I'm afraid not," Joyce replied, "only what I told you on the telephone."

"If only they could find his body then maybe…"

"Look Mrs Frazer, about this theory of yours, don't you think it's just a little far fetched?" said Joyce.

66

"Well Peter was involved in undercover work, espionage, you said so," Mother whispered. "Did you find anything from the War Office? I thought perhaps with your working there…"

"Yes Mrs Frazer, but even if the British wanted the Germans to think Peter was dead…"

"When he was really still alive."

"He wouldn't want Annabelle to think he was dead," Joyce whispered intently. "He would have found some way to tell her, surely?"

I could not make out Mother's reply. The next thing I heard her say was, "Go through to the parlour now Joyce dear, she's in there."

I could barely believe what I had heard, and on several counts. My mother going behind my back to try to find something out about Peter, and involving my best friend in the process was shocking enough.

But that she thought Peter's death might have been faked was simply boggling, the stuff of nightmares. I did not move from the couch as Joyce gently opened the parlour door.

"Hello," she said. "Your mum said you were asleep Annie."

"Well I'm not, why don't you ask me how I'm feeling? Everyone else does." Joyce smiled and sat down beside me.

I didn't want her to be emotional, but to be strong. She seemed to sense this. I desperately wanted to ask her about Peter and the conversation in the hall, but at the same time I was afraid.

"I'm in a dark place Joyce," my voice trembled. "Can't escape. I want Peter to come back, hold me in his arms again and tell me he loves me, but he won't. In my dreams I hear him, I see him, but the darkness returns and he's gone. I might as well be dead, at least it would stop this pain."

It was no good. The next second I had crumpled into Joyce's arms and we sat, holding one another, in a desperate embrace, both of us crying.

When the tears were spent we began to talk. Joyce told me about her job in London. She made it sound quite an adventure, dodging bombs and rushing for the air-raid shelters. This was Joyce's way; not one of endless handkerchiefs, and 'there-there dear', but reminding me there was a world out there, with things going on, taking me out of myself.

"And we have quite a good social life considering there's a war on," she said.

"Trust you to make a state of emergency an excuse for fun dear!"

"Good heavens yes - R and R is most important to the war effort!" she laughed. "Food's tight and I've had my share of nights sleeping down the underground, but there's plenty of dances and no end of nice looking men…" Joyce stopped short. "Sorry Annie. I mean…"

I smiled and squeezed her hand.

"Don't be silly," I said. "You mustn't walk on tiptoe around me. I was about to ask if you'd had any intrigues of that sort."

Joyce then looked thoughtful.

"Annie," she said, "I know its early days but, well, might you consider a change of scene?"

"Where to?" I said.

"It's just a thought, but the department – the War Office – are always looking for people with certain skills. Your French is pretty good, you could get a job."

"What in London, as a translator you mean?"

"Perhaps – but there's other work too."

I could feel her watching me as she said this.

"   I mean you're not going to spend your whole life in Kingsford are you."

"I had rather intended to." I replied with some abruptness

"Anyway, I can't leave Mum and Dad. Mummy needs help around the house."

Joyce gave me a wry smile. "Arranging flowers all day Annie?"

"No!" I said, "it's out of the question I'm afraid. I can't go."

A noise from the hallway made me turn. Mother had been listening. I got up and quietly closed the door. "

"Joyce," I said at last, "What were you and Mummy talking about? Is there something I should know about Peter?"

Joyce looked at me uneasily for a second then said,

"Look, all I know is this. Peter was in France, working with the resistance. They were on a mission and were ambushed. The reports say he was taken prisoner."

I felt a pounding sensation in my chest. The possibility that Peter was alive suddenly seemed more unspeakable than his death. Despair, grief, one could suffer. The idea of hope now was appalling. "Then no one is certain – I mean, he could be - "

"Annie, the Gestapo don't let people go. You mustn't entertain any - ideas - for your own sanity."

"So what *was* Mother talking about?"

"I really have no idea, and that's the truth. War affects people in peculiar ways."

"Yes, yes I suppose that's true, but…."

"Will you think about what I've said Annie, about coming to London? I'm sure you'd be worth your weight in gold to the department."

I was thinking all right, in fact my mind was racing. If there was the remotest chance that Peter was alive I had to find out, and the best place to do that was working in the War Office."

"I'll do it," I replied. "London here we come!"

Two weeks later Joyce met me off the train at Euston. Being a cold October day the first thing she said was that I should have wrapped up warmer, and asked where my gloves were. I said I appreciated the maternal gestures, laughed and told her to stop clucking.

We walked arm in arm down the wide streets. I hadn't visited London since the war began, and found the sight of bombed-out buildings and sandbags now quite sobering. The hustle and bustle of trams and buses and people all around however, suggested that the Londoners mood was very much business as usual.

As we reached Baker Street Joyce stopped and pointed across the street.

"It's the building over there," she said, "see the big wooden double doors? I've got to dash now Annie, see you about five eh, oh and the best of British!"

I watched as she disappeared around the corner, marvelling how at home she seemed in the big city. Being early for my appointment I sat on a bench to wait. Two young lovers strolled by arm in arm, she inclining her head against his shoulder. I felt a lump in my throat, the hint of tears behind my eyes.

Pull yourself together I told myself; London was full of courting couples and I would have to get used to it. It wasn't only couples though. In the other direction a young man was walking away from me. He was tall, as tall as Peter, with the same blonde hair visible beneath his army officer's cap. I rose from the bench and began following, breaking into a run to catch up with him. The closer I got the more convinced I was that it was Peter. My heart was beating so hard I could barely breath.

As I approached he seemed to slow down. I reached out to touch his shoulder, but he turned and waved to a young lady across the road. Then he saw me. "Are you alright miss?" he asked. "Is there anything I can do?"

I drew back. It wasn't Peter, not even the faintest resemblance to him. I apologised and ran back to the bench. I felt suddenly very sick. I took some deep breaths, and the nausea began to pass. What an idiot I was. I looked at my watch and saw that it was almost time. I straightened my coat, tidied my hair and applied more lipstick. I wanted this job and had made up my mind to get it."

CHAPTER TWELVE

"Mrs Parker did you say?"

The elderly clerk peered at me over his half-moon spectacles.

"Barker. I've an appointment. This is 64 Baker Street isn't it? The War Widows Pension Office?"

"Yes, but you're not down on my list. Have you filled out your forms?"

"Oh, no – I'm here regarding a position? I was told to see Colonel Heath."

The clerk put down his papers, took off his spectacles and looked at me more intently. "I see. May I trouble you for some identification please madam?"

I took out my marriage certificate and handed it to him. After examining the document he gave it back and rose from his desk. "I'm so sorry Mrs Barker. Come with me please."

Following him across the lobby we stepped into a lift. A moment later we were on the third floor. The clerk pointed down the corridor. "First on the left – the Colonel is expecting you."

I tapped lightly on the door indicated. "Please enter," came a voice from within. I found myself in a spacious, wood-panelled room, where behind an enormous desk sat an affable-looking middle-aged man in officer's uniform. He was rummaging in the desk drawers.

"Ah, Mrs Barker, do sit down won't you. I'm Colonel Heath, I won't keep you a moment."

It's funny what you notice. I remember the room was a larger, grander version of Mr Oakes senior's office in Kingsford. The furniture was bigger, the windows taller, and the carpet thicker. The ceiling was considerably higher and in one corner there was even a cobweb in roughly the same place as in Mr Oakes's room. This gave me a kind of contentment, something tangible to hold on to in this strange place, far away from home.

Having at last extracted a file from the drawer, the Colonel rose to shake my hand. He offered me a cigarette, which I declined. Then lighting one for himself he took a long hard draw on it and sat on the corner of the desk.

"I see you've done office work."

"Yes but I have other skills," I replied. "A language, if it's any use at all."

"Such skills are admirable Mrs Barker. We're also looking for people with certain – qualities. How good is your French though?"

"A little rusty, but I can brush it up pretty quickly."

"I understand your mother was born near Dieppe?"

"Yes. She doesn't know I'm here I have to say. I thought it better to tell her when – I mean if, I get the job. She tends to worry unnecessarily about things."

"Quite right."

"How did you know my mother was born in Dieppe?" I said, "I didn't mention it in my application."

Ignoring my question he said, "Have you ever done any acting?"

"Acting?"

"Does that seem a strange question?"

"For a translating post, yes. But then I did wonder why translators were needed in the Pensions Office."

"Quite. But what's the answer? The acting I mean."

"Only an Oscar Wilde play, with our local amateur theatre."

"I'm sure you were splendid!"

"It was a very small part."

"Then perhaps it's time you had a larger one," said the Colonel, smiling. "Each man – and woman – in their time plays many parts Mrs Barker. Isn't that what the Bard taught us?"

I smiled. "Yes, my father often quotes that one. Though without the women of course."

The Colonel then began talking to me about Kingsford, looking through the file he had taken from the desk as he did so. When he asked if I would mind being away from the village and my friends and family for a while, I told him about Joyce and that I could stay with her at her digs in Kensington. Hearing this he looked up from the file. "If you come to work for us," he said, "you won't be in London for very long."

"But this is the War Widows Pension Office?" I said.

Colonel Heath smiled. "They're downstairs."

"Then what do you do up here?"

He smiled again. "All in good time Mrs Barker, all in good time. Listen, I'm going to have some tea sent up for us and then we'll chat a little further. In the meantime, I wonder if you'd mind reading this, and then just putting your signature along the bottom there."

He got up and handed me some papers then crossed to the door.

"You'll find a pen on the desk"

"What is this?" I said.

"A copy of the Official Secrets Act. Milk and sugar Mrs Barker?"

CHAPTER THIRTEEN

On the way home I decided it would be best to tell my parents sooner rather than later that I had been offered a job in London, and since I was required to leave the following day, there was really no other way. Mother began to cry but Daddy managed to calm her a little, and wished me well. That evening I packed quietly and went to bed early.

Arriving at the station gate I was relieved to see the platform empty. Today of all days I needed to be alone. My parents had wanted to come and see me off, but I had told them I didn't want any fuss. Putting down my suitcase however, I heard someone call my name. Turning I saw Michael.

"Michael – hello - how did you…?"

"Your ma, but never mind about that," he said, grabbing my case and taking my arm. "Let's go to the waiting room, we have to talk."

"There's no time." I protested, "My train will be here in a moment."

"Your train's been delayed." He ushered me into the little waiting room then shut the door behind us. "I've checked."

We stood awkwardly facing each other with the suitcase between us.

"You never said you were coming to see me off," I said.

"You wouldn't have allowed it."

He smiled now, digging his hands into in his trouser pockets. I looked at him, and felt I was seeing him for the first time. He was lovely, a kind man.

Suddenly I thought: we should have been together. How easy at that moment it would have been for me to take his hand in mine and go back home with him, forget London and Peter and the whole damnable war. But I knew Michael was also going. He had joined the RAF, and was leaving Kingsford that following week. What then would be the point of my staying behind? And I could not ignore the terrible, unresolved doubt about Peter. I looked at Michael again."

"You've had your hair cut" I laughed, "It suits you, really."

Michael ran his hand over the back of his neck. It looked still prickly from the clippers.

"Regulation job," he frowned. "In a few days I'll be in a flying jacket, with a big sheepskin collar around my neck."

"I wish I could see you in it!"

"So do I."

"Will you be flying straight away?"

"Good lord I hope not. There's a thing called training you know, though my A.T.C. stuff should give me a head start. How about you?"

"A few days in London then off somewhere for training before… they've told me so little. I'm nervous as hell if you must know."

"Annie," said Michael solemnly, "Why didn't you want me to see you off today?"

I hesitated, the tears were never far away, and I could feel them pricking my eyes. "You might have asked me not to go," I said softly.

"And if I had - what would your answer have been?"

As Michael inclined his head towards me a train whistle sounded in the distance.

"I…I must go Michael," I said, opening the waiting room door.

I wanted him to kiss me, to hold me and kiss me, as he had done that night at the Manor House, but now without pretence or excuse; perhaps it was what I had always wanted. As I turned again to leave he took me by the shoulders, and I inhaled his masculine aroma. With one hand I cupped the back of his neck as we pressed against each other. Through the open door I heard voices outside on the platform.

"Well I never," said Mabel Jarvis the teashop proprietor, in supposedly discreet tones. "Young Michael Oakes and Doctor Frazer's girl - and her poor husband not yet cold in the ground!"

CHAPTER FOURTEEN

"So you and Michael…" Sally hesitated.

"Courted?" I said. "That word meant so much then."

"Nan you're such a tease!"

I smiled at Sally, "After our kiss I boarded the train to London. From there I was sent to Wanborough Manor."

"Wanborough Manor?" said Nicholas "Isn't that down in Surrey?"

"Just outside Guildford, a grand old place, it had been commandeered along with a number of big houses up and down the country. It was there I was to learn my unlovely new trade."

"You were already a trained secretary," Sally remarked.

"Yes Sally I was, But this house was being used as a school for SOE - The Special Operations Executive. It was Churchill's idea after Dunkirk to train people from all walks of life as field agents…."

"And what happened when they found out you were nothing more than a shorthand typist?" grinned Laura, "Packed off back to dear old Kingsford and arranging the flowers with chez Mamma I suppose."

I glanced towards my daughter, " My, my Laura, when had she become so cynical?"

Laura scowled at me but said nothing,

"Mother! Do be quiet and let Nan carry on." Sally smiled encouragingly. I took a deep breath and continued my story. "Our role was to covertly harass and thwart the enemy behind the lines. The whole operation was hush-hush at the time. Officially we did not exist."

"Are you really telling us you'd been recruited as some sort of spy Mum?" said Laura; a dismissive, disbelieving tone was in her voice.

"Spy, saboteur, undercover agent – yes."

"How thrilling!" Sally said.

"How ridiculous." Said Laura.

This time it was Nicholas who came to my rescue. "Laura, will you please be quiet and let Mother finish her story; she obviously wants us to know…"

Laura sighed heavily; and threw me a terrible, dismissive glance. "Very well, carry on with this charade if you must."

76

"I must Laura, I really must tell you all, its a part of my life that you don't know. "

Laura turned away from me, Nicholas and Sally looked on in surprise and wonder, and in that momentary silence, I took my cue.

"Our superiors discouraged us from thinking in any such *romantic* terms. The instruction we received was practical in every sense. They didn't fill our heads with the idea we were special, it was the job that mattered. We were given fictitious new identities, and everything about it had to be right, from the labels in our clothing to the fillings in our teeth, it all had to be genuine, or appear so. The first thing each of us learnt was the cover story of the character we would be playing night and day from the minute we were dropped behind enemy lines."

"Wow – and who was your cover Nan?" asked Sally.

I smiled recalling the memory. "I became Claudette Simonais, the unmarried niece of a chocolate maker located just outside Paris. My story was, I'd travelled up from my home in the Loire valley to help in my Aunt with her business. I was also to have various sick relatives dotted around France, which would explain any journeys I might have to make. Each of these relatives would have real identities among the resistance in case my story was ever checked. Those four weeks of training were rather like going back to school. I never thought that by the time I was your age Sally I would know how to kill a man with my bare hands. And then of course there was the cyanide pill…"

"Oh Mum!" said Nicholas queasily. "Would you ever have taken it?"

"I was never quite sure of that. Given certain alternatives, I think yes."

"Gosh how gruesome!" grimaced Sally. "And did you ever kill anyone?""

"Now who's being gruesome!" said Nicholas.

"If you don't stop asking those sort of questions young lady," Laura said, "we're going home. And are we ever going to have lunch today, Time is getting on."

"Laura's right Mum, we should go eat soon if we're going," said Nicholas.

"Yes, that's a good idea. Could one of you fetch my cardigan?" I said, "I feel slight chilly."

Sally took my cardigan from the wardrobe and draped it around my shoulders.

"Are we ready then?" Asked Nicholas, "Here's your handbag Mum"

"Thanks you dear," I said tucking it down the side of the wheelchair, "I'm ready, but oh! but I've just remembered, there's one thing I must tell you about first."

"Maybe we could have some lunch sent in?" said Laura, not entirely flippantly.

"There's plenty of time Laura," said Nicholas, "This is Mum's day, remember." They all sat down again. "Carry on Nan, I'm enjoying this."

"Well, there was something that had always baffled me, about Peter's Aunt and Uncle, the people that brought him up.
When I arrived at Wanborough Manor, I realised it was only a couple of miles from where they lived. Peter and I had been to stay with them you see, just the once, soon after we were married. It was so odd not getting a reply from them after the telegram."

"Families can be strange," said Nicholas.

"Tell me about it," chimed in Laura.

"Had they seemed close to Peter?" asked Sally, "I mean, when you visited?

"Kind of, but it was hard to tell. After the telegram, even if they'd disliked me, you would have thought Peter being their adopted son to all intents and purposes there'd have been some communication but no, nothing from them. Anyway, now I was on the doorstep, I thought I'd investigate a little."

"You mean spy on them?" said Sally enthralled. "Your first mission!"
I smiled, "I didn't really have any plan, other than to see if they were still living there. Had they received my letter, and if not, did they even know about the telegram? Since I was his official next of kin, it was a possibility. It was all so unresolved and played on my mind. I wanted some answers from them. No one was allowed outside the grounds while at Wanborough.

But I was so curious about the strange silence of dear Aunt Bertha and Uncle Hubert that one night I purloined a bicycle from the shed, squeezed through a gap in the hedge, and set out to find their house. It proved more difficult than I had imagined. Peter had driven us down before; now it was dark, and what's more the civil defence had removed all the road signs. After a few wrong turnings however, I saw a large pair of gates with a distinctive floral pattern in the wrought iron that I remembered."

"And did it look like they were they there," Sally asked "Aunt Bertha and Uncle thingy I mean?"

"Hubert." Prompted Nicholas, now very attentive.

" No. There were weeds everywhere, and the house was boarded up."

"They had moved away?"

"It seemed so, but, tell me this: when a family moves, does the house get boarded up?"

"Not usually," said Nicholas. "Unless it's due to be demolished."

"Exactly."

"I imagine it was condemned, structurally unsound," said Nicholas.

"It was a fine property, in excellent repair."

"Something a bit fishy you thought?" Sally said.

"Yes, I was even more curious now. I found a garden bench to climb up on then slid a cycle spanner behind the board on one of the windows. Unfortunately I slipped and fell back into the overgrown garden. I stood still for a moment, but all seemed quiet so I tried again. The spanner gave little leverage. Something longer was needed to prise the board away from the window. I was nervous now, too nervous to use the torch I had brought, but by the light of the moon I made out a wooden pole leaning against the wall. I picked my way through the grass and found that the implement was a spade. I took it over to the window and stood up on the bench again.

Feeling with my fingers for a space where the board wasn't nailed quite flat and finding a gap, I dug the edge of the spade in and leant heavily on the handle. As my weight bore down the board fell away and dropped into the garden, the long grass silencing any impact.

Peering through the window I then got a terrible shock; someone was on the inside looking straight at me! Then I realised what I had seen. Caught in a shaft of moonlight was my own reflection in the windowpane. Composing myself I forced the bottom sash open with the spade and climbed in. The musty smell suggested the place had been unoccupied for some time. I felt for the curtains, closed them behind me and switched on the torch. The beam fell upon a painting on the wall. It was a portrait of Peter's grandfather; I recalled it from our visit. But also, their furniture was still there. They'd left everything behind."

"Perhaps they sold the house and contents included," said Nicholas.

"Ah, but what about the portrait," said Sally, "they wouldn't leave that behind."

"You'd think not but there it was. I went upstairs - beds, dressers and chairs were all there. But there was something more, and far more peculiar: their clothes were still hanging in the wardrobes. It was as if they had just got up and walked out leaving everything behind. ."

"I bet it felt a bit spooky Nan?"

"It did. I retraced my steps downstairs to the open window, dropped back into the garden and found my bicycle. I was just wheeling it towards the gate when I heard a cracking sound behind me. I turned, and straining my eyes towards the shrubbery at the bottom of the garden, I became convinced there was a figure standing there, watching me. I jumped on the cycle and pedalled away from the house as fast as I could. The figure in the garden had really scared me and the house - quite eerie."

"Ooh!" Sally gave a little shiver. "So what happened next?"

"Lunch?" said Laura.

"We're just getting to the exciting bit Mum!" said Sally

"Yes, lunch!" repeated Laura.

"Perhaps we could push on till teatime, or get an early dinner at the pub, if you you'd rather?" said Nicholas.

"Or an early breakfast at this rate," muttered Laura.

"I'm all right," I said. "But no, no, please, let me tell you, we'll go to lunch in a moment. Now where was I – oh yes, the course – at the end of the four weeks I had passed with flying colours, so they told me.

Colonel Heath asked to see me before I was sent out. I imagined he just wanted to say goodbye and good luck, I couldn't think of any other reason. He smiled as I entered his office, and invited me to sit down then asked if I had my new identity, which of course I did; he knew this. Then he told me I would receive further orders after I had landed in France. He sounded grave, almost apologetic as he spoke. Of course I already knew what awaited me out there, sooner or later."

"How do you mean Nan?" asked Sally.

"We had no illusions. Let's just say most SOE operatives flew out on a one-way ticket..." I paused, and looked at each one in turn, they were staring back at me.... now I had their attention... I smiled "And on that note" I said "We will now go to lunch. Wheel me out Nicholas, there's a dear."

Gestapo Headquarters Paris   November 1941

Kurt Gruber, in plain civilian suit, entered the building and strode briskly past the guard seated in the lobby. As he mounted the staircase the man sprang to his feet and shouted after him.

"Halt, halt – your papers - halt!"

Gruber turned to see the guard with a rifle aimed at him.

Retracing his steps, he took out his identity papers; the guard examined them.

"I'm sorry sir," he said, handing back the documents.

Gruber continued up the staircase. After a few seconds he stopped and looked back.

"Don't be. If you had not challenged me, I would have had you shot. No - I'd have shot you myself. Now get back to your post." His eyes were cold, expressionless. The guard fumbled nervously with his weapon, gave an awkward salute and clicked his heels to attention.

Reaching the top of the grand staircase, Gruber smiled to himself. He was looking forward to meeting the commandant.

CHAPTER FIFTEEN

"That was a lovely lunch, thank you Nicholas."

"Pleasure Mum, glad you enjoyed it," he smiled.

We were back at the home and it was now almost three.

"I enjoyed the change of scene as much as anything. Now I'm just glad to sink into my old armchair again."

"Can we continue now Nan?" said Sally.

"Your grandmother might be tired," said Laura.

"Tired of you telling her so I expect."

"Don't be rude Sally!" said Laura sharply.

"Sorry Mum, – but I don't know why you stopped us in the middle of the story over lunch…."

"Sally, there were other people there, and I'm sure they didn't want to listen to some gory wartime tale over their Ploughman's."

"It was more interesting than the conversation that family on the next table were having" quipped Nicholas "The weather and which supermarket does the best frozen asparagus – I ask you! The old boy with them was quietly all ears to your yarn Mum."

"It's not a 'yarn', Uncle Nick," protested Sally.

"No, I just meant it's exciting, I really do…"

"As I say – we're not all enamored with the war." Laura snapped. There was silence for a moment before Sally said,

"Do go on Nan, please."

"Yes Mum, do," said Nicholas. Laura turned and stared out of the window.

"Very well," I said and gave a little sigh. "I had finished my training and spent a few days waiting for orders. The cars brought the other agents and myself to the airfield in the mid afternoon.

In a small hangar were several trestle tables, with a handful of uniformed men and women stood behind them. Our identity papers and clothing had been checked and double-checked - the slightest thing out of place would have meant certain death for any of us so everything had to be right. And now, here was the moment we would leave behind our old selves, surrendering the last remaining artefacts of our lives into brown envelopes. For each of us, there was also a carefully worded letter addressed to our next of kin.

The hardest part for me was saying good-bye to Peter. As I dropped his photograph into the envelope, I realised that I might never look at his face again. All I had now was the memory of his face, and I did not want it to fade.

For several minutes I turned my wedding ring around and around on my finger, not wanting to remove it. When I finally relinquished it, a young soldier sealed the envelope and placed it in a wire tray with the others, to be posted along with the letter to my parents, if anything should... I imagined them, opening their front door one day; just as I had done ....

We drank tea, smoked, played cards and chatted aimlessly till it was time to leave. No one spoke of the future, or of why they were there. I was told I was going in alone. As the only female I preferred it that way.

After take-off, my mind lulled by the drone of the engines I thought: soon I may be with Peter again. It wasn't a death wish exactly, just a feeling that I wouldn't mind, not if it meant I could see him. I had no fear of the end itself, but of how it would come. The cyanide pill sewn into my handkerchief was constantly at the back of my mind, I'm sure it was for all of us. Then doubt, panic, suddenly leapt at me. Why was I doing this? Why had I been fool enough to volunteer? Perhaps I was as mad as everyone at home said, or what I suspected they thought. After all, who in their right mind would elect to die? I felt part of me was already dead I suppose, the day the telegram came.

My body still functioned, smiled in all the right places, laughed when I was supposed to and cried when alone. I ached for Peter, longed for him to hold me and tell me everything was all right, and it had all been a ghastly mistake. What I would have given to hear his voice.

The moon in that crisp and clear November night was almost full. Coming up ahead of us, long and glistening, was the Loire.

"There's our welcome mat," came the co-pilot's voice over the radio.

The river, vast, ghostly, rose quickly up, skimming the plane a hairsbreadth beneath us, then was gone.

I wondered what it was like down there now. Maison Vert, already far behind us, St Jacques, …I couldn't think about it, there was so much I couldn't think about, not now. I stared at the moon again. Soon it would be time to jump. Maybe tonight will end it I thought, a single shot from a sniper's bullet, or tomorrow, sometime soon.

In the far distance, on the ground, a row of tiny lights flickered. As the fuselage door was wrenched open, the whole roaring sky seemed to blast into the cabin. "Time to go." The young airman guided me forward, towards the black space.

The rushing air leapt up to embrace me. I felt a sharp tap on my shoulder. Checking the parachute straps and tightening the belt holding the radio around my waist, I closed my eyes and jumped.

Counting one - two – three, I pulled the cord. My armpits jerked upwards, I heard a frump – the 'chute was open. Everything slowed, quietened.

The unseen plane was already a dying hum, replaced now by a soft breeze and the flap-flap of the "chute, like the soft wings of a bird above me, black, like a raven, despatching its cargo, to life or to death. With a thud, I hit the ground. As I scrambled the parachute into a tight bundle, a figure emerged from the darkness, coming towards me. I searched my pocket for the revolver.

"The owl in winter is a pretty sight." The voice was female.

"But not as clear as a silver fox," I replied.

The girl gave a signal, whereupon others appeared from the trees and began quickly extinguishing the flares.

"You must come with me," said the girl, grabbing me by the arms, half dragging me to a waiting lorry.

"Put her in the back," said a man.

In the back were half a dozen more resistance. Arms reached down to pull me aboard. I saw the girl's face properly now, and realised I wasn't the only one scared. They all seemed on edge, hurrying, chaotic. The engine started but then almost immediately fell silent again. Someone at the front shouted. "Everyone out! – Trucks coming!"

Jumping from the lorry we ran for the ditches at the side of the road. The first girl and an older woman grabbed my arms. Then I felt the girl's grip slacken as she fell. The other woman continued dragging me across the road and into the ditch.

"Stay here" she whispered, leaving me squashed tightly between two of the men.

As the engine noises grew louder, the men and women moved their guns into position. The vehicles drew nearer, slowed and stopped. There was a slamming of doors as the soldiers alighted to investigate the truck. From further up the ditch someone shouted, "Now!"

The night air shook with gunfire. I screamed, cramming my hands over my ears and burying myself as far down in the ditch as I could go. The shadows beside me were leaping upwards, firing, some hurling grenades and bombs. Intermittently there came flashes of light, a blast, then screaming. Nothing could blot out the screams, one after another. I lay rigid, too terrified to even lift my head.

I do not know how long I remained there, my body pressing itself against the wet earth, my face buried under my arms.

Suddenly I felt something heavy bearing down on me from above, crushing the breath from my lungs, and forcing my body into the sodden ground. I heard someone call the retreat. Everything went quiet now save for my own laboured breathing, gasping for air beneath the burden smothering me.

Voices, German voices, rang out intermittently above. I heard the tread of boots, which took a few paces then stopped. Someone was standing above me, just a few short yards away. Shattering the silence came a single shot. The body pressing down on me jolted momentarily then was still again. I felt something warm trickle onto my cheek, and closed my eyes more tightly.

"Schnell, Schnell!" The shout came from further along the road. Another voice joined in, followed by a flaring sound then laughter. I smelled a familiar aroma, cigarette smoke.

After a few minutes the footsteps retreated, the voices faded. There was a snarl of engines, a crunch of gears, and soon, silence.

Trying to move, the weight on top of me felt immense. I stopped pushing, and attempted instead to squirm free from underneath. Any space I found however simply dropped the weight lower, wedging me more firmly. I was now face down, could barely breathe let alone move. The mud was now rapidly becoming water. Panicking, and with visions of drowning, I tried to call out but no sound would come. I don't want to die like this; I thought, not here, not now, no, please God no!

When I opened my eyes it was daylight, and I was lying stretched out in some sort of barn. There were piles of straw around me, and somewhere a sizzling sound.

"Welcome to France." A handsome, smiling face was looking down at me.

"Thank you" I said automatically. I moved to get up, wincing as a pain stabbed my side.

"They're not broken," he said, indicating my ribs.

"Well they feel it," I grimaced, "what happened?"

"Our comrade fell on top of you. Pardon his manners, but he was dead. You would be too if we hadn't gone back and pulled you out. Simone persuaded us, she was convinced you hadn't been killed."

I noticed a slim dark-haired girl behind him, the one who had met me at the drop. She wore a concerned expression, though on hearing her name looked away. The other, slightly older woman now came over, introducing herself as Monique. She gestured towards some straw bales, where a group of half a dozen men nodded dourly at me.

"My name's Francois," said the man who had spoken first. I believe you are Collette Simonais?"

I felt a spasm of fear. This had to be the test, but if not, what? They were all watching me now.

"No, monsieur," I said, looking him straight in the eye. "I am Claudette Simonais."

There was a pause. Then Francois smiled,

"Excuse me. I'm sorry." He said, "We lost three people. It was a bad night."

"Why say sorry to her. I said we shouldn't have taken a dozen people to meet an English operative. And a woman at that."

It was a dark-skinned, tough-looking man who had spoken. He glowered at me as he drew on a cigarette.

"Orders, Paul." said Francois "And, you misunderstand me, I am sorry for our comrades who died last night. No one could have foreseen it. Now, let's eat."

One of the men bent over a small paraffin stove and a jumble of pans. The group gathered round as he handed out tin plates of hot stew. I managed to sit up, wincing again from the pain in my ribcage.

As we ate I turned to the man who seemed to have taken against me.

"Do you dislike all women Paul?" I asked him. "Or is it just me?"

Paul snorted into his stew as he made some sullen, incoherent reply.

"Ignore him," Monique said. He's an ignorant bastard. Have you got your orders?"

"No", I said "I was told I would get them when I landed."

She glanced across to Françoise,

"All I know is," he said, "we have to take her to Paris. As soon as possible."

"She could be an informer," muttered Paul sourly, mopping up his now empty plate with a hunk of bread.

Monique responded angrily. "She gave the password, idiot!"

"Did you hear it? No – only Simone did. Whose idea was it to ask a girl we hardly know to get a password from a girl who drops from the sky that we don't know at all?" He lit a cigarette and leaned back, looking at us all through narrowed eyes.

"You suspect everyone," said Monique hotly. "You want to know what I think, I think it's you that's the informer, yes, what do we know about you eh?"

"Don't talk rubbish just because you can't think straight," he replied coolly. "Instead, look at the facts."

"Suppose you tell me what they are, since you're so clever."

"Someone knew we were going to be on that road last night… we lost some good men ……but who survived? *She did!!"* Paul hissed the words out.

"So did you for that matter!" Monique shouted at him. "Where were you when…"

"Be quiet both of you," said Francois sternly. "This is not the time to argue. We leave in fifteen minutes."

CHAPTER SIXTEEN

Francois took me to a small farmhouse. The elderly farmer and his wife were very kind, and offered me a bed, which I gratefully accepted.

Though exhausted however, my sleep was fitful. I could hear in my head still the noise of the guns the night before, the screams of dying men.

Next morning at seven, he returned, and we set out for Paris. Keeping to the side roads, this meant a slow journey. Approaching the outskirts of the city, Francois pulled over and beckoned me out of the cab. I was to travel out of sight in the back from this point.

When we finally came to a halt I squinted through the little window in the door of the truck. We were parked in a narrow street, opposite some steps and an arched doorway. It looked like a church. Francois came round to let me out

"Come on, get out!" he said abruptly. Without replying I jumped quickly down.

"Come and meet your new hostess."

He led me across the street to a pretty little shop with a red and white awning. Above the door a sign read: "Dupont – Vin, Tabac et Chocolatier Excellence." Francois rang the bell, peered through the window then rang again.

Standing beside him, I too looked in. Beautifully shaped individual chocolates were arranged one upon the other in elegant spiralling displays, some wrapped in shiny gold and silver papers, others packed into gift boxes tied tantalisingly with bright ribbons and bows. I remembered how much I loved chocolate.

Since rationing it had become a rare commodity in England. The thought of home brought a sudden rush of emotion.

"Claudette, are you all right." Francois nudged my arm.

"Yes, oh yes - I was just thinking…"

"Well, don't." He rang the bell again.

The door opened and a large middle-aged woman appeared. She smiled courteously.

"Good morning, how can I help you?" she enquired.

"I have a special order to collect for the Restaurant des Amies" Francois replied. The woman stood aside and waved her arm.

"Ah yes, come in. come in."

From inside the shop came first the nutty smell of tobacco, then a delicious aroma of melting chocolate. Glass shelves laden with elegant boxes of all kinds of confectionery lined the walls, and a glass fronted counter held an array of smoking paraphernalia. At the far end stood three large wine vats, with rows of bottles lining the walls above.

The woman glanced quickly up and down the street then closed and bolted the door behind us. Ignoring me she turned to Francois.

"You should have been here at nine," she snapped. Her smile had vanished, replaced by an air of suspicious authority.

"We had some bad luck last night - three lost, Maurice and Henri, and one of the locals."

"Ah no! What of Monique and the new girl?"

"They're fine, Paul too."

"He would be! Maurice and Henri killed – how could that happen? You should not have gone there yourselves. It was against all the rules."

"London requested it," shrugged François." "Bad luck is bad luck."

The woman then looked sharply at me.

"Is this her?" she asked.

Françoise nodded. "Yes Madame. Claudette Simonais," Madame Dupont scrutinised me, her face pinched with suspicion. I felt afraid to say anything, or even to move.

"Come," she said at last. "Have some coffee." She led us along a passageway stacked with crates of wine and boxes of tobacco, into a neat little parlour.

"Sit down," ordered Madame Dupont, pouring two cups of coffee and handing them to us. I obeyed as if it were a life or death command. I felt tense, ready to burst into tears. The old woman seemed to read my mood. In a kinder tone she said,

"You'll be all right, as long as you don't do anything stupid. Have you been briefed?"

"No," I said, wondering what qualified as stupid in the strange world I was now in. "They said I'd get my orders when I arrived."

Madame Dupont glanced furtively at Francois.

"Well that's good in one way," she said, "you can do the delivery first thing tomorrow."

"What will I be delivering?"

"Chocolates of course!" Madame Dupont beamed as she said this, her face like that of a benevolent fairy godmother.

"Chocolates?" I said incredulously and suddenly indignant, "I didn't come here to deliver chocolates!"

Madame Dupont's eyes narrowed.

"Chocolates," she said slowly, "Are a vital part of our communications, and until we find out from London exactly what you're supposed to be doing, I suggest you help us."

"I meant no offence Madame," I said. "It just seems such a strange request."

"On the contrary. What could be more ordinary than delivering chocolates? Ordinary, and innocent, you understand?"

"Yes, yes, of course," " I said.

"And there's no offence taken my dear. Tomorrow it is chocolates, another day it may be tobacco, or wine. We have to vary things a little – if Major Strauss is seen receiving only expensive confectionary each week, someone might ask questions."

"Who's Major Strauss?" I asked. Madame Dupont looked at Francois for a moment then they gave each other a nod of agreement.

"Our tame German," said Madame Dupont with a smile. "He is a member of German intelligentsia. They don't like what Hitler is doing, and so they help us. High Command seems to have forgotten about Straus. He took a piece of shrapnel in the leg and is hoping to sit out the rest of the war at the Hotel Juno. He gives his fellow officers the impression he's a wealthy aristocrat. In truth he's a penniless nobody - that is, until he started selling information to the Allies. I don't know exactly how much they're paying him, but enough to keep him in fine cigars and cognac. And the chocolates of course - his lady friends are very appreciative."

"Madame Dupont appreciates the Major's money too – or should I say the Allies money," smiled Francois. Madame Dupont shrugged and spread her hands out.

"He's my best customer it's true, and he's helping our cause."

"So the deliveries, how do they help?"

"It's quite simple," she said as she refilled our coffee cups. "They're a means of passing messages avoiding any direct contact."

"What kind of messages?"

"We tell him about all the important Maquis operations being planned. Strauss has friends in the German upper echelon all over France, including the Gestapo, old roistering pals from his days in Berlin. He spends hours on the phone to them, and entertains them lavishly at the hotel when they're in Paris. Oh yes, they have a high old time it's a scandal really. When they drink their tongues loosen. And like all such men they love to tell each other about their wonderful careers, where they're going with their unit next month, who's said what to whom about the next big push, and how they're going to crush the resistance like flies. They even say where and at what time!

It's amazing the things Strauss hears just by opening his ears - and a few bottles of Champagne. Troop deployments, special operations, generals arriving or leaving, even the German catering corps" movements – Straus hears it all."

"And he tells us," said Francois. "If we learn of any likely threat to our operations, we can revise them."

"Or plan new ones!" said the Madame with a girlish twinkle of mischief in her eye.

"But aren't these friends of Strauss worried their careless talk will be overheard by the hotel staff?"

"That's the beauty of it Claudette," said Francois, "they think they're completely safe to say whatever they wish - the Juno is owned by a family of staunch Vichy sympathisers; collaborators."

"Vermin in other words," said Madame Dupont haughtily, her eyes ablaze.

I was reminded of my Grandfather; picturing him that day in the farmhouse with his shotgun vowing no German invader would cross his threshold alive. I felt a sudden spasm of longing for the old man, wondering if I should I ever see him again. Forcing my mind back to the present, I said, "And these messages are concealed in the chocolate, or the cigar boxes?"

"Of course," said the Madame.

"Isn't that dangerous?"

"I write very small, on the insides of the wrappers. You have to break open the wrappers to read anything."

"You're right, it is dangerous," said Francois. "If a delivery were ever to get into the wrong hands…."

"I agree a code would be better," interrupted Madame Dupont, "but no one has ever got together with Strauss to devise one. It would be far more dangerous to meet him, the Juno staff are observant and often around in the town."

"And how does Strauss pass his reports back to you?"

"When you deliver, he may give you a tip, a folded 5-franc note. If he does, on no account unfold it, but put it straight in your pocket, thank him and leave. Inside the banknote will be a small slip of paper bearing whatever information he has obtained."

Francois was looking ruminative.

"I still say it's a wild system," he said, frowning into the coffee cup. "Writing our operations down in black and white for anyone to see...."

"There is always a risk," said Madame Dupont, "but the information he provides is worth the risk! If Strauss only hears the night before about a big operation, how else is he to let us know? The phone can be listened in to either at the Hotel, or tapped by the Gestapo. Strauss cannot be seen conversing socially with any of us."

Francois shrugged and lifted his hands.

"Strauss's notes are destroyed as soon as I have seen them," said the Madame.

"It would be safer for the deliverer to memorise and destroy them as soon as they leave the hotel." said Francois.

"Be seen setting fire to a piece of paper or tearing it into fragments in an alley? I don't think so Francois!" she said. Francois shrugged again and shook his head.

"Strauss's little notes have served our us well. Only last week we were able to destroy a whole trainload of munitions, with four Gestapo agents and a general on board. But that was only a rehearsal."

"What do you mean Madame," I said.

Madame Dupont's eyes widened, and in a lowered voice she said, "Soon my dears we are going to fry a bigger fish, yes, a very much bigger fish indeed."

CHAPTER SEVENTEEN

"Remember," said Madame Dupont. "This is for Major Strauss at the Hotel Juno. Don't leave it at the reception desk - insist they call him down to the lobby to sign the receipt. Most important, on no account allow anyone else to open the boxes."
My hand trembled as she passed me the package.

"This is your first time over here isn't it?" she said. I couldn't speak, only nod. My mouth now very dry, I tensed my hands to try to prevent the shaking. The old lady sighed as if in charge of a clumsy child.

"Just keep your eyes and ears open, your mouth shut and remember your story. You're Claudette Simonais, my niece, running a simple errand for me."

"Madame?" I said. "What if I get it wrong?"

"You will be arrested and tortured until you break. If *we're* lucky you'll keep your mouth shut. If not - you'll get us all killed. What else did you want me to say – never mind, it won't matter?" She then took hold of my arm. "This is not a game Claudette," she said. "If you cannot do the job, I will arrange to get you out of here. I will understand. There will be no blame if you go. Ah, you are a child, you should not be here perhaps. I say that sincerely my dear, I am not the ogre; war has given me the ogre's mask that's all. Come, I will ask Francois to take you back, you can return to England…"

"No."

"No?"

"I want to stay," I said, "I'll make the delivery. I won't foul up. I promise."

Still holding my arm Madame stared into my eyes, searching out my soul. I knew if I faltered now it would be worse, everything would be worse.

"Come," she said at last, "I will show you the bicycle. Get your papers?"

A wooden crate on the back of the bicycle contained the carton of chocolates. The job was simple, I kept telling myself, take the carton to the Hotel Juno in the Boulevard de Sevres, ask for Major Strauss and hand it over. If he gives me a tip, I pocket it immediately and leave.

Unfolding the map Madame Dupont had given me I studied the location. It didn't look far but there were lots of twists and turns. I tucked the map into my coat and mounted the bicycle. The little streets were quite busy, with cars, horse-drawn carts and several other cyclists journeying back and forth.

A little old man in a crumpled suit took off his hat and bowed politely to me. I smiled at him and pedalled on. The fear was easing a little now I was on the move.

A boy on a butcher's cycle seemed to be taking the same route for a while, shadowing me at each bend. Just as he turned off at a corner, I found I was at the hotel. Situated at the end of a quiet street, it was a rather scruffy-looking establishment, the paintwork peeling.

Leaning the bicycle against the rusty railings, I took out the carton and went up the steps. Peering into the hotel lounge I saw a group of German officers seated around a table drinking. I realised it was the first time I had seen the enemy at close quarters, and in daylight.

Alarmed, I stepped back out of sight. The gunfire, the voices in the night still haunted me. I leaned against the wall to catch my breath, anxiety coursing through me again. There was the sound of loud laughter from the table. If Major Strauss were among them it would be quick and easy. He would accept the chocolates and I would be away.

I strode into the lounge. Fixing my eyes on the reception desk I crossed straight to it. There seemed to be no one in attendance. This was not something I had planned for. My heartbeat quickened as the laughter at the table grew louder. Terrified of drawing attention to myself, I dared not look round.

Noticing a bell on the desk I reached out and pressed it decisively. Immediately, a door at the side of the lobby opened and a middle-aged man with a drooping moustache appeared.

"Yes Madame?"

"I have a package for Major Strauss. I need him to sign for it," I announced, feeling as though I were delivering the opening line of a play. Perhaps this was the best way, I thought; treat the whole thing as a theatrical performance.

"From the Chocolatier Excellence?" he enquired. I nodded.

"Thought I recognised the paper. You're new aren't you? The Major likes your merchandise – if it's not cognac it's cigars. I tell him I can get both cheaper for him - I'd like to know what your secret is at that shop! Though, Dupont's Chocolate is known all over France. The Major can't get enough of it – almost every week he gets a box. I wonder he's not the size of a barrel."

The man laughed as he picked up the house phone. I gave a rather stilted smile; then heard someone behind call out,

"Not another of his sweethearts are you?" It was one of the German officers at the table, speaking in perfect French. I stiffened. "Do tell us," said the officer in an amused voice - are you one of the major's girls?"

"I am sorry monsieur, I don't understand." The words tumbled nervously out.

"Hey," another officer yelled drunkenly, rising from the table, " she doesn't understand. Maybe we'll have to show her!" His colleagues roared with laughter.

"Actually I doubt she's one of his women Carl," said the first officer "Bit stupid getting her to deliver chocolates so he can hand them straight back to her!"

"I'll bet she's giving Straus more than chocolates!" bellowed yet another member of the party. "What say there's a little billet-doux, a little romantic note, inside? Let's have a look!"

I knew in that instant I had to get out, not wait for the Major, just turn, walk smartly out of the hotel and then run like hell. But I couldn't.

Five German officers were already surrounding me, trading witticisms and clamouring for my attention. As one of them made a grab for the carton I snatched it away, turning desperately towards the concierge in hope of assistance. The man merely raised his eyebrows, flapped his arms and called out vaguely, "Gentlemen, gentlemen."

At this point, a dark bespectacled man, who had so far remained seated at the table, now came over. In a voice of deadly earnest he said,

"I think you should all be extremely careful. I think it's quite possible she's a member of the Maquis – and that package could very well be a bomb."

They all then fell silent, staring at me. My mind was racing. Had I been set up - if so, by whom, and why? My pulse quickening I eyed the door. What chance did I have of reaching it? Perhaps if I threw the carton in the air and made them dive for cover, I might make it through. Then I remembered something someone had said during our training – talk your way out, talk your way out…

"Non Monsieur," I said, "Non, I only deliver the chocolates."

I thought any second now I am going to be taken away. Then, the officer who had just come over suddenly guffawed with laughter, whereupon the others immediately joined in.

"Or maybe those chocolates are spiked," said one.

"Who'd want to poison dear old Strauss?" laughed another.

"If you'd been romanced by Straus, wouldn't you?"

"If I'd been romanced by Strauss I'd want to poison myself!" rejoined his friend. This last remark brought uproar. Even the concierge's shoulders began to shake with ribald amusement. Next, one of the officers declared with mock grandeur.

"As Major Strauss's subordinate I insist on sampling these suspicious chocolates," and wrenching the carton from my hands began un-tying the ribbon.

As I reached out to retrieve it, he immediately tossed it to his nearest comrade, who quickly had it open. I watched helplessly as he took out one of the chocolates. Removing the gold wrapper, he dropped the chocolate elegantly into his mouth.

"Exquisite!" he exclaimed, "just like the young lady who brought it." He then glanced at the wrapper. "Why there appears to be some writing …………"

"What's going on here?" All eyes turned towards the stairs. A tall, uniformed figure was surveying the scene in the lobby.

"Strauss old man…" uttered his comrade in surprise, the wrapper fluttering from his hands.

"I'm sorry Major Strauss," said the concierge. "This package is for you – your friends are - in high spirits this morning." He retrieved the carton, closed the lid and placed it on the desk. Major Strauss strode towards them. As he did so the concierge stooped to retrieve the chocolate wrapper from the floor. The Major however stepped forward, placing his foot deftly over it.

"No, no, Jean I won't allow you to clean up after my comrades. I do apologise for their rowdiness," he said, picking up the wrapper and putting it in his pocket. Seizing my moment, I turned quickly to leave.

"Just a moment," called the Major, stopping me in my tracks. "I've not seen you before. Don't worry my dear - Heinrich here was fooling when he said you might be Maquis. His sense of humour is a legend from Berlin to Paris. He is always the first to laugh at his jokes – often the last!" Everyone laughed, Heinrich the loudest.

"But like all fools," continued the Major, "he reminds us of serious things. Who can forget the cake at General Von Stiller's party? A beautiful cake, three feet tall! With an unusual filling – a thirty pound bomb. The resistance have also tried using poison against us numerous times. Not so funny now is it. Where are your papers?"

Trying to steady my hand I passed him my documents.

"You are from Rennes," said the Major, studying my photograph, "Why did you want to come to Paris?"

"My…aunt needed my help…in her shop."

"Not to kill Germans?" The Major smiled and took a folded banknote from his pocket. "Here's for your trouble," he said, "Sorry about these marauders. They drink too much that's their trouble. Mine too come to that."

Slapping Heinrich heartily on the shoulder, and with a cry of "Let's have lunch!" the Major then steered the noisy group of friends back over to the wine laden table.

Pushing the 5 Franc note tight in my pocket, I walked quickly from the lobby and into the street. Riding off I saw the butcher's boy again, pedalling steadily his head bent low over the handlebars.

Back at the shop Madame Dupont eagerly unfolded the piece of paper that Major Strauss had secreted into the banknote. On reading it an excited glint appeared in her eye.

"You did well my dear," she said warmly, rubbing her hands with satisfaction. "We'll send you again."

I didn't reply. I felt sick to the stomach. Never before had I been so frightened as those few minutes in the hotel. How could ever I go through it again?

Madame Dupont must have read my thoughts. "It's natural to be afraid," she said, "the trick is not to show it, and from all accounts you did that very well."

"How do you know that?"

"Sit down dear." The old lady pointed to the armchair, "I know more than you think. The butchers boy – you noticed him?" I nodded.

"That was Etienne, we sent him to watch you, just in case you should have needed help."

"And to make sure I'm not a traitor?"

"That too, yes." Madame Dupont gave me a kindly smile. "We have to be sure. These are dangerous times. We have lived in fear since the occupation. It does not get easier. Every knock at the door may be the Gestapo - our neighbours may be collaborators. I saw the fear in your eyes, today. If you still want to return to England we will understand."

"I was afraid Madame," I said. "But I came here to do a job, to help. I know the odds on my survival, six weeks if I'm very lucky."

"Who told you that?"

"Oh that's not official of course," I smiled grimly. "London aren't so stupid as to give us any statistics, but we hear what people say... Tell me Madame, who do we trust."

"No one my dear, no one."

I looked at the old lady's face, a beautiful face, hardened and lined from resolve.

" Claudette," she said, "let me ask – you are a young girl, from the safety of England and I think a loving family yes? So, why are you here?"

There was a quiet concern in Madame Dupont's voice, hinting at something more than she was telling me. I said, "I don't have to wait for London to send my orders, do I?"

For the briefest second the old lady seemed caught unawares.

"Why do you say that?" she asked.

"Because Madame, you know why I'm here."

My bedroom was in the small attic above the shop. I supposed it was the safest place in the house. If the Germans came I could climb from the window onto the roof and run. How far I might get was another matter. I sat on the side of the bed, and closing my eyes saw the faces of Major Strauss and the German officers, the concierge with the drooping moustache, circling in my mind, a gallery of laughing, menacing devils. Forcing my thoughts elsewhere, I curled up, and after a while fell into a sort of half-sleep. I was awakened by voices downstairs. For a moment I was disoriented, unable to make sense of my surroundings. A small alarm clock beside the bed showed 1 a.m. I got up and opened the bedroom door, listened for a moment then stepped quietly out onto the landing. An argument was in full flow in the kitchen, between Madame Dupont and Francois.

"She must not be captured, at least not until her job is done," the old lady was saying heatedly. "These are their orders. Today was only a test."

"Damn you!" yelled Francois. "And damn them. It's hard enough for us to survive but to have to look out for some newcomer just because *they* say so…this is the last time Madame - they dictate to us no longer!"

"You will do as I say," said Madame Dupont coldly.

"And if I don't?"

"That's your choice. But remember young man to whom you speak."

There followed silence for a few seconds. Peering cautiously over the banister, I saw Francois standing just below. Attempting a more reasonable tone he said,

"It won't be easy – few of them ever make it back…look, what's so special about this one?"

"She's different, her role is different and…" Madame Dupont broke off suddenly. Leaning back from the banister, a loose floorboard had creaked beneath my feet.

"Claudette is that you?" called Madame Dupont.

I stepped forward again. "Were you talking about me?"

"We thought you were asleep child," said Madame Dupont, coming up a few stairs.

"Obviously,"

She glanced at Francois for a moment. "Come down and talk, the pan has boiled for coffee, Francois is just leaving."

"Yes - I am," the young man said, and glared at Madame Dupont.

I felt angry now, as well as afraid. The secret glances, the whisperings and furtive conversations – I could bear them no longer.

"Don't leave on my account," I said, "I'm sure you and Madame have not finished discussing me. Don't worry, I won't eavesdrop again!"

I returned to my room and slammed the door, tears brimming.

"Claudette…" I could hear the old lady coming up the stairs. "You have misunderstood child. Our conversation was not about you."

Fearful now, I turned the key in the lock. "Then who Madame? Why won't you tell me anything?"

"I know you want to help us," she panted through the door, her breathing laboured from climbing the stairs.

"And soon you will be able to, but for now my child, be patient and sleep. We will speak in the morning."

When I had heard her shuffle back downstairs I laid down on the bed again. But sleep would not come. I realised how resigned I had been up until now; afraid yes, but with a kind of numbed acceptance of whatever my fate might be. With a shock I suddenly saw myself – my grim notion of being a condemned woman.

Madame Dupont's words replayed in my head - "She's different." Why had she denied they had been talking about me? I was still the condemned prisoner – condemned not only to die, but as some terrible sacrifice for the resistance, a disposable and willing pawn in their game. How was my end to come, what nightmarish scene were they planning for me? I had heard stories back in England of agents being fed false information then deliberately led into the clutches of the Gestapo. That information, when obtained through torture was more likely to be believed by the enemy. I could not go through that, I could no longer stand any of it.

Taking my handkerchief from the bedside table I felt for the cyanide pill sewn into the corner. I went over to the washstand and poured some water from the enamel jug into the bowl. I splashed my face thoroughly, the cold water tightening my skin. As the droplets fell into the bowl I looked in the small oval mirror that hung on the wall. In a few short weeks my appearance had altered, my eyes fearful and haunted, my mouth turned down at the corners. Perhaps, I thought, I am dead already. Surely though with death, came peace? I still felt terror, misery; obviously, I was not quite there.

I took the clean white towel from the rail, inhaling its freshness. It reminded me of home, of a summer's day with newly laundered washing blowing on the line in the garden of my parent's home, the home I dearly missed, and where all this had begun.

I thought of Peter. "Why God have you taken him from me?" I said out loud. "I can't live without him, and you know this." No answer came.

I picked up the handkerchief again, and felt the little pill hidden inside. Then, I lay on the bed, and clutching the handkerchief to my heart, fell asleep.

CHAPTER EIGHTEEN

It was nearly Christmas, and Madame Dupont and I had been busy in the shop since early morning. Where she obtained the unending supplies of sugar and cocoa I didn't like to ask. From what I could gather the Germans had some hand in it, or were content to turn a blind eye, all the while Madame supplied them with free Cognac.

Since the delivery to Major Strauss I had been given no further assignments, and was beginning to think my sole purpose was that of stirring chocolate and packing boxes. There was a sense of being kept at bay, protected until such time as my task, whatever it was, was to be carried out.

This particular day however, Madame had something else in store. As I turned the shop sign around to 'Closed', pulled down the blind and locked the door, she announced with a beaming smile, "Tonight Claudette, Francois is going to take you into the city!"

"What's brought this on?" I said, "I thought we'd be working through the evening as usual, ready for the morning rush."
Madame laughed. "It's time you had some fun."

The apparently gracious gesture took me by surprise, and unnerved me a little. Madame Dupont was a canny woman, not, I would have thought, that interested in my welfare. Why suddenly had she decided that I needed rest and relaxation? There had to be more to it. Perhaps my mission had arrived at last.

"Why now, Madame?" I asked, "I've been here nearly three weeks and apart from running errands, you've not let me out of your sight. Are you sure you want me to go?"
Madame Dupont's eyes bored into me; the kindly smile gone.

"Don't question me," she said. "Prepare yourself, he'll be here at six."

Linking arms with Françoise we alighted from the tram and walked the short distance to the Eiffel tower. It was a cold night but that didn't seem to deter the Parisians sitting out, eating, drinking and conversing in the cafés beneath the great monument.

"It seems so peculiar," I mused, "there are so many couples, young lovers, so playful and relaxed, and look - German soldiers marching past them, through their city."

Francois laughed. "This is the city of love after all Claudette, what else would you expect?"

The whole scene had an air of unreality. It was a week before Christmas, the shops were gaily decorated and the Parisians were carrying on as if the war didn't exist. Even the Germans, many of whom were sat around in the cafes, seemed part of some vast theatrical set.

"I don't know what to expect anymore." I said.

"Wait till curfew," replied Francois. "You'll see a difference then. This place will be deserted. Come on, would you like to see the famous Paris Carousel? "

As we crossed the bridge over the Seine a magnificent merry go round came into view, emblazoned with coloured lights, and with Arcadian fairground music blaring from its heart. Colourfully painted hobbyhorses rose and fell on their candy-striped poles in time to the melody, as round and round the carousel span.

Everyone seemed to be having fun; children's laughter rang out through the crisp night air, while families and old folk waved the circling young ones fondly on. In a surge of euphoria, as the carousel slowed I grabbed François's arm and dragged him forward.

"Come on," I laughed, "I want that black horse, with the gold reins."

At that moment, from over by the bridge, there came a screech of wheels. Three trucks came to a halt in front of the carousel. The laughter dissolved, and a silent, watchful tension gripped the assembled Parisians.

Only the carousel and its cargo of children, oblivious of the menace, continued on its merry way, its jangling notes now eerie and hollow in the baleful scene. The bystanders huddled close. The tailgates of the trucks fell away as the troops, their guns directed towards the crowd, jumped out. François pulled me close to him.

"They're looking for someone," he whispered, "just do what they say."

A dozen or so of the soldiers lined the pavement, covering the crowd with their weapons, the others came amongst us, and began herding and shoving the men and women into separate lines.

"Papers!" One of the officers was shouting. "Show your papers!"

Soon I knew they would get to me.

"Schnell – your papers!" The woman next to me held out a crumpled document. The officer scrutinised her face for a moment then handed her papers back without comment. He then turned to the two soldiers behind him.

"This one," he said casually. The woman gave a piercing scream, writhing in desperation as her captors dragged her out. A rifle was swung at her, there was a sickening thud, and her limp body was carried off, blood pouring from her forehead.

The officer now turned to me. I could smell his dry, foul breath.

"Papers." he drawled, his upper lip curling.

I froze, the panic rising, and as, my hand trembled at the clasp of my bag, I dropped it, causing the entire contents to spill out on the pavement.

"Slut!!" He shouted, grabbing my shoulder and forcing me to the ground. His gloved fist was crushing the back of my neck, the pain excruciating. When I had scraped my things together he dragged me upright again, and from my shaking hand snatched my identification paper. We had been told our IDs were flawless, even under a magnifying glass. I would find out soon enough.

"You are from Rennes?" asked the officer.

"Yes Sir?" my voice trembled.

"What are you doing in Paris?"

"Visiting my aunt Sir"

"Who is she?"

"Madame Dupont…"

"Ah! The chocolatier!" He smiled. "I shall be visiting your shop very soon - for some chocolates for my family."

Thank God for Madam's reputation, I thought. The officer handed my papers back and moved along the row.

A minute later an order was yelled, whereupon the troops doubled back to the waiting trucks and clambered noisily aboard.

François came back over to me. "Hold on." he whispered putting his arm around my shoulder. "They'll be gone soon." As the trucks sped off, my knees gave way and I sank further into his arms.

We crossed to a nearby café, and after ordering coffee he took my hand in his.

"Tonight," he whispered, "you have been reminded what it's really like over here."

I nodded, "I know, that was awful."

"This city wears a mask, the dancing goes on, but the mask, it slips." A wry smile creased his face. "How are you getting along with Madame?"

The coffee arrived and I took a grateful sip. "Oh, thank you for rescuing me – despite what just happened. I was dreading the thought of another evening cooped up in that shop. Since the business with Strauss she's kept me under wraps most of the time, - just the occasional tram ride or trip on the bike to fetch shopping. I feel like a prisoner let out for good behaviour!"

"She's trying to keep you safe, from the likes of them." Francois inclined his head towards a party of Germans sat a few tables away. To me they seemed to pose no threat; they looked relaxed, their collars undone, drinking beer, ordinary young men on a night out.

"They seem to be just enjoying themselves." I said.

"Who wouldn't in this beautiful city?" Francois agreed "But don't ever let your guard down. If they knew who you were they would enjoy taking you to Avenue Foch."

"What's there?"

"Gestapo headquarters. They've taken over numbers 84 and 86."

"Oh, yes. I see."

"Let's hope not." Francois stirred his coffee thoughtfully. "By the way, how did you get on the other day, with Strauss?"

"I did the job all right, I suppose."

"Did he make a pass at you?"

"What?"

"You don't understand?"

"Yes – or rather no, he didn't. At least, well he tried to be charming…I supposed it was part of his cover."

"If you go to the Juno again, let us know what he says to you. He tried to get Simone into his room."

"Simone?"

"That's why we stopped her delivering there. Just in case."

"Of what?"

"In case Strauss is a German feed. He gains our confidence over time, gradually piecing together more names, faces, addresses, then one day we are all arrested just like in Lyon."

"What happened there?" I asked

Francois lit a cigarette. "We had a large network in Lyon. It was doing well until – we don't know all the details, but there was a traitor. The entire group were named." He took a deep draw on his cigarette and blew the smoke out in a long, slow plume.

"They were rounded up, dragged into the street for everyone to see and shot. If the same thing happened here we could lose half of the Paris network."

"You really think Simone might betray you?"

"Not deliberately perhaps, but maybe in some other way. We've no reason to doubt Strauss, but we must be aware of the possibility. Make no mistake these people are clever. And even if he's genuine now, remember - a man who has changed sides once can easily do so again, especially if the price is right, or if his life is at stake."

"Francois," I said, "if I'm going to be here, I've got to do something. What's the point otherwise? I might as well have stayed in England – I probably would have been more use there. I'm terrified sitting about looking over my shoulder, waiting for that knock at the door, to be taken away, and have achieved nothing."

"They won't come for you, not if you're careful"

"Don't treat me as a fool," I said coldly.

"Our work is all about timing Annabelle. We must wait for exactly the right moment. The information you collected from Major Strauss is soon to be used. You have already begun to play your part."

"Delivering a box of chocolates! It wasn't exactly what I've spent weeks training for, preparing myself for, my whole…"

"You're looking for glory Claudette? There is nothing that's glorious going on here. It's hard and miserable, ugly and sordid, day after day, month after month. Those that do their bit and don't survive are maybe the fortunate ones. But as for glory - " He made an empty gesture with his hands, and smiled his wry, sad smile again.

"You don't think I'm going to survive." I said, searching his face for some sign, some reaction. He stared down into his coffee and said nothing, his features inscrutable.

"One day," I continued, "they will find me, come for me and take me away and you will say, 'She was one of the fortunate ones.' Francois, I want to do something before that happens, something to prove I existed here, not be kept like a dumb waitress in that damn shop. So tell me - what is going on?"

Francois leaned forward and stubbed out his cigarette

"Don't worry," he whispered, "your moment may be coming sooner than you think."

"There's an operation?" I asked

"The others didn't want you involved. After what happened - at your drop - a number of the organisation suspected you were a plant. They still do."

"I heard what Paul said. You don't suspect me?"

"Would I be telling you this?"

"So what convinces you I'm genuine?"

"Instinct, at first."

"And now?"

"You've seen enough to have betrayed us."

"You're sure I haven't? I could easily have made telephone calls while out on the bike."

"Not with Etienne watching."

"Madame mentioned him."

"He delivers for the butcher though even he has to be careful – the butcher is a Nazi lover - Etienne is one of us. He has followed you everywhere since you arrived in Paris. He'd have prevented you contacting anyone."

"I did notice him, though I don't see how such a skinny boy could be much use to you."

"Others have made the same mistake, to their cost. Etienne carries the tools of his trade with him – just in case any special cuts are required. If you had got past him, which is unlikely, and informed the Germans, we would all be at Avenue Foch by now, either that or floating down the Seine, Straus too."

From the table of Germans there came a burst of ribald laughter. The café door opened momentarily, and from the street I felt the touch of cold air like fingers round my heart. Turning my collar up I said,

"So what is this operation – is it the 'big fish' Madame Dupont keeps hinting at?"

Francois averted his eyes and fiddled nervously with his coffee cup.

"Ok listen," he said, "I'm trying to persuade the others to use you. The fact is after losing Henri we simply can't pull it off without you. No one else is as good with explosives. And the rest of us will be otherwise engaged when the time comes."

"Francois" I said looking him straight in the eye, "just how big is it?

"All our work is important. Madame's called a meeting. We must be there for 8.30."

I glanced at the clock behind the counter; there was an hour to go. "That's just before curfew."

Francois nodded. "We'll be there in plenty of time…"

"More coffee sir?" I looked up to see the Maitre De standing beside us. "Allow me to give you fresh cups." Leaning over the table he whispered something very softly into François's ear.

"No thank you Hugo," Francois said, standing swiftly and picking up his coat. "We're just going - Claudette don't forget your bag."

Whatever the Maitre De had said had made Francois suddenly edgy. "We have to go," he said again.

As I turned towards the exit however, Francois took my hand and steered me over to the counter. To the side was a small service door.

"This way sir, madam," said the Maitre De in a casual manner.

The door opened onto an unlit alleyway.

"Come," said Francois, as, taking my hand again, he led me further into the darkness.

Paris - December 1941 - One week before Christmas

Kurt Gruber, his uniform newly pressed and immaculate, strode into the café, flanked on either side by a unit of four armed infantrymen. The group of young Germans at the table stood immediately to attention.

Gruber ignored them. His eyes were fixed on the service door by the counter, which he seen closing as he entered the premises. He turned to the Maitre De who was behind the counter. "Where does that lead to?"

"Only to the alleyway at the rear of the café sir," replied Hugo.

"Who has been out there recently?"

"Me sir," said Hugo. "I've just put the empty wine bottles out there for collection. The door sticks, it closes very slowly."
Gruber walked to the service door, opened it and let it close. The door shut without any hesitation.

"It seems not to be sticking now. You two," he said, turning to his men, "Check outside."

Turning to Hugo he said, "We are informed a British agent has arrived, here in Paris. A woman. Have you heard anything?"
Hugo shook his head "No Sir, nothing."

"Then maybe you have seen *this* girl." Gruber produced a photograph from his pocket. "We suspect she is working with the resistance."

"No sir," Hugo said handing the photo back to Gruber. " I have not seen her."
Gruber's smile was icily courteous.

"My friend," he said," We know you have dealings with the resistance…."

"No, no, sir…"

"Quiet. I should arrest you and hand you over to the Gestapo. But, if you can help me."

"Anything to help our friends in the Reich sir…"

"Then tell me where she is."

"Herr Gruber, I have not seen this girl, I swear." Hugo pleaded, "I would of course tell you if I had."
Gruber's eyes glinted "Well, I'll just have to ask elsewhere. Perhaps we'll have a word with your wife instead."

"Oh but sir, she could not possibly…"

110

"I'll ask the Gestapo to collect her - they'll arrange a car, it's no trouble, really."

"I'm telling you the truth Herr Gruber," said Hugo.

"The alley is clear sir," reported one of the soldiers, returning from the service door.

Putting the photograph back in his pocket, Gruber smoothed his gloves and put them on.

"Very well my friend, we'll leave her be for the time being."

"Thank you, sir." Hugo gave a sigh of relief.

"But you will come with us now." Gruber snapped his fingers. Hugo's arms were seized and he was led out.

CHAPTER NINETEEN

"The train leaves Gare Du Nord at ten minutes to midnight January 10th, destination Marseilles. All military trains are now checked for explosive devices before departure, so…"
Madame Dupont stopped as the cellar door flew open and Francois came running down the stone steps

"Hugo's been arrested!" he exclaimed gasping for breath. "We saw them take him away. He'd tipped us off that the Germans were on their way, got us out through the alley. We hid there till we saw them leaving. It was that new officer, Gruber…"

"Who is we?" said Madame Dupont.

"Claudette and me," said Francois.
All eyes turned to me. After escaping from the café, Francois had taken me back to the shop, and finding Madame Dupont absent, gone off to try to find her.

"Claudette said nothing to me," said Madame Dupont.

"I thought it best to wait for – I mean…" I faltered.

"No matter. Etienne," snapped Madame Dupont. "See what you can find out."

Almost invisible in a dark corner of the cellar, Etienne unfolded his legs from beneath his body and glided noiselessly up the steps. When Francois had sat down, the old woman continued with her briefing.

"So, we must mine the track."

"How?" said Paul, "Ever since we hit that ammunition train they check the track as well, always. They'll have an advance guard inspecting every inch between here and Marseilles."

"No they won't," said Monique. "That's an impossible task."

"They'll do it for this train, believe me," said Madame Dupont.

"So what do we do – and where?" said Paul

"We must make our move in-between the advance guard and the train. Francois has the location - he'll brief you all in a moment, but no one else will be told exactly where we strike till he takes you there on the night."

"If you don't tell us beforehand, how are we to prepare?" Paul said, "It's not going to work."

"I agree with Paul," said Monique.

Francois stood up. "When you've all finished conceding defeat," he said, "we'll tell you how it's going to be done. This is the railway track." Francois chalked a line on the cellar wall. "Here's the train, and this, is the advance guard; about forty strong with an armoured vehicle travelling slowly on the line. They'll set out an hour or so ahead of the train and examine the track with flashlights."

"What then?" Monique asked.

"We position ourselves, and wait for them." He replied, "We are few in number, but we'll have grenades, machine guns. The location for the ambush has been carefully chosen."

There was silence as the group stared at the chalk lines on the wall. From the crude diagram, each began to form a picture of the plan Francois had just described; a plan which, if they assented to it, they could be acting out in reality in just over two weeks time.

"Ok – who does what?" Paul asked.

"You and Etienne will open fire on the armoured car." Francoise continued. "Simone, Monique, Claudette and I will set the explosives."

"Are you mad – they're women - and why are you taking her?" Paul nodded towards me. "Does it need four of you – or do you just want women around you all the time!"

"Simone and Monique are both nimble-fingered and light on their feet. To position the charges correctly we also need someone with specialist training, which none of us have had – we've relied on Henri and guesswork till now. I want Claudette."

At this, Paul gave a silent, withering look.

"No Francois." All eyes turned to Madame Dupont. "Claudette is not to go"

Before Francois could reply I was on my feet. I'd had enough – the remarks from Paul, this unsettling protection – or more likely mistrust – from Madame.

"What is wrong with all of you?" I asked, "I'm not the traitor, I'm here to help, put my life on the line. If you don't let me come with you I'm contacting London to get me out. It is pointless my being here any longer under such conditions."

"But it's dangerous," said Madame, "you are a young girl...."

"Don't patronise me," I interrupted. "You lot, and London, have been treating me as a complete idiot. They told me I'd get my orders when I landed. All I've done is run errands and potter around in this damn shop. For goodness sake, let me do what I've been trained for!"

Paul's hollow laugh reverberated around the cellar.

"So, the brave English agent wants to save the poor Parisians!" he mocked. "If you want to help us, keep out of the way, and leave warfare to the professionals. Once the Gestapo finds out you're here they'll be searching day and night for you, and that puts all our lives in jeopardy. Save your own pretty English skin - contact London now and do us all a favour."

This was the last straw. I walked slowly over to Paul, and stood very close to him.

"Your words don't frighten me Paul." I said,

"Well they should," he retaliated. "Remember you're the foreigner here, a self righteous, spoilt, child, with the arrogance to think you can parachute in and join our cause. If the Gestapo catch you, you deserve all you get."

My blood was up now. "How dare you speak to me like that?" I said, "You are the arrogant one! My husband gave his life for your damn cause, and I'm probably going to do the same. Tell me Paul, would you die for me? In fact, do you ever even think of anyone but yourself? I think we all know the answer. "

There was a silence that could be cut with a knife, and as Paul looked away I felt a surge of exhilaration in my veins. I was ready to take on all comers now. The others stared wide-eyed as I turned to face them.

"Well, Madame," I said, "you have the power - am I in?"

Madame Dupont shot a glance at Francois, who shrugged his shoulders.

"Very well Claudette, you are with us," she smiled. "But remember you are part of our group, and you work *with* us."

"I have no intention of doing otherwise Madame." I said.

"This is a massive train we're talking about," said Madame Dupont, "ten or more carriages. That requires several charges over a considerable length of track. We won't have much time and we need four people."

"I'll organise that," I said as I sat back down on the nearest up- turned barrel. This time no one challenged me.

"What's on the train?" said Monique.

"A consignment of anti-tank weapons bound for North Africa. Without them the Germans will almost certainly be defeated in the desert." Francois replied.

I've heard about these anti-tank devices –they're experimental, and not yet tested properly," said Paul.

"What's your point?" said Francois.

"My point - is that we are risking our lives to derail a train-load of useless weapons."

"The Germans have invested a great deal in them," said Francois. "Destroying them will be a significant propaganda coup"

"Seeing them fail miserably on the battlefield would be a greater one." said Paul.

Francois shook his head. "That, is impossible to know." he said slowly and patiently. "What is certain is that in one operation we can destroy a hugely valuable weapons consignment along with dozens of elite Nazi troops. Are you with us on this, or not?"

All eyes looked at Paul. "I'm - not sure."

Why for god's sake?" Monique said

"I think there's something you're not telling us"

Seeing, Madame Dupont about to speak, François continued hastily.

"All right - there's a rumour – and it's no more than that at present - of some high-ranking Nazis on board."

"So we're risking our lives for useless weapons, and a rumour now," Paul drawled. "Tell me Francois, where did the intelligence for this operation come from?"

"Strauss of course."

"And what about the train's departure details - I don't imagine they'll be displayed in the passenger timetable at Gare Du Nord – it'll be highly confidential."

Francois hesitated then said, "Simone – her father works on the railway. She'll find some innocent excuse to ask him about it."

"So now, information from a collaborator!"

"My father is neutral," said Simone quietly.

"No one is neutral…" began Paul.

Madam Dupont broke in authoritatively. "If he was a collaborator, he'd have been asked to work on this particular train. We know he's already been given the night off. They'll only be Germans and Vichy on board, including the driver."

Paul lit a cigarette and blew out a slow stream of smoke, which drifted in the yellow light of the candles around the cellar walls.

"Consider this," he said slowly, nodding towards Simone, "we know nothing about this girl - apart from the fact Francois has been trying to get her into bed as soon as he saw her."

"Take that back Paul," said Francois.

"We've all got eyes, why do you deny it? We could all end up in the hands of the Gestapo - because of your stupidity!"
Francois got up and strode towards Paul, his fist clenched.

"Francois!" said Madame Dupont sharply. "Sit down. Let us have some wine. Monique, fetch that crate over and find some glasses. Nothing has been decided yet.

We will talk this over again when I call our next meeting and we'll act only when everything is sure. Meanwhile – Paul, Francois, all of you, we will celebrate Christmas, the time of peace and goodwill to all men – and women." I give you a toast." The old lady raised her glass, her eyes gleaming in the candlelight, "La Belle France!"

Paris – December 1941

"There is a visitor for you Major Strauss."

"Ah - not that rogue Ernst? Ask if he has the 100 francs I won from him last night!"

Strauss opened the door of his room a little wider and grinned amiably at the concierge. Although almost ten a.m. the major was still in his vest, his braces hanging limply down from the waistband. His face was unshaven, and there was an aroma of stale cognac on his breath.

"No Herr Major, it's a Herr Gruber."

"Gruber…Gruber - now where the devil do I know that name from?" An expression of mild bewilderment crinkled the major's somnolent features.

The concierge, lowering his voice said, "I believe the gentleman is a representative of the office of the Gestapo Herr Major."

Hearing this, the Major's expression became suddenly more focused.

"Oh, I see. Well would you tell the, ah…Herr…

"Gruber sir."

"Yes. Tell him I'll be down in a few moments."

"Major Strauss?"

"Heil Hitler!"

Kurt Gruber, standing in the hotel lobby, returned the Nazi salute then clasped his hands behind his back and surveyed the Major, who, after some hasty grooming, now looked smart and alert.

"Can I offer you a drink, some coffee?" Strauss asked.

"Thank you, no. A late night Major?"

"Guilty as charged I'm afraid. Won't you sit down?" Strauss gestured towards a pair of leather armchairs positioned by the window looking out onto the street.

"Thank you" said Gruber.

When they had both sat he continued, "I understand you are invalided here for the time being."

"A shrapnel wound. How long my luck holds depends on the medical officer. I've a check-up scheduled soon."

"You consider it fortunate to be unable to serve the Fatherland?"

Strauss looked at the young man carefully. He then lit a cigarette and said languidly:

"Oh I do my bit for the Reich."

"Getting your fellow officers drunk and gambling and carousing into the small hours?"

"That's right. It's wonderful for morale, mine most of all – what the British call rest and relaxation I believe."

The young man smiled a cold chilling smile, "The British are decadent and disgusting in so many ways."

"You should try it sometime – come along and enjoy yourself one evening - it'll do you the world of good. You look a little tense if you don't mind my saying so. Perhaps some female companionship would lighten the load. Anything can be arranged, this is Paris after all."

Gruber's face was immobile.

"Do you consider such facetiousness amusing – or indeed wise Major?" he said coldly.

"On the contrary, I'm quite serious," replied Strauss. Leaning forward he said in a solicitous tone, "and don't worry, I can get old Von Staffen to give you time off whenever you want."

Gruber looked unsettled.

"You know my superior - the General?" he asked.

"Klaus is a scoundrel and an incorrigible gambler – he also has a heart of gold. He understands that men are men. Even you Herr Gruber."

"I have little time for – recreation," said Gruber.

"Then you must make some!" replied the Major expansively.

"Perhaps you're right. I'm having a taxing time with one particular line of enquiry at present - which brings me to the purpose of this visit. We believe that an active resistance unit is grouped somewhere in this area."

"How can I help?" said Strauss.

"I'd like you to keep your eyes and ears open for us."

"As I'm sure you know Herr Gruber, this hotel is owned and staffed by our friends - all loyal to the Reich."

"No one is ever beyond suspicion, replied Gruber quietly. "The Resistance are adept at concealment Major."

"Forgive me old chap, but your own undercover people are likely to observe rather more than a uniformed German Major!"

"I am of the belief Major, that the resistance are astute at identifying plainclothes agents lurking, however casually, in doorways. You on the other hand spend many hours each day seated here gazing idly from the window. Your face is as well known to passers-by as that potted palm. Clearly you are the enemy, but - forgive me saying so – you are regarded I believe as a harmless fellow. 'Oh there's the Major again' they say, 'never quite sober.'

"Do they really say that?" smiled Strauss, "well, well, who'd have thought it!"

"Certain persons may be - less than cautious in your vicinity. They may not take the same care about those they are seen speaking and consorting with, as when some quiet stranger is hanging around."

"I get it - I'll be the spy that's hidden in plain sight," the major laughed. "I'll be an associate member of the Gestapo – what an honour!"

"Yes Major, an honour indeed." said Gruber unblinkingly.

"I must confess I know little about such clever work," Strauss said. "Can you give me some pointers, particular people to look out for?"

The trace of sarcasm bypassed Gruber.

"Certainly," he replied. "For a start, we believe a British agent, recently dropped, has been assimilated into the local community."

"Any idea what he looks like?"

"The agent is a woman."

The Major gave a soft whistle. "Ooh la-la, as they say!"

Gruber made a disdainful face.

"Here's another woman we have identified and are watching." He handed the Major a photograph. "Maybe you know her?"

Strauss studied the portrait. "Um yes, I think I have noticed her passing by."

"She's been under suspicion for some time. We're hoping she'll lead us to the hornet's nest. Hold on to the picture for a while." said Gruber.

"I'll keep her by my bed."

"Memorise the face then destroy the photograph. Study anyone she is seen with, and give us a full description. Make notes of times and dates, how she is dressed, what she carries and her mood."

"If you suspect this girl," said Strauss, putting the picture into his breast pocket. "Why don't you pick her up?"

"That would immediately alert her co-conspirators. They'd vanish before we'd got her to talk."

"What makes you certain she would talk?"

"You know the Gestapo better than that. I must go now Herr Major. I'm sure we can rely upon your vigilance."

"Anything for the Gestapo Herr Gruber - I'm an amateur of course, but I'll do my best."

The two men walked towards the entrance hall of the hotel, the concierge appearing from nowhere to open the door.

"And do come over for that drink one evening," said Strauss, "I'll make sure you have a good time."

"I'll consider it Herr Major. But I won't play cards with you – I understand you always win"

"Usually."

"Perhaps you cheat."

"How did you guess?" smiled Strauss.

"Oh by the way," said Gruber, "you didn't ask the girl's name - the one we are watching. Perhaps you already know it?" He looked steadily at the Major.

"Oh – no, what is her name?"

"Armand – Simone Armand. Her father works on the railway. We may require you to become intimate with her. Think you can manage it? Well, good day Herr Major."

Strauss watched his visitor get into the waiting car. Then, laughing loudly, he called to the concierge for a bottle of wine.

Major Strauss stared thoughtfully into his wine glass. It was an hour before dinner and he was expecting his friends to join him shortly for aperitifs. He had been thinking about the visit he had had from Herr Gruber earlier that day. On the face of it the request seemed perfectly straightforward. The Gestapo were always sniffing around asking people to keep an eye on this or that Frenchman or pushing photos under one's nose. Gruber had probably visited half a dozen like himself that morning. There was no reason to think he'd been specially picked out, he just happened to be billeted in the area.

It was rather a coincidence that Simone Armand was the subject of the Gestapo officer's enquiry. She had visited the hotel several times to deliver and collect his information, though not recently. Was Gruber already aware he knew her? If so perhaps he too was under suspicion. If they already knew Simone was a possible agent, why were they asking him to watch her? Gruber's explanation didn't ring true somehow. Maybe it was an attempt to unnerve him. If he turned her in, he might implicate himself.

On the other hand if she were picked up anyway he'd be a dead man along with all the others. Perhaps it was best to do nothing. After all, what could he report about her? The fact he'd once tried to seduce her was neither here nor there. Not unless Gruber was aware of it. On the other hand it was a perfectly reasonable thing for a fellow to keep quiet about, especially having been rebuffed by the girl!

It was not the first time Strauss had had misgivings about selling information to the resistance. Mostly it was plain sailing, just passing on bits of operational tittle-tattle really. The money arrived regularly from London via a private bank account in Vienna. And there was a further substantial sum to be paid out later, assuming the Allies were victorious and he continued to play his part. The likelihood was of a very pleasant life waiting for him a few years down the line.

Indeed life was pretty good now he thought, as he refilled his glass. The only risk was getting caught. Then things would be far less pleasant. He had a tidy sum stashed already, perhaps it was time to cut and run. There was this business with the train in a few days. Perhaps he could tip off Gruber – it would either put a feather in his cap with the Gestapo, or draw their suspicion.

It was unthinkable to compromise the resistance group's safety - a man must have loyalties somewhere. Besides, his own name would surely be given to the Gestapo, irrespective of whether or not the resistance knew he'd betrayed them. Strauss hated complications that got in the way of enjoying life. This was a complication that had to be dealt with.

Perhaps he could stop this operation going ahead by some other means. He had to find out more. Why was this train so important? Gruber would know. There must be a way he could consolidate his own position and keep his money flowing in, while safeguarding the resistance. He would come up with something, a solution that would keep both sides happy. That was what diplomacy was all about. Smiling to himself, he called to the concierge for another bottle.

CHAPTER TWENTY

Christmas had been a mixed blessing. The colour and gaiety in the streets and shops were a pleasure to behold, and there seemed a true feeling of enchantment in the air. For me though it was a fragile magic, the sight of every laden tree, lighted candle, and sprig of holly reminding me of a past I was cut off from. Peter, my parents, home, I mourned for them all, the sense of loss re-sharpened in the collective urge for joy.

Madame had been almost comically jolly in her attempts to cheer me.

We went to church on Christmas morning and spent the rest of the day with Madame's friends who came to the shop. I was accepted without comment as her niece, though as I chatted away I felt Madam's keen eyes and ears attuned to my every word and gesture.

The New Year came and went, and the business of the train was now very much on the agenda again. Madame arranged another meeting. The mood of the group had changed since I had last seen them. An air of gloomy tolerance seemed to have settled on them, the sense that they were allowing me there under sufferance.

"Are there any questions?" asked Madame Dupont when she had gone through the plan. The meeting had been long and we had listened intently while she and Francois went over every detail again and again. There was no response. Even Paul kept quiet. Simone confirmed the train's date and schedule, information that had been double-checked by Paul, who had a contact of his own at the railway station.

It had been decided we would all travel separately to the rendezvous point on the line. Madame Dupont would drive the truck with the weapons strapped beneath the chassis and the others would take bicycles using separate routes. The operation was now scheduled for three days time, Saturday night. The whole thing seemed simple.

If not for the grim expressions, it could almost have been a social club outing that was being arranged. After a minute or so of quiet conversation among the group, Monique spoke up:

"Who carries the explosives?"

"I'll take them in the truck" said Madame Dupont.

"Isn't that risky?" said Simone.

"They'll be well hidden. They can't be concealed on a cycle."

"A truck's more likely to be stopped though."

"She'll have a forged night-pass, her cover is transporting shift-workers to the railway repair yards." said Francois.

"If there are no more questions," said Madame Dupont decisively, "I suggest we disperse now and avoid meeting again till the night; 21:00 hours, not a moment earlier or later. God will be with us. Goodnight all."

As people shuffled towards the stairs, Francois came to my side. "Are you alright?" he asked.
I thought this odd, but answered, "Fine - a bit nervous that's all."

"It would be strange if you weren't." Then when everyone was out of earshot he said quietly, "Listen, I don't want you spending the next few days fretting. Come and see me on Tuesday, at my house – no forget the rules - come at midday, I'll make some food, we can relax, talk. What do you say?"
I looked into his face, trying in vain to read his intentions. The thought of being alone with Madame Dupont for the next three days was not appealing.

"I'll come in the evening," I said. "Perhaps we can go to the carousel again. Would Simone come too?"

"No – she has to work that night. It will be just the two of us. I'll call for you about six. Don't tell Madame. Till six."

When Francois had gone I stood at the foot of the cellar steps for a while, blinking into the gloom, alone with my thoughts.

"Come my dear," called a voice from above. It was Madame Dupont. "I must lock up now."

As I mounted the steps I jumped in alarm as a figure emerged from the darkness behind and brushed hurriedly past me. I realised it was Simone.

"Wait," I called out, and ran after her. When I emerged into the shop however, she was gone.

"Don't worry about those two," Madame Dupont grabbed my arm. "There's more important business to deal with. Listen, I want you to take a radio to Albert Hannard; here is the address." I felt confused and frightened. Why this sudden activity I wondered?

"What about the curfew?" I said, " It's 10 o'clock already."

"That can't be helped." Madame lead me into the kitchen, "Hannard has to have the radio before Saturday to set up the signal. You will have to go tonight."

My nerves felt jangled; all sorts of anxieties were kicking in, the thought of being out on the streets of Paris on my own at night made me reel. I began to feel sick.

"Why couldn't Francois take it or one of the others?" I said trying to delay the inevitable.

Madame Dupont smiled "I thought you wanted something to do?" She put the kettle on to the hot stove. "Or were those just empty words?"

I didn't reply.

"Here is the address," she said, handing me a scrap of paper. "Memorise it before I put it on the fire."

"218 Rue de Famille?" I read aloud. "That's right in the centre Madame, it will be crawling with Germans. Have you a curfew pass for me?"

"There was not time. Take the alleyways; it should only take you an hour that way."

I was panicking now. "Why can't I go in the daytime, tomorrow when the streets are full of people?"

As the boiling kettle whistled Madame slowly rose from her chair.

"It has to be tonight, Hannard is leaving Paris in two hours." She poured the hot water into the coffee pot. "But if you don't want to do this Claudette. I will understand."

"No Madame. I will go, it's just that…"

"You're afraid…" The old lady interrupted. "Child, that's how you *should* feel, it will keep you alive. Don't take anything - or anyone - for granted."

I turned and stared into the glowing embers of the fire. A thought stirred, the same one that had been nagging at my brain since the visit to the carousel. "They know I'm here don't they."

The old lady nodded. "Yes child, they do. Etienne told me."

"So at the carousel, and the café, the person they were looking for was…"

"Claudette, the Germans are always looking for someone. Every night there are arrests. We have lost so many of our people through random raids or informers - we don't keep count any more."

"How long though, before it's my turn, before someone tells them who I really am?"

Looking at the old lady, for the first time I saw vulnerability in her eyes, and with it a sense of resignation."

"Nothing is certain Claudette," she said, summoning gentleness into her voice. "Believe me, I do not want to send you tonight, but there is no-one else. The others don't know about this, and I want it kept that way. You see Claudette, I too have my orders."

She took my hand and held it. In that moment I felt special, yet also humble. I saw now an immeasurable courage in the old woman, the sense deep within her of a fire of destiny, its intensity far exceeding my own.

"Where is the radio Madame?"

Madame Dupont handed me a small brown leather suitcase.

"Go child, and may God watch over you." I watched as she threw the scrap of paper on the fire. There was a quick burst of flame, and in an instant it was no more.

CHAPTER TWENTY-ONE

The suitcase containing the radio, though only small, had become after an hour on foot, immensely heavy and cumbersome. With only the moon for illumination along the network of winding alleyways from the chocolate shop to the Rue du Famille, I finally found the apartment. I knocked on the door, which immediately opened.

"About time," breathed a middle-aged man I assumed was Monsieur Hannard.

"Come inside – quickly, before anyone sees you." He glanced furtively up and down the corridor before locking the door behind us. "There's a lot of activity tonight."
I followed him into a large, elegantly furnished room, with a high, ornately decorated ceiling. Long red velvet curtains draped the windows, and opposite, a huge gilt mirror hung above the large white marble mantelpiece. A fire burned welcomingly in the hearth. I placed the suitcase on the dining table.

"This is for you Monsieur. Madame says you're leaving."

"None of your business." Hannard said abruptly, flicking open the case, and checking the headphone, single Morse key and wires.

"Its all here. Tell her I'll begin transmitting Friday night and I'll get a message to...Shush."
There was the sound of vehicles outside. Hannard went to the window.

"Oh God! The Gestapo are here again. Let's get out – now – and bring the radio!"

"But where..."

"Go!"
I quickly packed the radio into the case and headed for the front door. Hannard grabbed my arm.

"Not that way you fool," he hissed, pulling me towards the corner of the room. "Go! Go!"
Drawing back a curtain he opened a door and pushed me down some iron steps, slamming the door shut behind us. I ran blindly down the staircase, into an unlit alley below.

"Ok, give me the radio," he said snatching it from me.

"Where are we?" I said.

"At the back of the apartments. Follow me now, for god's sake, run!"

The next instant he was gone, his running footsteps echoing away in the dark. With no hope of catching him up, and fearful of getting lost now in the maze of alleyways I turned towards the street. Inching along the wall I peered around the corner. There were soldiers everywhere, some running in and out of the apartments, others standing guard along the footpath, voices shouting out orders. A flashlight suddenly lit up the alley. I shrank back in terror, squeezing myself behind a pile of wooden crates.

My heart pounding, I watched the beam of light move from wall to wall picking out every detail of the brickwork. I heard a slow tread of boots on the cobbles, then a noise above. Something came tumbling down from the top of the crates.

"Who's there? Come out or I shoot!" I saw the soldier now, his pistol pointed into the alley. A shape, moving slowly forward on the cobbles drew the torch beam. It was a black and white cat.

"Hey Kitty! What are doing there eh?" The boot steps came closer.

The torch beam swept back over the crates. I contemplated my chances of making a run for it. As the soldier drew close there was a shout from the street.

"Corporal! What in hell's name are you doing? Is there anyone there or not?" The beam dallied over the crates. "Corporal!"

"Nothing to report sir"

The beam flicked away as the soldier walked slowly back up the alley. As he did so there was a scrabbling sound from a dustbin, which made him stop and turn. He retraced his steps, and in doing so the torch beam fell across the crates again. This time the light pierced straight into my eyes. The soldier stopped in mid stride and aimed his pistol towards me.

"You, come out!" he barked.

I felt for the knife in my pocket.

"I said – come out!" he repeated.

Slowly I stood up and stepped out from behind the crates.

For a second the soldier looked at me, then said. "Why are you hiding there? We'll find out. Walk in front."

As I moved past him there was a sudden rattling noise from the dustbin. In the split second the soldier looked away I raised my knife and lunged.

We had been trained to go for the heart. He made no sound as he collapsed, his arms fluttering up momentarily before the strength left his body. It was very quick.

"Corporal!" a voice shouted from the street.

Without thinking I took to my heels, running blindly away and down into the narrow, enveloping alleyways.

How I found my way back to the shop I did not know. Madame's concern was written all over her face.

"What's happened to you? Look at your coat."

I looked down and saw for the first time blood splattered across the bottom of my overcoat.

"It, it...was either him or me." I said, "I had to, to get away...."

"Him?" demanded the old lady. I told her what had happened. She looked at me silently for a moment then went to the cupboard and poured out a large brandy.

"Drink this. Did anyone see you?"

I took a large gulp of the brandy, wincing as it hit my throat. . "I don't think so. I took the alleyways as you said, though a different way back"

Madam Dupont slumped into her large armchair by the fire, bidding me to sit opposite

"Well, let's hope not," she said, staring intently into the embers. I shivered now, feeling as if I might pass out at any moment. Madame looked up at me again. "Take deep breaths child," she said. I gulped in air and leaned back, trying to let go the knots in my body.

"You will say nothing of this to anyone Claudette do you understand." I nodded. "Hannard will have gone to ground," the old lady continued. "Take off your coat and shoes and give them to me."

When I had done as she asked, Madam Dupont placed both coat and shoes on to the fire, the flames instantly taking hold.

Then, without further questions she said, "Now get to bed and remember, this is our secret."

"Jacques – can you spare a moment?"

"What's the problem?" Jacques was crossing the station concourse on his way home. It was Friday evening and he was looking forward to doing nothing. His wife was cooking her famous casserole, and his daughter Simone would be finishing early at the factory to help her mother in the kitchen, a family evening for once. He hoped his manager wasn't going to ask him to take another shift now.

"Jacques we've been asked for an extra dining car waiter - one of the long runs, down to…"

"No, really, its too much Monsieur Gravois. I'm just off home, my wife will have started the dinner…"

"I wasn't going to stop you going home!" said the foreman smiling, "I know your nights are special. This is tomorrow night"

"Friday night?" said Jacques looking surprised.
"Yes it's an overnighter, you won't get back till the Sunday but the tips will be good"

"Officers?"

"Some high-ups I'm sure"

"Oh – well the money would be welcome – but Marie likes a bit of notice. She'll nag me all evening about it if I say yes - it would spoil her dinner – and mine!"

"Tell her in the morning" winked Gravois. "Then give her a big bunch of flowers tomorrow before you leave."
Jacques pursed his lips. On his last overnight shift he'd taken more in tips than his weekly wage. He'd be able to treat the family, buy some good black market Cognac, Simone some clothes maybe. He saw his daughter's face lighting up.

"All right Gravois, but if I come in with a black eye on Monday I'll be blaming you!"
The foreman laughed. "Your wife should be proud of you - it seems you've got a reputation as a good waiter."

"What do you mean?"

"Don't say anything, as you know I'm supposed to divide the overtime equally, but he specially asked for you to be on this train on Saturday"

"He?"

"The German that telephoned the office – some fellow called Gruber"

Having slept late, it was not until the mid-morning of Friday that Simone learned of her father's revised work schedule for that coming night, by which time, he had left the house.

"Why he couldn't tell me last night I don't know…" drawled her mother complainingly, as Simone, sick with fright, jumped up to fetch her coat. Her first impulse was to rush to the station and warn her father. A few seconds reflection however, told her this would be madness. He would want to know the reason, and even if she withheld that information, his sudden defection from the shift would place him under suspicion following the sabotage. In any case, once her father knew what was planned he would warn everyone else not to travel. It wasn't the Germans he cared about, but Simone knew he would never allow his work colleagues to ride to their deaths. But what was the alternative?

The obvious option was to call off the mission, if only the others agree to it. Perhaps this was a trap set by the Gestapo – her father had been "specially requested" to work tonight by this German, Herr Gruber, her mother had said. Could it be a ploy to link her to the resistance?

As her mother stood washing dishes and idly talking, Simone paced the kitchen in an agony of indecision. Perhaps she could alert her father then take the whole family into hiding somewhere, deep in the countryside. But they could only hide for so long. And besides, what of the others, her comrades – could she really desert them - and then there was Francois, she knew she could not be without him, not now.

Then suddenly she had an idea – Major Strauss. Could he not call the German authorities, to say he'd overheard a snippet of conversation, in a crowded café say, about a possible sabotage being planned on a train leaving Paris this evening? The train would then be rescheduled, surely - they would not take any risks, even on the slightest rumour. Major Strauss could certainly carry off such a thing, and it need not endanger him one jot whilst doing her the most immense service.

She remembered the last time she had seen Strauss, during a drop at the Juno, how he'd looked at her. He'd been quite charming, his little compliments, his offer to share a bottle of 'something special' upstairs in his rooms. The Major would help her, she felt sure of it. Her father's life was all that mattered.

CHAPTER TWENTY-TWO

Having purposely left the curtains open in the little attic room, I awoke to see the moon peeping out from behind a small cloud. The sleep had done me good and I felt quite rested. I had tried not to dwell on what happened in the alleyway, the life I had taken in cold blood. It was in the line of duty. That's what our trainer had drummed into us, everything was a target, an objective, nothing to do with blood and bones and killing real people. The thought of the cat had made me cry as I went off to sleep, a young man helping a small defenceless creature, and I had snuffed out his life in an instant. I knew he would have had no qualms about doing the same to me, but that gave little comfort. I had crossed a line as a human being, if that's what I still was.

Then, half-dreaming, I thought of Simone, and the jealous look she had given me on overhearing the conversation between Francois and myself. I knew she was in love with him, and I had wanted to tell her that nothing had happened, either during the afternoon I spent with Francois, or before or since. But since that incident Madame had for some reason reined me in tighter than ever, even forbidding me to serve in the shop. Francois did not call as often either. It was strange.

The clock showed 6am. Soon Madame Dupont would be knocking on the door; another day would begin. My thoughts turned to Francois. The way he had looked at me, the way he always looked, left me in no doubt about his feelings. He had wanted to make love, and how very nearly I had succumbed. 'No one knows what tomorrow will bring,' he had said, gazing into my face. How right he was. My life was a temporary thing, but how temporary was only for God to know. In any case there was Peter. Peter! But Peter was…

If for no other reason, I could not have betrayed Simone, who had saved my life. Francois belonged to her, and I had never stolen anything in my life. But since leaving Francois that day, with a kiss on the cheek and a fond wave, I had wondered: had I needlessly forsaken any chance to make love to a handsome man, to any man, ever again? There was a gentle knock on the attic room door. Tomorrow was here.

We arrived at the rendezvous point within minutes of each other. Francois dismounted from his bicycle and pushed it deep into the undergrowth at the base of the tree, then did likewise with mine.

"Remember the formation of the trees, the shapes, that broken gate," he said. "There won't be much time later"

It was now 20.30. We were a good half-hour early. Francois told me he liked to get a feel for the place before an operation – get a grasp of where he was. He took out a cigarette and lit it, shielding the match carefully. As he blew the smoke out he raised his eyes to the night sky.

"What are you looking at?" I asked,

"The stars."

The night was cold and sharp, the clear sky filled with thousands of tiny specks of light, millions of miles away, twinkling like diamonds on black velvet.

I thought: he is young and strong, and has a natural instinct for survival, yet he too is vulnerable. I knew he'd been on countless missions like this, and always come through without a scratch. I knew he felt fear like anyone else, but dealt with it through action.

The day before, we had been close together, sharing wine, sharing an afternoon of our lives.

"If you stop to think, they'll be a bullet in your back, do the job and get away," he had told me. This wasn't bravado, he explained, just a trick to get you through. At that moment I didn't feel very brave, quite the opposite. I had already drawn blood - I was a killer now. Surely I would find it easy to follow his advice?

We crouched together under the tree, peering down the slope in the direction of the railway line. It was hard to make anything out in the gloom.

Francois said: "As soon as Madame Dupont gets here with the truck we all head to the ambush point. It's just a few hundred yards further up the line. See where it's lit down there?"

I looked to where he was pointing. A solitary light glimmered in the blackness far below.

"You know what to do Claudette?"

"Yes," I answered, "Is that the little station?"

"Yes – it's deceptive, the line curves round. That station's our marker. There'll be guards hanging about but hopefully not more than a handful."

Francois must have sensed my worry. "What's troubling you?" he asked.

"When the others open fire," I said, "Won't the noise alert the train?"

"It might, but it'll all be happening on the other side of the tunnel."

"And if it doesn't?"

"Then the train will carry on," Francois said, "Taking them right over the charges. Claudette there's something else, what is it?"

I couldn't help myself. "Are you – are you in love with Simone?" I said. I could feel his discomfort in the silence. In that instant I had forced him to see what he had always known – and I had my answer. Yes, he loved her.

A low warbling sound came from the other side of the bushes. Looking round, I stared as a gaunt, hollow-eyed face, like an emaciated cat, appeared from out the branches.

"Good evening Sir – Miss," it hissed.

"Good evening Etienne," said Francois.

"The truck is here," said Etienne, his long body snaking noiselessly from the foliage.

"Where's your cycle Etienne?" I asked

"At night I go faster on foot. I go anywhere"

"It's true," affirmed Francois. "We call him the shadow, eh Etienne." But Etienne had already melted back into the night.

"Claudette…" began Francois, "you're right about Simone – I do care for her…"

Forestalling him, a sound of breaking twigs heralded Paul's arrival. He wore a thick, black leather jacket, and there was a broad, humourless grin on his face. Monique and Madame Dupont now followed swiftly behind. All three carried large sacks on their shoulders.

"Paul has the explosives and detonators," "said Madame Dupont, "here are machine guns – hide them in the bushes near the track for your retreat. When Francois is ready we take the truck to the ambush point on the other side of the tunnel."

"What about Etienne?" Monique asked.

"He's gone ahead to scout." Madame Dupont handed Francois the weapons. At the same time Paul thrust a heavy sack at me, making me lose my balance and stumble.

Paul sneered. "I hope you stay on your feet better down there," he said, indicating to the railway line below, "for your sake."

"Give it a rest Paul," snapped Francois

"Oh someone's in a foul temper – fallen out with one of your ladies?"

"Just shut up before I..." muttered Francois.

"Before what?" Paul snarled aggressively.

"Shut up both of you - are you mad!" hissed Madame Dupont. "And where is Simone anyway?"

"Ask lover boy," droned Paul laconically.

"I'm asking you Paul," said Madame Dupont, "you are supposed to be liaison man."

Paul shrugged. "She had her instructions like the rest of us. I don't hold her hand."

"She's usually one of the first to arrive," said Monique.

"Relax for heaven's sake" said Francois, "She's got over fifteen minutes yet"

"In fifteen minutes the train leaves Gare du Nord," said Madame Dupont. "It could be here in just over half an hour." The group exchanged uncertain glances.

"Don't say I didn't warn you about that girl," said Paul.

Gare Du Nord – Paris 1941

Simone looked at her watch; it was almost 8 pm. She peered casually around the brick pillar again. The station concourse was less busy now, several trains having departed in the last hour.

The "special" was easy to pick out. Large crates had been loaded onto the open trucks and German guards were standing conspicuously close by. A self-important looking officer was pacing up and down the carriages, checking his watch and issuing orders. Maybe this was Gruber, the man who had caused her so much anguish.

Up front the boiler was being stoked, building up steam, an occasional hiss escaping into the high atrium of the station. There was an air of expectancy. Simone bit her nails again. Still there was no sign of her father. She knew he would be there though, working away dutifully. Panic gripped her heart. She would have to make a decision soon.

After arriving at the Hotel Juno and asking the concierge to summon Major Strauss, a sudden uncertainty had made her change her mind, and she had slipped away before he came down. She then decided to run to Madam Dupont, throw herself on her mercy, and beg her to call off the mission. But on the way to the chocolate shop she demurred yet again; this would be no guarantee of her father's safety. Even assuming Madam Dupont agreed, she in turn would have to convince the others to cancel the operation, and the others included Paul. She therefore ran home, shut herself in her room, and tried to focus her mind objectively on the problem.

There were a few hours yet; if she made the wrong decision she didn't want it to be because she'd acted too hastily. Already her aborted visit to the Juno might have dangerous consequences. Her curious antics at the hotel – she had heard him questioning the concierge just as she made her escape behind the potted palms – might even now have prompted him to contact Madame Dupont. She hoped not.

No nearer a solution, the hours had gone by and now she found herself at Gare Du Nord. She dared not approach her father, but felt that all the while she could keep an eye on the fateful train, that fate itself might yet intervene in some innocent way to save him – a postponement of the service, a fault with the engine, an air raid even. But it had not happened.

And now she must leave for the rendezvous with Francois and the others. Resolved she could not involve her father, or tell her comrades, she knew there was now only one course of action open to her.

Alongside the station concourse a German staff car had just arrived, followed by another. The self-important officer strode up and saluted the occupants. Taking a last look at the train, Simone turned and ran quickly away across the square.

CHAPTER TWENTY-THREE

"We can't wait any longer for Simone."
Madame Dupont's tone did not invite discussion. Francois and I exchanged a concerned look, then filed out of the bushes with the others.

"Something must have happened," Francois confided to me, "I just pray she's alright."

"Hurry now," called Madame from the truck. "We must go now, the other groups will be in place - no more hold-ups...."
Then, as the truck's engine growled into life, I saw a figure, running out of the darkness towards us.

"Wait," I called, "She's here, its Simone - Madame Dupont, wait, please..."
Simone came panting to my side. She squeezed my arm, then that of Francois, who guided her quickly in front of him towards the truck.

"I'm sorry," she said, still breathless, "I was stopped. ..."
I could hear the relief in François's voice, as, putting his arm round her he said, "Come on," there's not much time."

After a few minutes drive Madame Dupont stopped the truck. We were amid a thick clump of trees on the side of a hill. Francois and I got out, and without further word from anyone the truck moved off.

Looking down I saw we were now much closer to the little station. Two soldiers were clearly visible on the platform, illuminated by a bright overhead lamp. There was no sound apart from an occasional night owl hooting far away.

"Don't worry about those guards." Francoise whispered. "See where the track curves? We'll be hidden by the bend once we're down there. Right – got the charges?"
I nodded and followed him down the slope. We quickly reached the bottom, and settled behind a thick patch of gorse, getting our breath back. Francois leaned forward, carefully parted the bush and peered out along the track. Through a gap I could see the faint gleam of bare steel, the smooth crest of the rail. Francois looked at his watch. "Could be anytime now."

I tried to focus on what I would have to do in the next few moments - rigging the charges, setting the timers. Francois took out a bundled blanket, unwrapped it to reveal two machine guns, and handed one of them to me. From far off, there came the whistle of a train. Francois nodded to me then, bent low, left the gorse and ran swiftly down the bank to the line.

Clutching the bag of explosives in one hand, and with the machine gun slung over my shoulder, I followed. I shrank further into the bracken as the boot heels and flickering lights went by. Gradually, as they neared the tunnel, the German voices dwindled away into silence.

"Now!" hissed Francois. A second later we were on the line. I glanced towards the dark mouth of the tunnel; the inspection unit had already disappeared inside. It felt safe.

We set swiftly to work, fixing the charges carefully on the underside of the track then mounding up shingle to cover them. When the wheels of the train triggered the first charge, it would set off the others to explode at timed intervals, assuming everything went according to plan. Before adjusting the separate timers, we waited for the next sound of the train. Crouching against the track, I put my ear to the rail. There was a faint tremble.

"Delay the timers," I whispered. "It's here."
We moved quickly back along the track, staggering the settings. Francois looked at me for the go-ahead this time. "Yes, that's it," I said.

We ran to the edge of the cutting and began clambering back up the grassy bank. Reaching a broad expanse of rock, from which a huge tree-root arched out, Francois stopped, and signalled to me to come over.

"This is ideal cover," he said, bidding me to kneel down, "and a good sweep along the line. Now we wait."

Train Station outside Paris - 1941

Simone dropped to her knees. No one seemed to notice her, but it was better to be sure.

Madame Dupont, Monique and Paul had all secreted themselves along the embankment. Etienne had as usual become invisible. If she were quick, Simone thought, she could get over the other side of the bridge, alert the guards at the little station and be back in her position before the train arrived.

Quite how she would get away from the guards on the platform was another matter. With any luck, on hearing what she had to say they would be busy radioing ahead and rushing up the track waving their arms, and forget all about her. The main thing was her father would be safe. One German train more or less counted for nothing besides that.

Confident she was out of sight of her comrades, Simone rose to her full height and began running as fast as she could through the dense trees. She was not however, out of sight of everyone. Paul, who had observed her slinking away from the group, now followed swiftly behind her.

Simone had now reached the bottom of the incline. Approaching the track she paused for breath. Paul, hidden by a line of trees, saw her hesitation and rushed forward.

Simone, hearing the approach, spun round, and on seeing the flash of steel in Paul's hand, sped off in the direction of the station. Paul hurtled on to the track after her.

As he did so however, his foot struck one of the metal pins securing the rail, which sent him sprawling on the ground. Paul was quickly on his feet again, but the delay had been enough for Simone to sprint ahead, putting a good dozen yards between them. She was now within sight of the station, Hearing the whistle of the approaching train, she put on a tremendous spurt.

The two guards on the platform, who had also heard the train, were stubbing out their cigarettes and making ready for the arrival.

Simone waved her arms and opened her mouth to shout. But no sound came.

A shadowy, cat-like shape had sprung from the darkness and wrapped a sinewy arm around her neck. A knife slid once across her throat. Etienne dragged the body swiftly into the trees.

CHAPTER TWENTY-FOUR

It had begun to rain heavily as the train emerged from the tunnel and slowly rounded the bend. As it rolled over the first detonator there was a flash of light and a single loud blast echoed across the cutting.

Like a wounded beast the huge engine left the track and careered into the platform, ploughing on almost majestically through the station building.

As the engine and leading caboose smashed, splintered and overturned, the timed charges along the line began to go off, upending several of the following carriages in a cacophony of grinding metal and shattering glass.

Flames roared from the busted windows, the noise reverberating like thunder along the valley. The train, much of it an unrecognisable heap, finally lay still, every carriage either on its side or slewed at an angle across the track. Then could be heard the terrible screams and moaning of the injured and dying.

Slowly, soldiers began to emerge from the chaos. From the cover of the bushes Francois, his arm raised, prepared to signal the attack.

"Wait for it - now!"

I pointed my gun towards the track, squeezed the trigger and fired randomly. One soldier fell, another staggered away. The rest melted back into the darkness.

Francois was firing furiously, moving across the outcrop to improve his advantage. Then suddenly everything changed, as the hillside was doused in a blinding light. There was a loud rat-a-tat of a heavy machine gun from somewhere beneath us. Crouching low I ran for cover.

"Aim for that searchlight!" shouted Francois. I could see nothing, in the glare. I pointed my gun over the edge of a rock, but before I could fire there was a sharp zinging noise and the branch above my head splintered. The Germans voices below us seemed to be getting closer.

"They're climbing the bank," said Francois, "Come on, let's go!" He was already some way ahead as I struggled up after him. The rain was now teeming down, making it hard to get a foothold. With each step forward I felt myself slipping back. Francois, realising I was not behind him, turned and grabbed hold of me.

At that moment machine-gun fire raked the trees again, showering us with foliage. An amplified voice rang out. "Give yourselves up, you are surrounded."

The searchlight swept the bank and back again, and with horror I saw my legs lit by the glare. To left and right, the Germans appeared from the trees, their weapons trained on us. Francois and I dropped our guns, slowly raised our arms. From below came another explosion, then another, this time from high above.

All eyes, the Germans' included, looked skywards. A low drone grew louder as the dark shape of a plane appeared between the clouds. It was followed by a second, then a third, a fourth.

The leading plane went into a sharp dive, its engine whining, heading for the railway line. The Germans threw themselves to the ground. The planes opened fire one after another, raining their fire over the tangled train carriages. The German machine gun retaliated. The planes circled and came in again, swooping low they dropped their bombs and repeated bursts of fire hit the searchlight, and the incline was suddenly shrouded in darkness again.

The Germans scattered, some running down towards the train, others diving behind rocks, intent on avoiding the attacking aircraft at all costs. Seizing the moment, Francois tugged at my arm. I followed him behind some rocks and from there we began to climb, making towards the wooded area higher up.

Aftermath of The train Crash

When the planes had left there was an eerie calm. Among the wreckage of the shattered train carriages, splintered wood creaked and burned quietly. Here and there a door swung or the wheel of an upturned chassis moved. Smoke drifted from little fires, with occasional bursts of flame as upholstery or shreds of fabric caught light. The wooden crates, that had concealed the consignment of weaponry lay strewn about, their contents mangled and useless.

Two dead generals and one high-ranking Nazi party official lay sprawled in the centre carriage. From this same carriage now staggered another German, also a General. Easing his bloodied body down onto the track, his legs buckled beneath him.

From the far end of the train another figure emerged, a civilian. With one hand he held an apron to his head, in the other was an electric torch.

On seeing the General fall he hurried forward and knelt down, tending the officer to stem further bleeding. The General looked up gratefully. He recognised him as Armand, the dining-car waiter who had served him on previous journeys. Armand reassured the General that help would soon be on its way. He was going to check for further survivors. He would also try to find them both some brandy.

After some time investigating the wreckage however, Armand found only dead bodies. A few German soldiers were now making their way back down the hill. He decided to try and locate his flask of brandy before someone else did.

As he walked back along the carriages something fluttered across the beam of his torch. It was a headscarf, but something about it was familiar. In fact it looked very like one worn by his daughter Simone.

He shone his torch where the scarf seemed to have blown from, and walked over to the patch of trees at the side of the track. Here he stopped abruptly. Simone was stretched face up on the ground. A large bloodstain covered the top of her coat and her eyes, wide open, stared innocently at the sky.

Kurt Gruber shone his flashlight on the girl's face. It was her all right, Simone Armand. He wondered who had cut her throat.

"These damn peasants – nothing more than savages!" He kicked at a portly form lying next to her and turned it over. The dead man was wearing a waiter's uniform.

"Good lord!" exclaimed a railway man who was clearing wreckage nearby. "It's Jacques!"

"Jacques?"

"Yes Sir – Jacques Armand, one of our stewards - and heavens no, that's his daughter too! Holy Mother of God! Dear old Armand – there doesn't seem to be a mark on him, only the wound on his head – I suppose the shock did for his heart poor fellow."
Gruber left the bodies and returned to his car.

"Get HQ on the field telephone, immediately." he snapped at his driver.

"Yes Herr Gruber."

"Someone will pay a heavy price for this."

"HQ on the telephone now Herr Gruber"
He snatched the receiver from the young man. "This is Gruber. I want you to arrest Strauss, now."

CHAPTER TWENTY-FIVE

Françoise and I took our places in the cellar. Madame Dupont was about to begin the debriefing. Before she had spoken, Paul stood up. "All right, who knew about the planes?" he demanded.

"Me". All eyes turned back to Madame Dupont. "There were some very high-ranking Germans on board that train, vital to the Nazi war effort. The Allies wanted to make sure of things."

"They almost 'made sure' of us. We should have been told," said Paul firmly.

"For once I agree with Paul." Francois was sounding heated now. "Why the hell weren't we told? And, I thought Strauss said the train wouldn't be heavily guarded?"

Madame shook her head. "It wasn't. The soldiers came from the road, someone must have tipped them off."

"So, another piece of false information from Strauss," said Francois.

"Maybe the planes saved us" Madame Dupont said "I couldn't tell you about them, I'm sorry. Air co-ordinated attacks have failed in the past because someone gave the Germans a warning."

Francois threw his cigarette end down and drove his heel into it.

"Surely you trust all of us!"

Paul gave a sardonic snort. Madame Dupont looked faintly uncomfortable. She was not used to sustained criticism from Francois, and never in front of Paul.

"The main thing is we all survived, and a crucial target was destroyed," said Monique.

"I saw two generals on their feet afterwards," said Paul.

Monique rose to the bait. "You couldn't possibly have done! Don't be absurd Paul…"

"Paul sees many things that escape us mere mortals," said Madame Dupont, glad to find an ally in Monique.

Paul stood up and walked slowly to the front of the group, the candlelight throwing his shadow large on the cellar wall.

"I'll tell you what I did see," he hissed through narrow lips. "Simone."

"Where is Simone?" said Madame Dupont.

"She must have gone straight home," said Francois."

"No, she didn't go home," said Paul quietly.

"Then where is she – what are you saying?" said Francois.

"Don't ask me, I bungled the job. Etienne finished it."

Deep in the shadows, Etienne's eyes glinted. Francois leapt to his feet, looked murderously towards Etienne then flung himself headlong at Paul seizing him by the throat. Madame Dupont and the others rushed forward to prise them apart.

"You bastard!" roared Francois, "I'm going to kill you…"

"Before you do that," wheezed Paul, "you'd better know this - she was going to get us all killed. She was on the track by the station, waving her arms at the Germans as the train came through. I warned you, all of you, that she was an informer."

Francois stared at him for a moment, then, shrugging off the restraining arms of Madame Dupont, ran from the cellar.

I immediately got up and hurried after him.

Outside I heard François's running footsteps, and followed the sound. Fleetingly I saw him, sprinting wildly, in and out between the houses. Just as I thought I had lost him, he slowed then came to halt, slumped on a step, his head in his hands.

Neither of us spoke. Francois remained motionless, his face hidden. It was several minutes before he turned to me.

"Do you believe Simone was a traitor?" he said quietly.

"Of course not," I said, wanting to weep.

"How can you be sure?" he asked with some urgency in his voice

I held his hand.

"You just know things about people sometimes." I answered

"She's dead Claudette, dead!" he shouted, "I let her down, should have looked after her…"

"Don't Francois– It's not your fault …"

Francois sat up. "I too know she wasn't a traitor."

"She'd never betray us, least of all you …"

He shook his head. "I don't know if that makes it worse or not. Perhaps it would be better if I could hate her. One thing I know - someone has her blood on their hands - and they will pay."

"You mean Paul – and Etienne…but why?"

"Paul thought he was doing his duty," Francois said, "and killing is like clearing his throat to Etienne. No, I'm talking about Strauss"

"But Strauss is our agent."

"He had some kind of hold over Simone, something to do with her father – you know he works on the railways…."

"Well if that's true…" I said.

"It's the only possible explanation. I've never liked Strauss – he must have done something to really frighten her this time."

"Francois – let's go back and talk about this. The curfew's on – it's dangerous out here."

"You go back. I've work to do. At the Hotel Juno."

"Francois this is madness…"

He rose to his feet, walked to the house on the corner and peered cautiously round the wall. Across the street the Hotel Juno stood in silence. No one was about. I pulled at François's sleeve, but he pushed me away and stepped into the road. Before he had taken more than a couple of strides he came running back.

A car had appeared suddenly from around the corner and pulled up sharply outside the hotel. From the shadows we watched as two German soldiers stepped out. Two other men, in civilian clothes also emerged.

"Gestapo," whispered Francois.

All four men mounted the steps of the hotel and disappeared inside. In a few moments they re-emerged, closely escorting a fifth man. Francois strained his eyes.

"They've got Strauss."

"Strauss? Then he can't have betrayed us," I whispered, "not if the Gestapo are arresting him."

Major Strauss was put into the back of the car, which drove swiftly off, and the hotel descended into silence again.

Francois stood staring for a moment then grabbed my hand.

"Come on," he said, "If Strauss talks to the Gestapo, we're finished – every one of us."

We told Madame Dupont the news. She sat in her large armchair her eyes narrowed.

"Hmm, we've probably got twenty four hours. They'll try the gentlemanly approach first – cigars, cognac, and 'help us out with some names if you don't mind Major' – that sort of thing. If that doesn't work they'll bring in the fist men. Only, it won't be just fists. Then he'll talk."

"Then surely we've got to try to get him out, rescue him…" I began in alarm.

"Don't worry; we'll attend to him. Etienne will take care of it. I will visit the butcher's shop when it is light. Etienne begins his early-morning deliveries in one hour."

I stared at Madame Dupont. Not a trace of panic or fear had crossed her features, only a cold, clear appraisal of the situation and a decisive remedy. Etienne would take care of it. There was to be no rescue for the Major.

Hotel Juno - Paris 1941

"There's a call for you Herr Gruber – it's Herr Mencken"
Gruber rose from the armchair, an uncustomary smile on his face. He was in the lobby of the Hotel Juno having just conducted an exhaustive search of Major Strauss's room. Mencken was the head of the Paris Gestapo, and presently away in Berlin. He must have heard about Strauss. This would no doubt be a call of congratulation. Gruber took the phone.

"Good morning sir"

"Gruber what the hell are you playing at?"

"I beg your pardon sir?"

"Didn't you search this fellow you brought in?"

"Strauss? Of course – I'm just on my way back to HQ to interrogate him now. We'll soon have the whole bunch rounded up and…"

"Then tell me Gruber, ow the devil did he get hold of a cyanide tablet?"

"There must be some misunderstanding sir. There are often crossed lines from Berlin…"

"I'm back at HQ you fool!"

"I thought…"

"I flew back as soon as I heard about this bloody sabotage last night. Why are you idling in some hotel when you should be here?"

"This is where we picked up Strauss. Sir, what is this about cyanide?"

"Strauss was found dead in his cell from cyanide poisoning a few moments ago. Why was he not searched?"

Gruber gulped. "He was – sir, I cannot understand - all prisoners are thoroughly searched. Someone must have got into the building, and given him the pill."

Mencken, as head of the Gestapo in the city, was ultimately responsible for the building's security. Gruber's inference was not lost. "Impossible! No one could get in, unless they were invisible. Why on earth was this man not interrogated immediately?"

"It's good to let them stew for a while. It's my method…"

"Your methods, Gruber are going to come under some scrutiny from now on. And that goes for your position here in Paris. Do I make myself clear?"

"Yes Sir."

"Now get back here immediately and tell me how you're going to catch those responsible for what happened last night."

"Yes Sir"

The line went dead. Gruber slowly twisted the telephone cord around his hand in silent fury. How dare the man speak to him like that? It was he, Mencken who should be accountable. He was simply trying to pass on the blame.

The situation was serious of course - these peasants had made fools of everyone. There would have to be reprisals. Yes, he would take Mencken's advice; it was time to change his methods.

With a sweep of his arm, the telephone crashed to the floor and Gruber stormed out of the hotel.

CHAPTER TWENTY-SIX

I stood at the window of the attic room and gazed out over Paris. It was now three weeks since the mission. During that time Françoise had been calling at the shop frequently, and escorting me about town, much it seemed to the approval of Madame Dupont.

Simone, the girl who had saved my life, and been loved by Francois was gone, yet while I felt bereaved, I had found it hard to judge his mood. 'Live for the moment Claudette,' he would say. Was this how he really felt? More likely it was bravado, whistling in the dark the only way to face his loss.

Since Simone's death I had thought more about Peter. Was Francois now in the grip of that same sense of utter desolation that had descended on me? I felt now that I loved Peter more than ever in death. In my more disturbing dreams I recalled what Joyce had told me, about his body having never been found, and the uncertainty, the mind boggling, horrifying uncertainty that went with that knowledge.

The previous evening Françoise and I had visited the Moulin Rouge. 'A special treat' he had said as we dined, laughed, and flirted with one other; and in the small hours, here in my tiny attic room, I had surrendered myself to him. We had made love with an unbridled urgency, his tender gentleness arousing me in a way I had never experienced before. I responded to his touch with such passion, and wept with pure pleasure.

Afterwards we lay back in silence, François's black, tousled hair falling across his forehead, his strong muscular arms stretched above his head. As he closed his eyes, I watched the gentle rise and fall of his shoulders as he drifted to sleep. Perhaps, I thought, we never need talk of this, never mention it to anyone. It had happened, a necessary thing for both of us.

Now, here was the new day and I had to get away, to be alone to clear my head. I did not want Francois to wake, to have to speak with him, so I dressed quietly and crept downstairs.

The shop was quiet, Madame having apparently gone out. Not wanting to face her either at that moment, I grabbed my coat and bag and left. It was a bright morning, and people were taking advantage of the winter sunshine. In the city, in the daytime like this I felt comfortable on my own, flitting among the crowds.

I decided to take a tram and hopped on the first one that came along, not caring about its destination, just glad to be away from the shop, going somewhere. There would be time later to deal with what had happened, to face Madame and François. For now I wanted to be on my own.

As the tram bumped and rattled along I gazed absently at the passing shops and cafes, Joyce came suddenly into my mind. How good it would be I thought to be in London and bump into her right this minute, and go off for tea and cakes together at Lyons. What a lot I would have to tell her!

It was while the tram was waiting at a junction, that I noticed an old man, sitting hunched over some object. At first I wasn't sure what it was about this scene, which so drew my attention. The old man seemed to be scratching the back of his head with something. I then realised this was a paintbrush, and that he was twirling the handle in his hair.

I stared in amazement – it was exactly what Peter used to do when painting. I leaned forward to get a closer look, and sure enough the old man did it again. Not only was the mannerism the same - the angle of the head, the slope of the neck, everything was identical.

The tram was now very full, but I had to get off. Just as I got to the steps however, the bell rang and the tram lurched forward. Losing my balance, I fell forward, and into the arms of a young man.

Do be careful mademoiselle," he said politely, helping me to my feet. "You should not get off while were moving - you will get hurt!"

"I'm so sorry – but I must get off, please excuse me…"

"The next stop is just around the corner, why not wait?"

I had no choice. As the tram trundled on, I peered back but could see nothing through the crowd of passengers.

When the tram rounded the corner and came to a halt, I barged my way out and ran back. Reaching the spot where I had seen the old man there was now no sign of him. Had this been the spot, I wondered? There was a small roadside café and a sign advertising cognac. But then there were any number of these. I was starting to doubt everything now.

I could no longer amble around the city. That instant on the tram, everything had changed. After pacing up and down the street for several minutes I decided to return to the shop Francois would almost certainly have left now, and I could go up to my room and rest. I needed to be alone. At the same time I desperately wanted to tell someone what had had happened. Oh for Joyce and that Lyons corner house!

The pleasant, homely smell of baking greeted me as I opened the kitchen door and found Madame Dupont, vigorously rolling out pastry. She gave me a cheery smile.

"How are you feeling today my child? Did you enjoy the Moulin Rouge last night?"

By the look in her eye I knew she knew what had happened after the Moulin Rouge. The thought even occurred to me, that through her unseen power, some kind of ancient Gallic witchcraft perhaps, she had even brought it about. But that was ridiculous.

"Yes Madame, very much. Is Francois still here?"

Madame laid down her rolling pin. "He left an hour ago. Are you sure you're all right Cherie? You're as white as a sheet. Perhaps you have seen a ghost!"

I shivered, thinking about witchcraft again. It wasn't hard to picture Madame in a pointed hat, astride a broomstick, and for a crazy surreal moment I almost laughed. I sat down at the kitchen table.

"Almost," I said, feeling like I was coming to a precipice.

"What do you mean?"

I began to explain, telling her about Peter, everything I shouldn't, expecting her to stop me at every second. Instead she listened intently.

"I'm being foolish Madame, I know. It was a silly trick of the light. I suppose I just desperately wanted to see Peter. It's happened before, I used to see him everywhere."

Madam Dupont nodded, though looked thoughtful.

"My dear," she said, "I should not have let you tell me this."

"I know, I'm sorry."

"You poor thing, to lose your husband so young – and now this today, it is enough to take your reason I think."

I began to cry. "What an idiot I am - please forgive me."

"There, there." She laid her hand on my arm then went to the cupboard and took out the brandy bottle.

"Where was it exactly you saw this old man?" she said, pouring brandy and handing me a glass.

"By a café – it had a name I couldn't remember when I got off the tram and went back, oh what was it?

" Café Janvier maybe?" Her voice was strangely ruminative.

"Yes, that was it, the Café Janvier, I did see that name. The old man was just outside. I should have known it couldn't be Peter."

"Why so my dear?"

"You see my Peter loved to paint only trees and the open countryside, always natural scenery. I couldn't see so much as a blade of grass let alone a tree in this particular spot. Do you know this café?"

"Yes, I do." She replied, "And besides, why would he dress as an old man?"

I nodded in agreement. Why indeed would he? Of course it hadn't been Peter. Peter was dead – dead, dead, dead.

"I feel so stupid Madam…"

"Nonsense, you've been through a lot. And what happened here to Simone, that was hard for you too I know."

"You don't think she was a traitor do you?"

"Certainly not – someone had a hold over her. The Gestapo are cunning. We'll find out in time. Listen my dear you've had a great shock, why don't you go and lie down. I'll bring you some food in a while"

As I got up, Madame Dupont did an unexpected thing. She hugged me tight, and kissed my forehead.

"God bless you my child. Sleep now."

I went up, but paused outside my room, some vague sense of unease keeping me there. Peering over the banister rail I saw Madame Dupont go into the back room and close the door behind her. The back room was where the telephone was.

I crept down a few stairs and heard Madame Dupont's voice.

"Herr Commandant? We're in luck – yes, she's found him…"

Who had been found I wondered – a traitor in the group as Paul had suspected? – Oh poor Simone… Perhaps it wasn't that at all, Madame had many irons in the fire – possibly this commandant was one of her black market cohorts. I strained to hear more, but there was nothing.

Once in bed I fell immediately asleep, and dreamed of Peter. He was dressed as the big bad wolf in the Kingsford pantomime. Daddy was the Dame. Cornelius laughed so loud he fell off his seat.

That evening Madam Dupont announced she had a job for me. I was to deliver a package in the morning, another radio transmitter recently dropped by the British, to an address on the other side of the city. The plan was to relay it via a chain of agents to a resistance group in Dieppe, desperate for a radio. On hearing this, I asked where in Dieppe, thinking it may be near my grandparents' farm. Madame Dupont said she knew nothing more than she had told me.

"And don't worry," she said, seeing my look of trepidation. "What happened last time – Hugo, was unlucky. As you English say – the lightning does not strike twice."

It was just after 9am when I boarded the tram. There were no seats available, and I stood with the brown paper parcel between my feet, feeling all eyes on me.

As the tram set off it swayed over to one side. I reached out instinctively to steady myself. At the same time I heard someone say. "Madame – would you come over here please." A German officer was beckoning to me. I glanced quickly up and down the tram for a possible escape route if I needed one, but the exits at both ends were jammed with passengers. Trying to stay calm, I picked up the parcel and made my way forward.

"Is there something wrong?" I asked.

"I am afraid so Madame."

My heart began thumping like a steam hammer. "Yes – what is it please?" I said.

"I must insist that you take my seat." He indicated the seat beside him. "I was not aware that you were standing. Please accept my apologies."

"Oh – well that's very kind," I said, "thank you."

As I sat, setting my parcel on the floor he smiled and gave a little bow. The tram then suddenly lurched again, this time sending the parcel sliding along the floor. I froze. The young officer leapt forward to retrieve it.

"Goodness what have you got in here?" He said feeling the weight. "It feels too heavy for you."

"Books," I said without missing a beat. "For my aunt, she loves to read."

"I can see!" he said, testing the weight by holding the string. Well, be careful. Too many books might hurt you!" He smiled and placed the parcel at my side.

"Thank-you again," I said.

At your service Mademoiselle." he said, clicking his heels.

I turned to look out of the window, but could sense the young officer still looking at me. A few stops later he got off, biding me farewell as he left. I then realised we were passing the place where I had seen the old man painting the day before. The Café Janvier was much busier now.

As the tram pulled up outside, I looked all round but could see no one painting, old or young. Then, as a couple rose from one of the pavement tables, I saw, seated at his easel, the same old man.

Holding my breath in anticipation, I waited, hoping for the figure to make some movement, but the bell rang and we were moving slowly off.

Forgetting everything else I leapt from my seat and hurried to the rear door of the tram. Pushing between two German privates hanging on to the handrails, I jumped clear of the steps and landed heavily, tumbling over on the road. The soldiers gave a little cheer, waving as I regained my balance. Then with a spasm of alarm I had realised I left the parcel on the tram, and began to sprint after it.

"Looking for this Fraulein?" one of the soldiers shouted jovially.

From the back of the tram an object came hurtling out. The brown paper parcel containing the radio hit the cobbles a few feet away from me. Running over I saw that the side was gaping open, and quickly bundled it up. As I did so I noticed something sticking out where the paper was torn. It was the spine of a heavy book. Further investigation revealed more books – the entire parcel comprising half a dozen of them – large, dull looking textbooks – with absolutely no sign of a radio.

CHAPTER TWENTY-SEVEN

The pounding in my ears grew more intense as I stared at the old man. Could it really be Peter? I waited for some sign, some clue, anything to show me I was mistaken. His face still turned away, the rhythmical movements with the paintbrush continued.

Each step as I crossed the road seemed unending, till finally I stood there, close enough to reach out and touch him.

"Peter?" I whispered, as my hand brushed his shoulder.
The reaction was like a bolt of electricity had struck him. As he swung around I stared into a strange, mottled face, fringed with wisps of grey hair. Though the features were ancient, decrepit, the blue eyes that stared out at me were incapable of disguise.

"Oh - Peter...!"

"Keep your mouth shut you little fool." The voice was low, growling. "Do you want to get us both killed?"

"But I...please, tell me I'm not mad..."

"You're not. Now help me pick up these things and let's get away from here."

Like an automaton I stooped to gather up brushes, rags, boxes of paints, as he folded the easel. The next moment I was being dragged across the street to a narrow doorway, then up some stairs. A heavy wooden door was unlocked and we entered an apartment.

"In here - sit down, don't move." He crossed quickly to the window and peered through a slit in the curtains. "Two men outside - Gestapo - this is what your stupidity has done."
Grabbing my arm he pushed me back out onto the landing. From below could be heard banging. "They're at the front door – come on."

We ran back down the stairs and out along another alley, emerging after a few yards in what looked like the rear of a shop. A man chopping some meat stopped in mid swing as we entered. Nodding at Peter, he indicated some narrow wooden stairs.

On the first floor we entered a small bedroom. Peter closed and bolted the door.

"Who is that man," I asked.

"A friend."
His voice was gentler now, more his old self. Apart from the strange disguise on his face, time could have stood still.

"We can remain here till it's safe," he said.

I looked around the room. There was a rocking chair in the corner with an old suitcase on it, a rickety wardrobe, a washstand with a basin, a jug of water and two glasses, and in the centre an iron-framed bed. On the bedside cabinet stood a single oil lamp.

It felt cold, and I noticed sticks and coal laid ready in the fireplace. I had the bizarre thought of how nice it would be to light a fire right now, and pretend we were on a weekend away together. Peter seemed to have read my mind. Taking off his hat and coat, he knelt at the hearth and struck a match. The fire took quickly, the wood spitting, crackling in the flames. He turned to me.

"Well," he said, "don't you want to kiss your husband?"

"Peter I…"

"I know, you probably think I'm my grandfather. Wait." He poured some water into the basin, then cupped his hands and splashed his face and hair several times. He rummaged in one of the drawers, took out a large towel and buried his face in it.

When the towel was lowered the old man had gone. The golden hair I knew so well was there again, the blue eyes stared piercingly out, and the vision I had seen a thousand times in my dreams now stood alive and well before me.

"Better?"

"Yes, oh yes! But – oh I'm so sorry - it's more like I'm looking at…"

"A ghost?"

"Yes. I'm sorry."

"Come here." He threw aside the towel and took me in his arms. "There," he said a moment later. "Do ghosts kiss like that?"

I broke down in tears. "Peter – oh Peter – I never really believed you were dead. Part of me did - wanted to, I wanted to put you away, to face it – but deep down I – it wasn't even hope, just a feeling – we had no information you see, no facts, there was always doubt and it has been such a nightmare Peter, oh Peter…!"

He enfolded me in his arms once more.

"I'm sorry darling I didn't mean any of it to happen like this. If there was any way I could have let you know I was alive, I would have done it, please believe that. But it was impossible."

"Oh Peter – I've been so unhappy – and so afraid…"

"There, there." He stroked my hair. "And listen, I'm sorry if I didn't seem very pleased to see you just now."

"Perhaps you thought I was a ghost too?"

"You were the last person I expected to see in Paris that's for sure. You certainly gave me a shock."

"Well aren't you going to ask me – what I'm doing here?"

"You mean you didn't come to look for me?"

"No – well in a way yes, but there's more."

I told him everything – right from Joyce's suggestion that I take a job, the interview with Colonel Heath, joining the SOE, and all that happened since.

"Peter, I killed a man – probably others too."

"Then you are a soldier, like me."

"You have killed?"

"Of course."

"The first time – did it make you feel…"?

"Bad? Yes. Killing is always bad. But at the same time it can be the right thing to do. For me it has to be right."

"I don't think I'll ever accept that." I began crying again. Peter led me to the bed and we held each other close. After we had lay there for a while he said, "Who are you with?"

"What? Oh, Madame Dupont, she has the chocolate shop, perhaps you know her?"

Peter got up and went to the dressing table.

"Yes, I do – but I wasn't aware…it's so strange - I can't believe you're here. You of all people…"

He poured water into a glass and sipped it very slowly, watching me in the mirror as he did so.

"Well I am here." I said rather indignantly, "Doing my bit for the war effort. I'm not completely useless as you all seem to think. You're as bad as Madame, I had to persuade her to let me help with sabotaging the train."

I saw his reflection smile.

"My darling girl." The smile broke into a laugh as he said, "what a brave soul you are!"

He placed something on the dressing table. It was a gun. He then returned to the bed, took me in his arms and kissed me passionately.

It was almost dark in the room, only the firelight glimmering and a shaft of moonlight filtering through the curtains. We had made love with a savage urgency and afterwards I had fallen asleep in his arms. I realised Peter was no longer beside me.

"Peter, where are you?" I called out.

"Here." Peter emerged from the shadows smoking a cigarette. Walking to the window he adjusted the curtains, switched on the lamp and sat beside me on the bed. He was dressed, and seemed nervous.

"Get your clothes on," he said. "We have to go."

"Where to?"

He stubbed out the cigarette. "Just do as I say", he said tersely, getting up again."

I dressed quickly. "Don't worry my love," I said, slipping my arms around his waist. "Everything will be alright."

"Don't be so naïve," he said. He moved away from me and went to the window.

I looked at him for a moment then said, "Peter, who are you expecting?"

"I don't know," he said. "Look I'm sorry but we must get out of here." Then almost with a leap he came and took me in his arms.

"Oh Annie, why are you here? You don't know what danger you are in. If only you had stayed in Kingsford!" His eyes had a desperate, almost haunted look I had never seen before. "Listen - you've got to leave Paris. It's not safe. I'll take you back to Madame Dupont, she will get you out."

"And you, Peter, we'll go together."

He shook his head. "No, my work here is not yet finished. I'll come home later, for now we must...shush!" He broke off and pointed to the door. There were footsteps on the stairs, then a single knock on the door.

"Yes, who is it?" Peter's tone was casual.

"Henri Juneau - I have a message for you."

Peter seemed visibly relieved. "The butcher," he said. Something in the disembodied voice however made me uneasy. I reached for my gun in my coat pocket.

"It's alright - I told you, he's a friend."

"Peter don't open the door yet," I whispered.

Peter smiled and took the gun from my hand, placing it beside his own on the dresser. "Don't shoot Henri – he can be trusted."

Peter unlocked the door and opened it. The man I seen with the meat cleaver was framed against the landing.

"Yes Henri, what's the matter?" Peter asked.

"I...have a message," he stammered"

161

"Out of the way you fool," said another voice, as from behind the butcher a tall man, clad in a leather jacket and gloves, pushed his way into the room, closely followed by three armed German guards.

"Good evening Monsieur," said the leading man. "My name is Mencken; I am head of the Gestapo here in Paris. Sorry to break up this little soiree but we would like you to come with us."

"Peter moved towards him. "No wait - you're making a mistake here – I must speak to you...."

The Gestapo officer swung the back of his hand hard across Peter's face, knocking him to the floor.

"Well, well - two rats in the trap how fortunate."

I moved nearer to the dressing table to mask the two guns. One was only inches away. I edged my hand towards the weapon's handle and folded my fingers around it.

"Him first," said Mencken, "and her in the other car." One of the soldiers dragged Peter to his feet and pushed him towards the door.

I raised the gun and squeezed the trigger. In the confines of the small room the blast was tremendous. The soldier by the door gasped and held his shoulder.

Before I could fire again something hit my arm. I dropped the gun, and saw it skid across the floor, stopping at Mencken's feet. The pain in my arm was unbearable. Mencken picked up the gun.

"That, was foolish," he said, grabbing me where the rifle butt had struck. I winced as he gave my elbow a twist, thrusting his face close to mine. On an impulse I spat, sending a gob of saliva into his eye. For a second Mencken jerked his head instinctively away. He then hit me in the face with such force that I fell to my knees.

Minutes later I was wedged between two hulking Germans, the car travelling at speed. My arm and face throbbed, and I could taste blood oozing from my nose. I tried to keep my eyes on the car in front, the one they had put Peter in. It was late evening and I could see people at pavement cafes, young men and women arm in arm. Pausing at a junction, the sound of accordion music drifted from a restaurant. Next to me, one of the soldiers hummed the melody.

Iron gates came into view. The car passed through and stopped in a cobbled courtyard by a building hung with Swastikas. A wall plaque bore the address: 84 Avenue Foch. I was bundled from the car towards stone steps. Mencken issued orders and disappeared through tall double doors. Then I saw Peter being taken in the opposite direction.

I called hoarsely, "Peter...!"

As he turned to look at me I stumbled, and was immediately hauled upright again by the guards. In doing so I caught sight of an upper floor window, a man was looking down into the courtyard. I wrenched my neck round in search of Peter again, but he was gone.

"Keep walking," ordered the guard. A rifle rammed into my back, pushing me along a corridor till we stopped outside a wooden door with a small observation grille. The door was opened and I was thrown headlong in, my face slamming against the wall. The door closed behind me, and the key turned in the lock. I lay on a cold stone floor, quite unable to move.

Gestapo Headquarters Avenue Foch - January 1942

Kurt Gruber turned from the window of the Commandant's office as the door opened.

"Ah, Commandant - my name is Gruber." He held out his hand. "I don't think we have been introduced."

"No Herr Gruber." the commandant replied, "We have not. I have replaced Captain Muller."

"I know." Gruber smiled coldly. "I hope Muller likes the Russian front. The British woman agent you have in the cells, would you mind if I observe the interrogation? I would like to see the new methods in operation."

The Commandant nodded.

"And something else," continued Gruber, "that woman at the chocolate shop, Madame Dupont – she's involved in the resistance? I want her arrested."

"I will give the order," the Commandant replied, reaching for the telephone. "You go on ahead Herr Gruber - I will follow later then we can get started on the girl. Herr Mencken is already down there. You do know where the interrogation rooms are?"

Gruber nodded and smiled. "Of course."

Mencken was sitting behind his large desk when Gruber entered. The room was hot, and smelled of sweat and cigarette smoke. It was dark save for a small lamp on the desk. Gruber was glad he didn't have to look directly at Mencken, whom he considered an odious man. He had little respect for him or his methods.

"Ah! Gruber, glad you could join us. I have some news for you."

"For me?"

"Yes, Gruber the wonder boy…"

"Come to the point Mencken."

Mencken laughed and lit a cigarette. "You have been recalled to Berlin. Finally your incompetence has prevailed."

Gruber flinched, his fists tightening. Then he thought: this could be a lie. Mencken was mocking him, waiting for him to squirm, be humiliated. Well, he wasn't going to give him that satisfaction.

"On whose orders?" he asked.

"The Fuhrer!" Mencken laughed again. "You must have really upset someone."

Gruber breathed hard. If he went back to Berlin it could mean one thing - he was as good as dead. He knew he should have protected the train. If his informant had given him the right locations he could have done so. It was too late to worry about that now. He had to think carefully, think of a way out.

"We will leave as soon as we have broken the girl," said Mencken.

"Suppose she doesn't talk - what then?"

"Don't worry about her. She *will* talk." Mencken laughed again. "If I were you I'd worry about yourself. There's no getting out of this one wonder boy!"

CHAPTER TWENTY-EIGHT

The rope cut into my wrists, I was tied to a chair behind a large desk. All around was darkness, in the centre a pool of bright light. Someone was holding my head and shoulders.

Once captured, death would be a release, some of the SOE people had confided. At that moment I would gladly have welcomed it. My eyes were closing up, swollen from the beating I had just received.

Opposite sat Mencken. To avoid other thoughts I put a question to myself, trying to make it almost an interesting problem: could I bear further pain long enough before oblivion came? I had been trained not to talk, groomed for this event, and now it was here, happening to me. No one survived Avenue Foch. Who had told me that? Francois probably. I felt dizzy again - perhaps this was it, blessed relief, and Peter...

"A pity," Mencken was saying, "such a pretty girl too - don't you think so Gruber? Now tell me my dear, who arranged to sabotage the train? We know all about Madame Dupont, so we'll find out anyway - one way or another. But we don't want to arrest innocent people – give us the names of your fellow conspirators and you can stop that happening – if not, many poor people who have done nothing will be shot."

Appealing to my conscience now, we'd been told about that too. I didn't, couldn't answer. Blood trickled from a wound on my cheek, down into my mouth. Every bone in my body felt broken. Mencken's hand swept viciously across my face again - this way, that way, back and forth. I could feel hard lumps moving around in my mouth, and realised they must be my teeth.

The hands holding my shoulders released and I slumped forward, my head hitting the desk.

"Herr Gruber, your information was very good, but we have a stubborn one here as you can see."

A movement caused me to turn my head. Gruber was standing behind me. I wanted to face him but the pain made it impossible. Through delirium I heard a door opening. Another man seemed to have arrived. The three men were speaking in German. I understood little, only that they seemed to be arguing. An open hand slammed down on the desk. Again and again the hand hit the desk.

Mesmerised, I focused on the hand, on the little finger of which was an unusual gold ring with an engraving: a panther's head. I concentrated on the ring, staring at its detail. As it moved with the hand I saw only the ring. It was as if I was shrinking, and being drawn into the intricate design, which correspondingly grew larger, disappearing escaping into it's mysterious, sheltering heart.

The arguing voices abated. Mencken began speaking in English. "Madam, you cannot endure much more. For your own sake tell us what you know. Then you will be free to go. If not you will be executed by firing squad – as will the agent who was accompanying you at the time of your arrest. There will be no further – discussion. The choice is yours.

I knew Mencken was probably lying. As for the threat to Peter, he was probably dead already. But suppose not? What if there was just a chance that Peter was still alive; all I had to do was say the names. And maybe Mencken would keep me alive too – not out of honour or compassion, but because I might be useful to him in some way. I heard a voice inside my head, my own voice, telling Madame Dupont I would never betray them, that I was not a traitor.

"Well Madame?" said Mencken. "We must have your answer?"
I slowly raised my head. "I can tell you – nothing."

"So be it." He said "Herr Commandant you must give the order," I heard a door at the far end of the room open. A few second later, from somewhere outside came the sound of a gunshot. The sentence of death I had passed on Peter had been carried out. Immediately I felt something hard pushed against my temple.

"Pull the trigger and get it over with Gruber," said Mencken, as the gun pressed closer, boring its way into my skull. Mencken laughed. "Ha, they sent a boy to do a man's job! Give it to me…"
I began praying.
Then another voice rang out authoritatively. It was the Commandant: "No Herr Gruber," he said, "put that gun away. She is not to die today."

Gestapo Headquarters Avenue Foch - January 1942

Kurt Gruber, Mencken and the Commandant were stood on the steps of the Gestapo HQ.

"I am glad that all went well - so far," said Gruber shaking the Commandant's hand. "We still need that information from her about the other agents involved of course. Are you sure you can get it? I will handle the matter myself if necessary."

"You are needed in Berlin Herr Gruber," smiled Mencken. "Or had you forgotten?"

Gruber fixed Mencken with a stare. "I forget nothing Herr Mencken – and no one. But I think I would like to finish the job here myself first."

"We will get the information from the girl," interposed the Commandant. "You should go to Berlin as you have been ordered. Who knows what may be in store for you."

Gruber brushed down his uniform.

"Herr Mencken, he said, "I would like to speak to the Commandant privately. Would you wait in the car for me?"

Mencken glared for a moment then said unctuously, "Of course Herr Gruber."

When the two men were alone Gruber straightened his hat and turned to the Commandant. "I will endeavour to see you are rewarded for what you have done for me," he said. "The Fuhrer will be grateful, I know this."

"Gruber!" shouted Mencken from the car. "We are due in Berlin!"

"I am in your debt." Gruber saluted the Commandant, walked down the steps to the staff car and got in next to Mencken.

"Heil Hitler!" called Gruber through the open window as they sped off.

In a quiet, tree lined side road some distance from the city, Mencken's driver brought the car to a halt.

Mencken leaned forward. "What is it?" he said impatiently, why have you stopped?"

"A roadblock ahead sir, but it seems to be unmanned."

"Then drive on you fool – we must get to Berlin."

Gruber had already taken out his pistol. He aimed it deftly at Mencken's temple and squeezed the trigger. With a grunt Mencken slumped towards him, his startled, bulbous eyes staring out. As the driver turned in horrified disbelief Gruber swiftly put a bullet in his forehead, making a neat round hole.

He dragged the body of the driver to the ditch then went back for Mencken.

Hearing a noise from the trees Gruber stopped and crouched, his pistol at the ready. The figure that emerged was carrying a brown paper parcel. It was someone he despised even more than Mencken - any man who betrayed his friends was in Gruber's eyes despicable. However, right now this was one particular traitor that he needed.

"Put the gun away Gruber," called Paul. Have you got the money?"

Gruber nodded, drew his hand slowly from his jacket and showed some banknotes. Paul walked cautiously towards him, snatched the money and counted it.

"I need more than this."

"That's all you're getting, Where's the body?"

Paul indicated a small clearing. "Why did the boy have to die? He wouldn't have talked."

"Three bodies were needed," Gruber said meaningfully. "If not him, it would have been you."

"Ah but you couldn't have done it without me – this roadblock."

"True," conceded Gruber, wiping blood off his hands. "But a word of warning - be careful who you talk to. Give these to Francois," From his pocket he took out an envelope and gave it to Paul, "I'm sure he'll be glad of them."

"What is it?"

"Identity papers."

"What do you care of any of us?" Paul sneered." You'll soon be out of all this.

"Not soon enough - get rid of these bodies, and make sure they are dead."

"Don't give me orders Gruber! I could get you shot just by…"

Paul did not get further as Gruber's bloodied hands had closed round his throat.

"Be careful," he whispered through clenched teeth, his face close to Paul's. "Your friends would be very interested to learn who the real traitor is. Some of them would not like you to die too quickly." He released his grip and Paul sank to the ground wheezing for air.

Gruber went to the ditch, aimed his pistol at Mencken's head and pulled the trigger. The body briefly shuddered. He then did the same with the driver.

Opening the parcel Paul had brought, he took out clean clothes and changed swiftly into them. He tossed his uniform to Paul.

"Put this on the boy," he said, "and put him with the others."
Paul dragged the young boy's body from the clearing and flung it into the ditch. Gruber took a can of petrol from the boot of the car and handed it to Paul.

"Burn them."
Paul gave a sickened look. "No…no not the boy - he deserves a burial…"

"Do it or join them." Gruber raised his pistol.
Paul opened the can and poured some petrol over the three bodies. Gruber took out a lighter, struck the wheel, and with a well-aimed throw tossed it into the ditch. He stepped back as the smell hit his nostrils. Paul turned away.

"Have you the address?"
Paul took out a crumpled piece of paper, Gruber snatched it and quickly scrutinised.

"Now you must run – run, run, run and keep on running!"
Paul obeyed and was quickly gone.

Gruber tossed his pistol onto the passenger seat and turned the key in the ignition. The car fired into life. Sitting in the driver's seat, he looked in the rear view mirror and laughed.

CHAPTER TWENTY-NINE

I did not know how long I had been in the cell, perhaps an hour, maybe two, when I heard footsteps, then the rattle of the lock. Shielding my eyes from a splinter of bright light, I saw two guards. It was either time for my execution, or further interrogation.

The guards shouted at me to get up, which, after several awkward attempts I managed to do. "Schnell, Schnell!" As the command was issued again, I felt a stab of pain and fell against the door. One of the guards had jabbed his rifle butt into my back. I was dragged from the cell and along the corridor, through several doors, then bumped down some steps.

Suddenly there was daylight. The all round glare hurt my swollen eyes, but at a distance something caught my attention; a man wearing a blood stained butchers apron, his bicycle leant against the wall. Etienne the butcher was here for me too.

It was raining as the car left the city. The windscreen wipers swishing rhythmically back and forth on the glass rendered everything oddly normal, the kind of humdrum afternoon when time hangs heavy.

After maybe twenty minutes the open countryside came in view. The storm clouds had dispersed, and a cold winter sun was visible. I stared from the window at the tree-lined road, watching the water splash out as the tyres sliced through puddles. When would it end? Where they were taking me I had no idea. Woods were said to be usual. The Gestapo liked to play games, dark, terrible games. They would amuse themselves till they grew bored with me.

Perhaps that time had come. They had seen me cry, vomit, scream for mercy, abase myself, what more was there? Like a broken clockwork toy, I had run out of tricks. I was fearful again, but not as I had expected. What had I expected? No one had ever told of these last moments. Now it felt almost like something medical. Was that what death was; a few hours hell in a waiting room, then nothing?

The car halted. A tree had fallen across the road. Switching off the engine the driver went to investigate.

The tree was too big to move. The guard beside me now got out, shouted something and laughed. The driver returned the banter, but only for a moment, before, without a sound, he crumpled and fell to the ground. The other guard jumped from the car and raced forward.

From out of nowhere, a cat like figure leapt on him, something glinting was drawn across his throat and he too dropped lifelessly. The cat was Etienne. Having dealt with the Germans I knew he was now going to kill me. As he stood next to me with the car door open, I could see the blood on his knife.

"Get out," he said, his mirror-like eyes looking past me. "Get out now, and go to the trees."

Shivering, I obeyed. He would come from behind, his favoured method, the blade severing my jugular. Death was near, but it would be quick. I was almost at the trees.

"Etienne, get it over with." I heard my voice as exasperated, almost tetchy. Did he want to see my face, was that what this was about? I felt a hard tug at the bindings - they fell to the floor. I turned around - Etienne had gone. I limped back towards the road, and on hearing a vehicle approach, dropped into the ditch. Through the bracken I watched as a truck slowed, then pulled up.

"Get in," called a voice. It was Francoise. Too weak for questions I struggled from the ditch and took his hand. Helping me into the truck he said, "you're safe now. We have been warned to get out. Madame Dupont has already gone, so will we as soon as we have got you on your way."

"On my way?"

"Via the safe house," he replied, "you'll rest for a few days then we'll get you to the coast. You're going home."

Two days passed in the safe house. I was feeling a little better for the rest. Although my body still felt broken all over, I could at least walk more steadily. The farmer and his family had fed me and tended my wounds, risking their lives in doing so, a gift I could not repay.

Francois and Monique had arrived early morning, and we were due to leave together in the evening. The rendezvous point had been changed; Dieppe was now heavily guarded.

"We will take you to St Jacques;" Francois said. "You know the area. From there you must make your own way. Your rendezvous is a few miles on, we'll give you the details later."

Curious, I asked where Paul was.

"Dead," said Francois, in a tone that precluded further questions. Monique was equally tight lipped on the subject.

"Is there something more I should know?" I asked. Francoise shrugged and turned away.

As dusk fell three other men joined us. Francois introduced them as our back up, who would go with us to St Jacques. We set off into the night, through the woods and along the small lanes. Monique and I lay in the back of the truck with two of the men.

"Monique - " I said. "How did Paul die?"

"He was sent on a mission. Only François and Madame Dupont knew about it. I should have gone but Paul insisted on taking the young lad, the new recruit. "

"And what happened to him?"

"Killed on the mission. Paul survived, he said they had been attacked."

"So who killed Paul?"

Monique looked towards the front of the truck, to where Francois was. "He did." she whispered.

The truck suddenly halted. "Come on," said Francois, who had already jumped out of the cab. "Soldiers."

From a distance came a rumble of vehicles. "Into the ditch!" shouted Francois.

Flattening ourselves in the undergrowth, weapons poised, we waited. The engine noise ceased. Francois signalled to the other men, then, turning to me whispered,

"You must go now - we will draw their fire, you know the rendezvous point- make for the trees – you'll find your way from there."

Francoise gave a sharp whistle and he, Monique and the others sprang from the ditch firing.

Without looking back, I ran. In that instant I realised I would almost certainly never see Françoise or Monique again. They might be dead before I reached the rendezvous. My war was coming to an end.

At the trees I stopped. The sound of the gunfire was petering out. Though a cold night, the sweat was pouring from me, and the exertion had drained me. I sat down against the trunk of a tree and looked across the fields. The landscape seemed anonymous. Then I saw it, the shape I had known since childhood, a presence that could not be mistaken.

Silhouetted in the moonlight, rising majestically out of the dark earth, were the huge walls of a once great church, the ruined abbey of St Jacques. Soon I would be safe.

CHAPTER THIRTY

Maison Vert lay silent in the moon's silver light. Walking the dirt road towards the farmhouse I passed the empty byres, the wooden barn where I'd left the old bicycle that last summer, and the hayloft, all of them weed-ridden and abandoned. Grandpa would have been sad to see it.

On reaching the farmhouse, I heard a faint sound behind me, like a snapping twig or a rustle of grass. I stopped and listened, concluding it was probably a fox. Finding the door to the kitchen unlocked, I slipped quietly in. The interior was partially lit by a shaft of moonlight filtering through the kitchen window. Judging by the cobwebs that trailed over my face, no one had entered the property since the day my grandparents left

Just at that moment the moon went behind a cloud. The relative darkness was no hindrance, since I knew every inch of the house. Memories flooded back; the rabbit stew simmering in the oven, dear Father smoking his dreadful pipe, and, amid the warmth and laughter, mother's gloomy forebodings of war.

Seating myself in Gramps's chair at the head of the table, with the black Breton kitchen range behind me, I looked along the room to the dresser at the end. The blue and white crockery was still in place, as Gran would have left it.

I was woken from my reverie by a noise outside, close to the house. This must be a bold fox. Then I remembered; Gramps had written instructing his neighbours to help themselves to all the chickens. The fox was on two legs. The kitchen door then creaked and began to open slowly. I shrank further back into the darkness as a figure appeared in the doorway. As the moon cast a brief light again I saw the uniform of a German soldier and the shape of a gun.

I realised what had happened. I had been seen running towards the trees during the engagement, a search had been ordered, patrols sent out. Quite possibly this soldier was alone, an eager young wolf, out to impress.

Slowly I moved my hand down towards the pocket containing my revolver.

My heart then gave a stab of alarm; the revolver was gone. It must have fallen out somewhere between the lorry and the farm. Rigid with fear and indecision, I knew I could stay put and hope to remain undiscovered, or try to get out. The only exit however was the kitchen door, now barred by an armed soldier ten feet away from me. Suddenly in my head I heard Gramps's voice:

If any German were to step through that door, I would have a present for him...

Slowly and carefully I felt beneath the table for the ancient gun that Gramps had shown us that day. Pray God he had not asked the neighbours to collect it along with the chickens. Finding the shelf, my hand touched against the butt of the shotgun.

Inserting my fingers against the triggers of the twin barrels I waited for the German to make a move, and with it some noise that would allow me to take out the gun unheard. It was then that some dust, finding its way into my throat, caused me to emit a tiny, involuntary gasp.

The next second the moon lit up the German's face. Though he still could not see me, he now knew I was there. There was no way I could remove the gun now. Praying it was loaded I shifted the angle of the barrel towards the door, cocked the weapon and squeezed both triggers.

The recoil sent me reeling backwards off the chair, hitting my head against the kitchen range. I remained there, not daring to move. All was silent. Had the wolf been alone? If with others, would they not be here by now? I got to my feet, then realised that the soldier might still be alive, and waiting to strike. My only chance was to run for the door. Then I saw his lifeless body slumped on the floor. The blast from the gun had thrown him against the dresser, shattering the crockery. I took a last look around the kitchen. The house had been my haven, my place of happiness. Forever now it would be a place of death.

With the likelihood of German patrols on the road, I struck out across the fields. A light drizzle turned to a heavy downpour as I walked. Apart from a gentle gurgling of the rain the gutters and drains, the village was silent when I got there, the shops and houses shuttered for the night. Keeping to the grassy path to stay out of sight and avoid making any sound on the cobbles, I crept along the street until I reached the little shop owned by Mademoiselle Barr. There was an alleyway at the side of the building and I hurried along and through to the rear of the shop. The gate was locked but with a hefty push it opened.

Somewhere nearby a dog barked. I made my way quietly into the yard, up to the back door, and tried the handle. Before the occupation no one in St Jacques had kept doors locked. Fortunately it seemed Mademoiselle Barr had not altered her habits, for the door opened smoothly.

As my eyes became accustomed to the dark I made out the table and chairs, the kitchen range and a door at the far end. I had just reached it when, from the opposite end of the room another door opened, and the kitchen was suddenly flooded with light. A commanding voice rang out: "Stay where you are!"
Mademoiselle Barr was standing in the doorway, the rifle in her hands aimed straight at me.

"Don't shoot Mademoiselle!" I pleaded, "I can explain – "

"You had better, now who are you? Answer before I blow your head off!"

"It's me Mademoiselle, Annabelle Frazer."

"Annabelle, is it really you?" The old lady lowered the gun. "But you're wet through child."

Taking my coat from me she sat me down at the table and began immediately bustling about the kitchen. A moment later a plate of bread, cheeses and pickles, together with a cup of warm milk was set before me. I ate ravenously while explaining to Mademoiselle Barr all that had happened, and why I was in St Jacques under such very different circumstances to the last time I had seen her. "The rendezvous is at 7 o'clock tomorrow morning."

"You mean this morning!" replied Mademoiselle Barr, pointing to the kitchen clock. "

"Yes, yes of course…" From her face it was obvious she was thinking of the implications of my being in her home.

"I had better go now, thank you for the food," I said, getting up to leave.

Mademoiselle Barr put her hand on my shoulder.

"Wait," she said. "You came here, to me - did someone mention...?"

"No, no," I said quickly, "I was in need of food and shelter. I'm sorry Mademoiselle; I should not have come to you. It's too dangerous."

"It is dangerous for us all Annabelle." The old lady held my arm. "Listen, I have a friend, someone who will help you. The Germans will be looking for you now if they have found their comrade. We have four hours to get you out – shush!" She quickly switched off the light

From outside came the sound of vehicles braking, followed by heavy, running footsteps, jackboots on cobbles. Frenzied orders screamed out. Mademoiselle Barr tugged at my arm and hissed: "Come!"

She took me behind the counter of the shop, and slid aside one of the wall cupboards to reveal a small door, then, lighting a candle led me down some stone steps. Flicking a switch on the wall she blew out the flame. A single light bulb hanging from the ceiling dimly illuminated what appeared to be a large cellar. The walls of the cellar were lined with shelves, crammed with all kinds of merchandise. Near the steps were several large wine barrels.

"In here, quickly," said Mademoiselle Barr, and pulled at one of the barrels, which opened at one side to reveal a small compartment, complete with a little wooden seat. I squeezed my body in and sat down. Mademoiselle Barr immediately closed the barrel with a thud; the wine sealed in the other half to sloshed audibly around. It was completely dark in the barrel, and any kind of movement in the confined space extremely difficult.

"I'll let you out as soon as it's safe," came the old lady's muffled voice, then I heard her footsteps returning upstairs.

The only sound now was that of my breathing. Then suddenly there came a commotion from above; Mademoiselle Barr was having a heated argument with someone. The Germans were here. I heard the door at the top of the steps opening, then the heavy thundering of boots.

"Start at the far end, search everywhere," a German voice shouted. There were repeated loud thuds, and soon a rich, sweet smell filled my nostrils, the aroma of fine wine, as the soldiers began smashing the barrels. I was trapped, a sitting duck awaiting capture. I cursed my foolishness: why had I not run, taken my chance while I had it? Now an innocent woman was going to die because of me.

Suddenly the barrel I was in shook violently, making my head spin and my knees scrape against the wooden sides. As each blow brought my discovery closer, through the noise and the racing of my own pulse I heard Mademoiselle Barr's voice.

"There is no one here, monsieur please stop - this is my livelihood you are destroying!"

For a moment the chaotic noise abated. I held my breath

"Very well Mademoiselle," said the German officer. The boots rattled loudly up the steps, the cellar door closed and all was silence once more. Soon Mademoiselle Barr would come back down to free me

As the minutes ticked by however there was still no sound of her approach. The relief at having evading discovery was replaced by a chilling thought: what if the Germans had taken Mademoiselle Barr away? Quite apart from the horror of what they would do to her, no one else knew I was here. I searched frantically for a handle to open the compartment but there was none; the thing was sealed tight from the outside. My heart began beating hard, all other fears vanishing at the thought of being trapped forever in the barrel. I began shouting for help and banging with as much force as I could muster on the wooden slats.

Hearing some other noise I stopped: the cellar door had opened again and someone was coming down the steps. With an awful sinking in my heart I realised I had fallen into a trap; the Germans had been waiting for me to betray my whereabouts. Now it really was all over. With a thud, the barrel split open. Looking up I saw Mademoiselle Barr. "Shush child. It's all right, they have gone." As she helped me to my feet, I fell sobbing into her arms.

It was almost dawn when we set off. Mademoiselle Barr, who had given me dry clothes and more food, told me we were going to meet a friend who would help me reach the rendezvous. Keeping to the back roads and fields we arrived at a small house at the edge of the village. Mademoiselle Barr tapped softly on the door, and a young man ushered us quickly in.

"We must be careful," he said, "the Germans are everywhere."

Mademoiselle Barr told him about our own recent encounter as we followed the young man along a darkened hallway to a small kitchen. An oil lamp stood in the centre of a wooden table, cast the room in a soft, amber light.

"Rest here for a while child," said Mademoiselle Barr, "Then Pierre will take you to the rendezvous."

Pierre nodded. "It's all arranged. A boat will pick you up, it's waiting off shore now."

The old lady took me in her arms and held me for a moment.

"God be on your side," she whispered, "you're going home."

Approximately two hours later I was sprawled among coiled ropes, out of sight under the tarpaulin of a small fishing boat, heading across the Channel to England. The smell of rubber and diesel, the rhythmic swaying of the vessel, and the chugging of the engine, were making me queasy. I desperately wanted to inhale the fresh sea air, feel the salt spray on my face, even, or especially on the wounds. It would be a cleansing reminder of how close I had come to death, of what I was now leaving behind. I *was* going home, I told myself again, to the safety of England.

Through a hole in the tarpaulin I surveyed the fast receding French coastline. Would the anxiety and dread I had lived with, the suffocating terror that had been my constant companion these long months, fade away as rapidly? If so, what would replace them? I was certain of but one thing: that my life as I had known it had changed, and that nothing would ever be the same.

CHAPTER THIRTY-ONE

Rounding the final bend before Kingsford, the train whistle blew, announcing its imminent arrival. Smoke from the stack blew in dancing swirls along the carriages. I was glad to be alone in the compartment. I didn't want conversation now, however trivial.

The old familiar sights flashed by - the patchwork fields, the red and cream signal box and the four railway cottages whose gardens met the embankment. It seemed time had somehow stood still, the war hadn't reached here yet, at least, not on the outside. It was all too amazing –in a way unreal as if I had emerged from hell and was arriving in heaven.

But I had left my friends to fight on in France and that saddened me. Most devastating of all, I now knew for sure that Peter was gone forever. Morbidly I had speculated on what had become of his body. The idea of a grave I could one day visit, was I knew too much to hope for.

After being in England a few weeks, and with rest and care, a strange thing had happened; I had found myself wanting to go back. I had pleaded, even begged, but ' *they'*, the faceless ones who decided the fate of others, had sent back but one answer down the mysterious chain of command – no.

Now I was almost home, and soon to be within the safe and loving confines of my family once more. The thought brought a great sense of comfort, like sinking down into a warm, enveloping blanket. To go back, return as if to childhood and one's time of innocence – I had never understood this urge before, now it needed no explanation.

I touched Peter's ring, once again on my finger. I sent a small prayer to God thanking him that my mother had never received my envelope. The wounds on my face were healing well and the bruises, having gone from blue to black were now yellowing. My attempts to cover them with face powder and overdo the rouge would not fool Mother. There would be searching questions, but what could I tell? The truth? Never.

The train was slowing now. Coming into view was the white wooden fence of the stationmaster's garden, Big Ben the station clock and the waiting room where Michael had seen me off, where we had kissed. If things had been different - but they were not I reminded myself, and it did not do to dwell on what might have been. What had happened could not be erased or altered. Kingsford and my old home might still be a place of innocence, but in a mere few weeks, I had changed beyond measure.

Lifting my case from the rack, I slid open the door of the compartment and made my way along the corridor. As the train squealed to a final halt I opened the door and stepped down onto the platform. Through the hissing steam I saw my family, my mother's hand moving to her mouth in the moment of recognition, my father at her side, Gran and Gramps shuffling behind them. They all came hurrying up to me.

"Annie!" cried Daddy, pushing forward and kissing my cheek. I opened my mouth to speak, but no words would come. The suitcase dropping from my hand, I fell, sobbing into his arms.

I had been home about three weeks, and still not had as my father put it 'a proper chat.' The fact was I really didn't feel like saying anything, couldn't say anything – not about France, and all that had happened there. And where would I begin? I could tell both Mother and Father found my reticence on the subject odd, not to say worrying, Daddy particularly so. The effects of my experiences spoke the volumes I did not, and Daddy was the one there when I woke up with the cold sweats, screaming from the nightmares, and who would sit by my bed till I went back to sleep.

One morning he emerged from behind his paper and announced he was taking me to Mabel's teashop in the village – 'just like we used to.' Afraid of being asked awkward questions, I said I didn't feel like going. There was no arguing with him however.

"Nonsense," said Daddy cheerily, helping me on with my coat. "A good strong cup of tea and a homemade scone with jam and cream - cure's all ills."

"I'm not ill Father," I said as we left the house.

"I know that dear," he smiled, looking at me nonetheless just like a patient, "but you're my girl, and I can't help thinking what you must have been through, and if you want to tell me Annie you know I'm here to listen...."

The look on my face silenced him. I could feel an unspeakable sadness descending, blotting out the light, blanking out my mind. It was like a wall of silence had surrounded me, beyond which no one could possibly hear, let alone understand my thoughts and emotions.

"Now then," began Daddy in a fresh attempt at heartiness as we sat down in the teashop, "what shall we talk about? Miss Dove and the wayward sea captain?"

I actually found myself smiling. The thought of Miss Dove romantically associated with anyone other than her famously staid fiancée was just so funny. My father beamed delightedly.

"I thought that would get your attention - want to know more?" he whispered conspiratorially.

"Daddy! And they say women gossip - I thought Mummy and her friends were bad enough!"

He laughed loudly, and proceeded to fill me in not only on Vera Dove's intrigues, but the goings-on of half of Kingsford during my absence. Mabel could plainly overhear, her expression one of embarrassment mixed with occasional salacious interest. She looked relieved when Daddy finally got up to pay the bill.

Linking his arm in mine we made our way along the High Street. As we passed the smithy, its old wooden doors now closed, I naturally thought of poor Joshua Bracegirdle, and the terrible accident that had befallen him.

"Does anyone use the smithy now," I asked.

"A young man from outside the village," said Daddy. "He comes in once a month or so. Not much work about nowadays."

"Joshua would have quite liked that – not being busy I mean - he could have spent more time poaching. You know Daddy, the last thing I recall about Joshua was that story of his – you remember – how he saw strange lights, down by the Colonel's river?"

My father laughed. "Yes, old Josh could certainly spin a good yarn."

"How did he die Daddy?"

"Accident – though some want to read more into it."

"A murder you mean - in sleepy Kingsford?"

"Quite. Note that's one subject I didn't gossip about. He'd probably been out tickling trout as usual and slipped. Must have gone down with a bang though."

"How do you mean?"

"To break his neck like that – and what with the rumours about the Colonel and his wife."

"Rumours?"

"The talk started shortly after you left in fact."

"Talk?"

"About them being - well, fascists."

"Fascists? But that couldn't possibly be true."

"Some people are still saying as much. Of course the colonel is denying any such involvement. They're both keeping their heads down though, until all this nonsense blows over. "

As we passed the Horse and Groom I paused and looked up to the room where Peter and I had spent our wedding night. We had made love there and then fallen asleep, wrapped in each other's arms. There was so much I wanted to tell him now. Turning away I found Daddy beside me. Without speaking he put his arm around me, and gently guided me home.

After France, and Peter, and all that had happened over there, I had come to think nothing remotely strange or shocking could ever happen again. I was wrong.

The 22nd of March began much like any other day. The first indication it was not going to end that way came with reports of smoke rising in the vicinity of Colonel Travers" home.

It was Cornelius who raised the alarm; he had seen the smoke as he was walking down the High Street early that morning. In a trice the Kingsford fire crew were mustered, and made their way swiftly to the Manor House to investigate.

On arrival they found the place completely engulfed by fire, flames leaping high from the gables, that were already beginning to splinter and crash to the ground. Despite pitching in manfully, the crew could do little to quell the advance of the blaze, the intense heat making it impossible to approach, let alone enter the house. There was no sign of the occupants.

It was an hour later before any search could be made, when, amid the charred and smoking timbers, the remains of Colonel and Mrs Travers were identified. While the police and other officials conducted their investigations, the village seemed suspended in disbelief. For the Colonel and his wife, such fixtures in their world, to have overnight been spirited away in flames, was hard to take in.

That evening Mother was due at her knitting circle. The other ladies had all agreed the best policy after such a tragedy was to proceed as normal and display the kind of stiff upper lip the Colonel would have approved of – 'keep calm and carry on knitting' as Daddy put it when he drove her down to the hall at around 7 o'clock.

"I'll walk back," said my mother as she waved him off.

After calling in for a quick pint at the Groom, Daddy made his way home, and together we sat and listened quietly to the radio.

At 10pm he looked up. "Where's your mother got to?" he said, "surely they've run out of wool by now."

"But probably not gossip," I yawned.

"True. Sounds like it's coming on to rain out there. I'll take the motor down."

"Shall I come?"

"Aren't you tired?"

"No – yes - oh I don't know…"

"Well, come on sleepy head! Lets get going or your Mother will be wet through."

With the decision made I quickly put on my coat and Daddy and I set off in the car towards the village.

22nd March - 1942

It was 9.10 pm when Kurt Gruber crossed the fields at Hunters Bridge. Following the wooded path, he came to a clearing in the trees, halted and looked up. Where previously had stood the sloping gables of the Manor House, now rose spindle-like outlines of blackened smoking timbers, the charred skeleton of a once fine old house.

Gruber took out a pair of binoculars, and scanned the ruin for several minutes. He hadn't intended to kill the colonel and his wife but their uncooperative attitude left him no choice, the colonel was becoming dangerous and a liability.

His escape from France had been dangerous enough and travelling through London now the war had started even more precarious. If only the colonel had been more willing to help him and given him a place to stay for a while this mess could have been avoided.

The two other agents were holed up in the barn. Gruber introduced himself and the three had meticulously set the house on fire. They had hidden most of the day but as darkness approached Gruber had had to make sure the job was done.

He looked at his watch; in half an hour he was to meet the other agents for the journey back to London. He scanned the ruins once again; Satisfied at last, he headed for the village.

Kingsford was quiet and in darkness as he approached from the fields. Upon reaching the high street Gruber quickly made his way to the rendezvous point, the corner of the alleyway leading to Millers Lane opposite the village hall.

It was 10 pm, the other two should have been there, if they didn't arrive soon he would have to go, catch the train without them and leave them to their own devices.

From behind him he heard footstep, the two agents emerged from the alleyway. Now it was time to leave, to get away. Just at that moment the village hall door opened. Instantly a bright light shone from within, several women emerged, laughing as they dispersed along the street.

One of the women crossed the road and came directly towards them. Gruber watched her - she was heading straight for them. He whispered orders for the other two to be silent. Momentarily she hesitated, Gruber bent his head, but as she came level with him the man opposite to him struck the lighter, the flare illuminated Gruber's face. Startled the woman hesitated. Gruber and the woman stared at each other. Their eyes lingered. Quickly she entered the alley. Gruber drew one last draw on the cigarette, threw it down onto the wet pavement, and followed her into the darkness.

CHAPTER THIRTY-TWO

As we pulled up outside the village hall it seemed to be all locked up.

"That's odd." Daddy remarked, "She must have left already."

"She often takes the back lane remember." I said.

"But we'd have passed her on the way down."

The rain was increasing now, blowing down the street and running into swift rivulets on the cobbles.

"We'll drive back up – see if we can catch her at the crossroads – she'll be a drowned rat in this lot."

Daddy turned the car around and we headed back the way we had come.

As we came to the junction where the High Street met the lane, something appeared in the headlights, someone was waving their arms. Daddy wound down his window.

"Cornelius old fellow," he said, "can we drop you home? We're just looking for Mrs Frazer – haven't seen her have you?"

Then I caught sight of the gravedigger's expression. It was a face stricken with horror.

"Come quick!" he cried.

"Stay here Annie." Daddy grabbed a torch from the glove compartment, stepped out of the car and followed Cornelius down the back lane.

A few seconds later I leapt out and went after them. I found Daddy and Cornelius hunched over something lying on the ground.

"I stumbled over her I swear – she was just lying there," wailed the gravedigger.

"Yes Cornie – yes, yes, yes."

"Daddy – what is it?"

Father turned to me, a pained expression in his eyes.

"Oh Annie, Annie" he said, "Your mother...she's dead!"

CHAPTER THIRTY-THREE

Since Mothers death there had been a stream of visitors and well-wishers, Miss Dove was just one of the latest.

"Oh Miss Dove – hello – do come in."

"Vera dear, please," said Miss Dove in a hushed voice.

"I won't stay long. I just had to come and see you, and your poor father. I didn't get the chance to speak to either of you properly at the funeral – he gave a lovely oration I must say – he's been so brave."

"Yes he has."

"You too of course - we're all so sad about what happened – and after losing your poor husband too. Has there been any word from the police?"

"Nothing. They seem to think a passing vagrant may have tried to rob her."

"But I understand her purse was still on her when you found her?"

"Yes – it's all a bit of a mystery."

"I'm so terribly sorry."

"Thank you – my father's resting upstairs."

"Oh you mustn't disturb him on my account."

"Please sit down," I said, leading the way into the sitting room.

Miss Dove settled herself on the couch. "What will you do now?"

"I want to stay here of course, but Daddy says if I do want to go back to work..."

"In London would that be?"

"Perhaps – anyway, he says that I mustn't fret too much about him."

"And will you – go to London I mean? Oh I'm sorry dear, that's really none of my business now is it. We do miss you at the office, though of course Michael's not there either, even though he could come back now if he chose..."

"But surely - Michael's still overseas - with the RAF," I said.

Vera's hand went to her mouth. "Oh I'm sorry – then no one's told you?"

"Told me what?"

"Michael's home dear."

"But he can't be – he wasn't at Mother's funeral."

"No, he…doesn't go out. His plane went down - he's all right, sort of, but…" Miss Dove looked at her shoes.

"Why did no one tell me – I must see him at once."

"I should warn you dear, he's – poorly."

"Even more reason to see him," I said.

"It's not just that…"

"What? Miss Dove - Vera - for goodness sake tell me."

At that moment my father entered the room. Somehow the subject of Michael was dropped, and before I knew it Vera Dove had taken her leave.

Mrs Oakes greeted me cordially. "I'm afraid you'll find him rather down Annabelle," she said ushering me into the sitting room.

A log fire crackled in the grate, and there was a strong smell of beeswax furniture polish.

"Naturally," I said, "I understand he was hurt?"

Mrs Oakes looked at me steadily for a moment.

"How much do you know?" she asked.

"Only that really."

This was true. After Vera's departure I had left the house without a word to Daddy and hurried straight round to Michael's home.

"You've known Michael a long time - I'm sorry you weren't informed."

"Informed of what?" I asked anxiously.

Before she could reply the door swung open. I saw a pair of feet, and the tartan pattern of a blanket. A wheelchair had glided silently into the room, and seated in it was Michael. It was not however, Michael as I remembered him. A momentary shaft of sunshine from the window bathed him in it's light as he turned to look not at me, but out towards the garden. His face was altered almost beyond recognition. The skin, pocked with craters, was a patchwork of leathery plateaus stretched taut between what remained of his features. The misshapen skin had the effect of pulling his left eye downwards, the pupil bulbous and enlarged. It was like looking at the face of a reptile.

Recoiling in horror, my mind at the same time raced to comprehend what I saw.

"Michael…how…good to see you," I stuttered.

"Really?" he murmured, still staring out of the window. "I wouldn't have thought so."

"Oh Michael…"

"You shouldn't have come - not you, not here."

"Don't you want to see me?" I said, straining for the right tone, the right words. But what were they, confronted with this? "Well I'm sorry we didn't meet in London," I said, attempting a roundabout entrée into some kind of conversation. "I've been rather busy myself. You're not the only one who's been licking Hitler you know!" I added boldly.

"I rather think the jackboot's on the other foot in my case don't you?" he said, and spun his chair round suddenly to face me. "Well come on, get it over with - take a good look at the freak and then you can be on your way."

"Michael I - I'm so sorry." I wanted to reach out and hug him, kiss him, but something other than revulsion – which in itself was strong enough - held me back.

"Yes, everyone's very sorry, isn't that nice of them." He turned his chair away again and wheeled it right up to the window.

Keeping his back to me, he said slowly, "I heard about your ma. A bad business, I'm sorry. I didn't make the funeral…God! - and here's me reeking of self-pity. Not very heroic is it, but then I suppose I was never cut out to be a hero, unlike your Peter - any news of him by the way?"

"Has no one told you?"

"No – you see they don't regard me as human anymore – rightly so…."

"Peter's dead Michael."

"Oh. Lucky blighter, wish I was." He said with a measured irony.

"Michael, you know you don't mean that."

"No - but for your sake not his. I mean you're the one who must be in agony."

I sighed heavily "I hardly know what I feel lately."

"How could you – the world just doesn't make sense any more. And what about old man Travers – do you suppose he was smoking in bed?"

"They're saying it was a suicide pact - after the rumours."

Michael laughed, "The Colonel; a Nazi? Never! - And not one to throw in the towel either. Those loose tongues want cutting off in my opinion. Well, anyway, I expect you have someone to meet, some smart, good looking chap to take you somewhere, so I won't keep you..."

"Do you really want me to go?" I asked.

He made no reply. I walked to the window and rested my hand on his shoulder. I stood there for a moment, listening to the ticking of the mantle clock, then turned

As I did so Michael's hand reached back and grabbed mine. In an instant we were both weeping, locked in an awkward, desperate embrace.

"I was the only one to survive." Michael said. After our tears had come words, conversation - even a little laughter.

"We were coming back from a bombing raid when the flack hit. Managed to get home but crashed on landing. The crate was alight – just had to get out."

"You did the right thing," I said.

"Did I hell!" Should have died with the others. Sorry."

"What do the doctors say – about your injuries?"

"That I'll make a full recovery, that's a joke. I might walk again a bit I suppose, but cricket's a thing of the past, and I'm going to be the elephant man for good."

"But Michael they can do wonderful things nowadays," I pleaded.

"Tell you anything to keep your pecker up you mean."

"Is that what you think I'm doing?"

Deep within the scorched wreckage of Michael's once handsome face, there came the flicker of a smile.

"We always did call you Pollyanna," he said. "What happened to your face if you don't mind my asking? Look as though you've been through it too - thought you'd got some ministry job?" He leaned forward and gently touched the red and blue bruise showing through the makeup on my cheek.

"Nothing serious," I smiled.

There was curiosity in his eyes now though.

Come on Annie," he said, "you don't" get that sort of damage sitting at a typewriter."

"You know my typing!" I replied jokily. But I felt uncomfortable now, fearful at where the conversation might go. I quickly finished my tea and put the cup back on the tray that Mrs Oakes had brought in earlier for us.

"Do you mind if I go home now Michael?" I said.

"Of course not – but come again, now that you've…"

"Seen the freak?" I finished off his sentence

"That's right." Behind the grotesque mask the smile flickered again. "We've both got time on our hands, now our war's over."

I leaned over and kissed his cheek.

"Goodbye Michael."

"Till we meet again," he said, and turned his wheelchair back towards the window.

As I was about to open the sitting room door he said,

"Peter lied to us you know."

I stopped, a strange, chill feeling inside me.

"Oh yes, he told us lies. And we believed him."

"What are you trying to say Michael," I said.

"That day he came back," Michael went on, still facing the window, "he told us he'd arrived on the two o'clock train."

"And so he did," I replied. I could see Michael shaking his head.

"He couldn't have done. You see Annie, that particular day, the two o'clock train to Kingsford was an hour late."

I suddenly felt very tired. "I'm sorry Michael, I don't understand. We'll talk about it another time. Goodbye."

Outside a gentle rain had begun to fall. I closed the front gate to Michael's house and began walking down the lane. Passing a familiar stile I paused and looked out across the fields to a single oak tree, standing tall beside a hedge.

Bare-branched now, I remembered it on a golden summer's day when Peter had set his easel under its leafy canopy, and I had attempted to paint it. 'Remember the shadows.' I recalled his words. There had been many shadows, even on that glorious day. I felt them now, creeping upon me as remorselessly as the darkening sky, the black clouds gathering overhead.

There was a flash of lightning then the thunder cracked. I shivered as the rain intensified, and quickened my step. Soon I was running.

"Why? I shouted to the raging storm, "why didn't I die?" In utter misery, I slumped to the ground.

The heavy coat, smelling of tobacco and soil, settled around my shoulders. The warmth soothed me. Someone was near me, showing me kindness.

"Here young Missy." a friendly voice was saying. "You'll catch the chills."

I looked up, and through my tears saw Cornelius. The gravedigger tucked the coat further around me and helped me to my feet.

"We all got a time to meet our maker Miss," he smiled. "But yours ain't yet a while."

As we walked back along the lane towards the village, I looked back at the tree. I knew it would flourish again, once the spring came. With a heavy heart I made my decision.

Two weeks later I was at Kingsford station again. I had asked Daddy and Gran and Gramps to be there. As the London train pulled slowly alongside the platform Gran tearfully handed me some sandwiches she had made.

"Now you will be careful dear," she said, "and write as soon as you can. We want to know you're safe." I kissed her cheek, then Gramps, and promised.

Since my mother's death they had both looked so small and sad, as if the grief had shrunk the life from their own bodies.

Then it was Daddy's turn, covering his feelings with bluster and funny remarks about the weight of my case as he hauled it into the carriage.

"Its only things I'll need Daddy."

"Rebuilding London this time are we? I'd swear you've got the first ton of bricks in there!" He gave an overly loud laugh then squeezed me tightly in his arms.

Looking over Daddy's shoulder I saw that two other people had come onto the platform. It was Mrs Oakes, and behind her, Michael. He was not in his wheelchair but walking with the aid of crutches. I realised how much I had been hoping to see him.

"Just like the first time I guess Annie," he called, hobbling towards me. He smiled and turned his face upwards. "But with certain obvious differences."

As I flung my arms about him, my head resting on his shoulders, he whispered, "You don't have to go you know."

"I know," I said, "it's just that my war isn't over yet."

194

CHAPTER THIRTY-FOUR

In the April of 1942 I accepted Joyce's offer to share her flat, situated on the Earls Court Road end of Kensington High Street, just above a dress shop.

"We're going to have so much fun!" She had made this remark so often in her letters and telephone calls leading up to my arrival, that I had almost begun to dread moving in. I knew what Joyce's fun meant - parties, dancing and generally out till all hours, or having people round. Once I would have been thrilled at this prospect, but not now. All I wanted was to live and work quietly and diligently, valuing, indeed craving, long periods of solitude.

"I'm sorry Annie, I didn't think, oh and so soon after your poor mother... I'm the most insensitive soul alive." Joyce said ruefully, when I asked if I might be spared some of the social whirlwind she was planning. Her reaction in turn then made me feel a little churlish – 'not thinking' I realised, was one of my friend's most endearing qualities.

I found the flat small, but Joyce had made it comfortable and homely, full of pictures and postcards and photographs, a vase of fresh flowers on the sideboard.

"It's charming Joyce," I said, setting my case down and looking around.

"You're on the left, the bedrooms are the same size but yours is quieter being at the back."

"Oh you shouldn't really have taken too much notice of what I said about wanting peace and quiet," I said, though relieved to know my room wouldn't be overlooking the street.

"I'll get the kettle on," said Joyce disappearing into the kitchen. I sat down on a rather tatty brown checked couch beside the hearth, which housed a small electric fire. On the oak sideboard beside the flowers, were arranged several photos of Joyce and her family.

Opposite was a bay window, a shapeless armchair in floral covers rested against thick net curtains. There was an oak bureau, which almost matched the sideboard, and in the centre of the room a dining table set with two places. Everything about the place seemed unfussy and relaxed.

Glancing up at the mantelpiece I noticed another photograph. Something about it made me curious, and getting up to take a closer look I saw that it was of Joyce and Michael. They looked very happy in each other's company.

"That was taken just before he went away for training." Joyce had come back in and set a tray down on the table. "We met up here, in London."

"Oh," I said, feeling vaguely unsettled. "I didn't know you and Michael were…"

"We were courting - until his discharge," Joyce said. "I've not seen him since. He doesn't want me to visit."

This was a revelation. After a pause I said, "I've seen him. I went to his house a couple of weeks ago." Now Joyce looked uneasy.

"You?"

"Well yes," I said. "I mean; we've always been friendly…"

"Yes, yes, of course dear – I'm sorry…"

"Nothing to be sorry about."

Does he look awfully bad?" Joyce asked, adding quickly, "not that it would matter to me."

"It's not pretty I'm afraid. But I told him, they can do ever such a lot nowadays, his face I mean – and when he came to see me off he didn't need the wheelchair."

"See you off?"

"Yes he came to the station yesterday – I wasn't expecting it."

I thought: why hadn't I seen this before? Looking at Joyce's expression in that moment, I realised she was deeply in love with Michael.

"You really like him, don't you," I said.

"More than that." she sighed. "But now you've confirmed my worst fears I'm afraid."

"Whatever do you mean dear?"

Joyce picked at the cover of the couch, her eyes misty now.

"It's always been you Annie – for Michael - I've just been playing second fiddle, I should have known better…"

"Tommy rot Joyce – Michael and I are more like – brother and sister, nothing more." I could feel myself blushing at this lie.

"In your eyes maybe, but for him it was always you, till Peter arrived and swept you off your feet. That was a bitter blow for him."

"How do you know all this? Did Michael tell you?"

Joyce nodded. "One night, while he was in London. We went up to the West End, we both got a little bit merry - that's when he poured out his heart to me."

Not knowing what to say next, I gave a little nervous laugh. Joyce carried on. "The ramblings of a drunk you might say, but I tell you Annie, that's when the truth comes out."

She got up from the couch and ignoring the tray of tea, took a bottle of sherry from the sideboard and poured two glasses.

"Here's mud in your eye," she said, handing me one.

"Thanks."

"Michael also told me how he hated the way Peter sometimes treated you, and that he couldn't always understand him."

"I can see what he meant," I said, "Peter could be a bit remote. What was your impression?"

"Wouldn't be for me to say, I mean I hardly knew him."

"But you normally have opinions on everybody," I smiled, "whether you know them or not – don't take that the wrong way!"

"Annie, Peter was your husband."

"Yes," I persisted, "but you're my best friend – and you can be honest with me. Did you think Peter and I we were suited?"

"You loved him and that's all that matters."

"Oh really Joyce you're impossible!" I laughed. "Perhaps some more sherry will loosen your tongue." I fetched the bottle and topped up her glass.

"No, some things are sacrosanct," she insisted, "even to a frightful gossip like me."

"Have it your own way," I smiled archly, the sherry already taking effect

"Not only that, you can't avoid fate – none of us can."

"Are you saying the future's mapped out for us?" I said.

"Everyone. You loved Peter but he's gone, I love Michael but he loves you. I don't intend to give up on him though."

I laughed. "So - not quite everything's mapped out?"

"Oh yes Annie, everything. But your map may not be the same as mine."

"This analogy's losing me – maybe I need a compass too!"

"Or another sherry."

"What happened to the tea?"

"Stewed."

"So will I be in a minute!"

"Anyway," said Joyce, "I've decided to see Michael whether he likes it or not, in a couple of weeks I shall go up there, tell him what's what."

I sipped some more sherry, wondering how, or if I should respond to this last piece of information.

Joyce then said, "Anyway enough of me, how are you feeling?"

"Exhausted, weary, numb – a bit empty inside if you must know."

"No wonder, with what you've been through, your mother, and before that France, and Peter…" Joyce stopped abruptly and fiddled with the couch cover again. "Of course, I'm only surmising about that." She looked down at the floor.

"Of course." I said. "You heard nothing more about him then – through your office I mean?"

"No."

"Well there's rather a lot to tell. "

"Don't feel you have to right now."

"No, no, I want to."

"Annie, you asked me earlier on to be honest, ok here goes. I know you've been though hell - just looking at you tells me that. For your sake, I wish you'd never met Peter. Never fallen in love with him, and never had to get that damn telegram telling you he was dead." Having said this she threw her hands up in shame

"Oh I'm so sorry Annie, I didn't mean that, its just I feel for you so, I wish I could have prevented it somehow, I feel so awful, please forgive me…!"

My tears began to fall. I could not hold them back. I had to tell Joyce, tell her I didn't resent her words, but make her understand too, why I had loved Peter, why I had gone to France - and that I had found him again.

"But he didn't die Joyce," I said, "At least, not then. You see, I found him again, in Paris, I found him, but we were arrested and they shot him, the Germans killed him…."

Joyce gathered me in her arms, and together we wept.

CHAPTER THIRTY-FIVE

It was December 1943. I had been living with Joyce in London for eighteen months. It had not been as I had originally thought, all dances and men; instead she had taken care of me. My mundane work, of typing letters and filing was a far cry from France and gratefully I buried myself into it. My reluctance to venture further than our flat must have been of great annoyance to Joyce, but she was not going to be beaten; and with a little gentle persuasion encouraged me to live again. Slowly I began to feel like my old self.

"What work did Joyce do Nan?" Sally asked

"I never knew; we couldn't talk about it. I presumed she did something similar to me - but the rages she came home in sometimes..........then there were the tears. She would rush straight to her room and lock the door then after a few hours emerge and the old Joyce would be back again. Stranger still were the telephone calls, mostly in the night. Never saying a word, she'd pack a few things in a bag and would be gone for days. I never asked her where she'd been and she didn't volunteer to tell me; I think it was her admirers; she had a few did Joyce and because I still missed Peter she kept that side of her life from me.

Christmas shopping in London was no longer the joyfully excessive annual ritual that for some it once had been. One felt lucky to obtain basics, never mind anything fancy. On the third Saturday before Christmas that year, I decided nonetheless to have a go. In the morning, as I was adjusting my beret to the jaunty angle favoured by certain film stars, Joyce appeared in the hall behind me and issued her now familiar reminder.

"Now don't forget your gas mask dear."

"Oh really Joyce, it's Saturday," I said, tilting the beret to the opposite side.

"Oh well in that case I'm sure Hitler will tell the Luftwaffe to stay at home too!"

"Yes, very funny, anyway I'm only going to Oxford Street to try and get a few gifts," I said. "Selfridges' have got a new batch of lipsticks in apparently."

Joyce put the string handle of the gas mask box over my shoulder.

"Careful, you'll spoil my look," I said, taking my keys from the hallstand.

"Sorry I'm sure Miss Dietrich. Pick me up a lipstick if there's any going cheap."

It was cold and drizzling at the bus stop. Luckily it wasn't long before a number 23 pulled up. It was already quite full, but I managed to squeeze into a seat on the lower deck next to a kind-faced old man and what looked like his young grandson on his lap.

"Hello there, Oxford Street please Violet," I said, handing the young blonde haired bus conductress the fare. I saw her most mornings on my way to work, and we had become acquainted.

"Doing overtime?" I asked.

"All the bloomin' time," she laughed. "Where you off to then duck?"

"Shopping."

"Anything special?" she enquired, handing me my ticket.

"Lipsticks. Christmas presents - I want to get in before the rush."

Violet's eyes widened. "Whew! Not seen any of that stuff for years. Don't suppose they got any nylons?"

I smiled and shook my head. "Not that I've heard."

"Best keep in with them yanks then I suppose." She winked and disappeared up to the top deck.

I looked out of the window. The London landmarks were a familiar sight to me now, many of the historic buildings overshadowed by barrages, monstrous, gas filled balloons, like huge fat cigars, floating high above Buckingham Palace, the Houses of Parliament and other important sites. Many places were noticeably bomb-damaged or with sandbags piled high in front of doors and windows.

The bus arrived in Oxford Street.

"See you soon dearie," called Violet, waving from the platform as I jumped down onto the crowded street. As I did so, I heard a noise like a lazy motorbike, droning through the air above me.

"Doodlebug!" shouted Violet. "Take cover duckie!"

Blindly I ran into a shop doorway and crouched down, burying my head in my arms. Then I felt something dragging me, pulling me into the shop. There was a deafening bang followed by the sound of crashing glass, which seemed to go on forever. When I opened my eyes, everything seemed dark. Some heavy shape was pressing down above me.

"So sorry," said a voice, "but under the counter seemed the safest place under the circumstances. Are you all right?" A hand took mine and helped me to my feet. The air was thick with a choking dust, and there was a rancid smell, like oil.

Outside there was a clanging of fire engine bells, mixed with the cries of the injured and voices, anxious voices calling out, shouting commands. Lumps of masonry and huge, jagged sections of plaster lay all around. Several people were sitting or stumbling about, some with blouses or kerchiefs held to wounds, or helping others. Heaps of garments half buried among the rubble suggested I was in what was left of a clothes shop, and I saw, flung askew amid shards of glass in the gaping space where the window had been, a signboard that read 'Bartholomew and Spooner, Gent's Outfitters'.

I turned to see who had spoken to me, and saw a young man brushing down his jacket.

"I only came in for a tie," he smiled. "I suggest we leave before the rest of that ceiling comes down." He took my arm and we picked our way over the rubble towards the doorway

Looking down I saw that the pavement I had been crouching on moments before had completely disappeared - in its place a huge crater stretched halfway across the road.

"Mind your step!" said my companion, and lifted me up through the window space, then down the other side onto solid ground.

Smoke was drifting up from the crater. Looking down I saw the twisted metal shell of a red double-decker bus with the number 23 visible. Its shattered windows gaped like empty eye-sockets. Hung from one of them was the lifeless body of Violet, her blonde hair curled over the collar of her uniform. I looked among the milling crowds for the old gentleman and his grandson, but there was no sign of them.

"Drink this," said the young man. We were sat in a pub called the King's Head, somewhere off Oxford Street. "Good for shock - by the way, I'm William Pearson."

"Annabelle Barker." We shook hands, my own still unsteady. I took a sip of the drink he had bought me and shivered.

"Don't tell me you've never had whisky before?" he laughed.

"Once or twice," I said.

"It's clear you know, whiskey, when it's first made, they add the colour later. Sorry, that must sound like awful small talk at a time like this Miss Barker."

"It's Mrs Barker actually, my husband was killed in action," I said.

"Oh I'm so terribly sorry, please forgive me."

"You weren't to know."

"This war changes so many lives."

"Sometimes small talk's a relief."

"You're too accommodating to a bore."

"You just saved my life Mr. Pearson, hardly boring."

"Nonsense, I was just desperate to buy a tie."

There seemed to me something familiar about his voice.

"Tell me Mr. Pearson," I said, "have we perhaps met before do you think?"

"I would have remembered if I had met *you*," he laughed.

"You have an English name but…"

"The foreign accent you mean? I was born in Warsaw, grew up there, my parents were English, Father was a diplomat with the Polish Embassy and my mother taught French, but when Hitler came to power Father sent Mother and I back to England, he was to follow later but he never did."

"I didn't mean to pry, Mr. Pearson," I said. "I'm sorry."

"I forgive you. And call me William – now, how about another drink?"

I looked at my watch, the glass had broken but it was still ticking.

"I should be getting back - Joyce will be worried. She's an old friend I share a flat with, and she's terribly sweet but fusses so, and mad as a March Hare sometimes…" I was rambling, one half of me saying I ought to go, that it was not right I should be out in a pub drinking with a strange man, the other half of me wanting desperately to stay.

William laughed. "Maybe some other time then - but let me at least walk you to the bus stop."

I sensed him being flirtatious, but not disagreeably so. Was it his smile, the gentleness of his voice, or the way his brown eyes looked softly into mine that made my pulse quicken. I returned his smile and accepted. What harm would it do to let him walk with me? After all, I wasn't ever going to see him again.

It was early evening when I finally reached the flat. After searching my handbag and my coat pocket vainly for my keys, I tapped lightly on the door. It was quickly opened.

"Annie!" Joyce exclaimed. "Where've you been? I've been worried sick."

I burst immediately into tears. Joyce sat me down, switched on the electric fire and administered sherry, whereupon I gushed out everything that had happened to me since I left the flat that morning, concluding my account with, "And this man saved my life."

"I knew I should have gone with you," said Joyce, rubbing my cold hands in a gesture of motherly concern.

"You couldn't have stopped the doodlebug. I owe my life to Violet too, poor love. I can't bear to think she's gone, and I'll never hear her cheery voice on the bus again – I hardly knew her, yet it was like we'd been friends forever, oh I know that makes no sense…" I was convulsed in another storm of tears.

Joyce stroked my hair. "The kindness of strangers, the ships that pass in the night – we make connections with people stronger than words can express sometimes. It's a mark of our humanity. It makes perfect sense dear."

Half and hour later, after some food and several cups of tea, Joyce said quietly, "So, who was he then, this chap in the shop?"

"He said his name was William Pearson."

"What was he like - tall, dark and handsome – or fair…?" Joyce stopped short.

"Like Peter you mean?" I said. "No, not at all like Peter."

"He seems to have made an impression. Are you seeing him again?"

"No of course not! He's probably married and in any case…"

"In any case what?"

"Joyce - he took me to a pub for a whisky, that's all, then walked me to the bus stop. He was just being a gentleman."

"Well, that's a shame, but probably for the best. After all, you can't go falling for everyone who saves your life." She winked at me and we both laughed.

That night I stood close to the window, staring down into the empty street. Sleep was impossible. The moment I closed my eyes, the events of the day replayed themselves over in my mind.

In France there had been the possibility of death at any hour of the day or night, and several times I had steeled myself, expecting it.

Back home I had found that in the peace of the English countryside or here on London, its streets teeming with life and energy, it was the same, a person could be snuffed out without warning – crossing the road, sitting in a café, riding a bus – one minute you were here, the next gone.

Pressing my cheek against the window, the cold glass chilled my skin. I peered into the darkness to conjure the image of Peter. But none would come. Instead another face looked out at me from the window. It was that of William Pearson.

CHAPTER THIRTY-SIX

A week later I was assigned to the Office for Administration, run by Sir James Metcalf. What was administered here I was as yet uncertain. All desk jobs seemed one and the same after SOE and France, and I was grateful for the safe, predictable nature of such work – telephone calls, typing and filing, the steady reassuring tick of the clock, the solid walls and equally solid hierarchy and daily routine of office life.

Every day at precisely noon, Sir James would leave his desk and go down to the executive dining room. One Friday therefore, noticing that the clock showed ten past the hour and he had still not emerged, I ventured to tap lightly on the half open door of his inner sanctum.

"It's gone twelve Sir James," I said, "are you lunching in today as usual?"

"No my dear," he replied, "I'm meeting Colonel Chalmers at two, I'll get something later."

"Oh, then I'll go to lunch now – if that's all right?"

"Yes, yes you run along – although..."

"Yes?"

"Could you type this first? I need it for this afternoon."

"Of course Sir James."

The typing turned out to be a long and detailed report. By the time I had finished, got it checked and gone downstairs, the NAFFI canteen was empty. The choice of food at best was limited, but all that remained now was a handful of vegetables, some curling sandwiches and a scoop of arid looking mashed potato. After picking the best of the wilting sandwiches and pouring a cup of stewed tea, I sat down at a table at the far end of the room by the window.

All morning thick grey clouds had hung low over the city and by lunchtime it had begun to snow. I watched the white flakes falling on the pavement, thickening the icy slush.

"Hello Mrs Barker," said a voice behind me. "May I sit here?"

Turning around I saw a smiling man carrying a tray of lunch. It was William Pearson. "I...hello...yes..." For some reason I was dumbstruck.

"Did I startle you?" he said.

"Yes."

"Well?"

"Well what?" I replied.

"May I sit here? It seemed rude to ignore you when there's no one else here. Or perhaps you'd prefer a bit of solitude? I won't be at all offended if you tell me to go away, I promise."

I laughed rather nervously. "Oh don't be silly, please join me. I'm sorry if I appeared offish – you were the last person I expected to see here."

"I might say the same thing about you," he smiled, setting down his tray and beginning his sandwiches. "I work here as a matter of fact, and I presume you do too. Ugh! Spam again."

"Why haven't I seen you here before?" I asked.

"Only started a couple of days ago. Just finding my feet. That's why I'm late for lunch, got lost on the third floor."

I laughed spontaneously now. "It's easily done, you'll have to get someone to show you around."

"Are you offering Mrs Barker?" he said, his soft brown eyes gazing at me.

The blush burst instantly onto my face. Fidgeting with my watch I said, "I really must be getting back, Sir James will be…wondering…" Still squirming I rose and pushed back my chair. William stood with me.

"Maybe I'll see you here again? If I can find my way!" He smiled, staring once more directly into my eyes.

"Maybe," I mumbled, moving awkwardly from the table and towards the exit.

"And what about that drink?" I heard him call as the canteen door closed.

Arriving that evening at the flat I was greeted by Joyce's shout from the kitchen. "It's corned beef hash - can you set the table?"

I hung my wet Macintosh and hat in the hall, and from the sideboard drawer took a folded white tablecloth, laid it on the table and arranged the cutlery, crockery and place mats for two.

"What's up?" asked Joyce setting down a casserole dish.

"Up?"

"You seem quiet."

"Nothing - only…"

"Come on, out with it."

"I saw him again."

"Who?"

"William."

"The one from Oxford Street?"

"He's just started at the War Office"

"No!" Joyce's eyes widened. "It can't be him…"

"What do you mean can't be him? He sat opposite me in the canteen, we spoke."

Joyce said excitedly, "Ooh fate must be taking a hand -what time was this?"

"Why?"

"I'd like to meet him."

"I bet you would," I said, trying not to sound ruffled. "He probably won't be there again so you'd be wasting your time. It was just a coincidence that's all. I don't…like him, in that way."

Joyce smiled impudently as she served out the food.

"So you won't mind if I meet him. He might be just my type."

I felt an attempt to draw me. Joyce could be mischievous.

"I doubt it," I said. "Anyway, what about Michael?"

Now Joyce was defensive. "Well… yes we are - but Michael's in Kingsford and I'm down here, for a while yet."

"So you might like some fun?" I said, pushing my advantage.

Joyce smiled boldly. "Yes," she replied, "some fun - and why not?"

I felt myself giving way to anger. "Well don't think you'll be having it with William," I said heatedly. "He's not that sort of chap!"

"So you do like him!" she laughed. "Maybe we could invite him for Christmas, a handsome man to look at over a glass of sherry. Cheer us both up. But don't worry I won't try to steal him." Joyce had got her response.

"Yes it would be, but first, all right yes, you've got to meet him – just to make sure."

"Sure of what dear?"

"I don't know exactly…"

"You mean like before Annie."

Now there was sadness in her voice.

Joyce was waiting outside the canteen as arranged. "Have a look around," she whispered, opening the door and nudging me gently in. "He might be here already."

"And he might have been and gone," I replied moodily, shrugging off Joyce's hand. "Let's just eat, it's not often we get our lunch hour together." We took some sandwiches to the table by the window where I had been previously.

"Oh this is nonsense," I said as we sat down. "I shouldn't have let you talk me into..." But as the canteen door opened I could feel myself reddening. Joyce knew at once and turned around to look. William was at the cutlery table.

"Not bad Annie, not bad at all," she whispered. "Shout him over."

"I will not *shout* anyone over," I hissed.

Ignoring me Joyce waved her arms and beckoned to William. Seeing me he came across.

"Hello again," he said. "This is becoming a habit."

I could feel my face burning up now. "Yes," I said weakly, and quickly introduced Joyce.

Shaking William's hand she winked at me. "He's as handsome as you said Annie."

I gasped, hoping the floor would open up and swallow me. This was forward even for Joyce.

"Is that right? William laughed.

"Yes, it is, and, on that note," she said getting up from her chair, "three's a crowd and I'd better be going."

When she had left I said, "Joyce gets a bit carried away sometimes. She means well."

"I like her," said William cheerfully tucking himself into the seat she had just vacated. "Have you been friends long?"

"Years. We're from the same village. She got me the job here. She's always been the same, coming out with the most outrageous things in front of strangers."

"But I'm not a stranger – not to you." William gave me the steady look again, his soft brown eyes innocent yet unflinching.

"Oh no, no," I replied quickly, I didn't mean..."

"Good," he laughed. "Then will you come out with me tonight?"

I blushed yet again. "Yes," I whispered, "I'd love to."

CHAPTER THIRTY-SEVEN

William and I had been courting for about a year before I decided to introduce him to my family. It was mid-October 1944, we had put in for some leave and both been granted three days. We agreed I should go up on the morning train to Kingsford and William follow on later the same day.

Over the preceding months I had worried a great deal about taking this step, but concluded the time was now right. Daddy, and Gran and Gramps would surely be overjoyed that I had found someone else. I decided to arrive unannounced.

"Darling!" Gran greeted me with a hug and we went into the kitchen. "This is a delightful surprise. Do you want some tea - it's a fresh pot? We never knew you were coming today - your father is in the surgery, and your grandfather at the village hall for some Home Guard business."

I settled at the table. "Yes please Gran. I'd love one."

Gran smiled as she poured the steaming tea into a china cup. "We could go shopping - I could do with a new hat, that's if the clothing coupons will stretch to it. How long are you here for?"

"Three days only I'm afraid."

She smiled again. "Then we'd better make the most of it. It will be just like old times, Annie." I could tell she was thinking of my mother.

"Yes Gran," I said, "just like old times."

"So tell me, how is it in the big city?" she asked, setting down the teacups and sitting close beside me.

"Pretty routine to tell the truth."

"And have you met any nice young men? It's been a long time now dear since…."

"You can say Peter's name," I said quietly. Gran reached out and squeezed my hand. "I'm sorry dear - I can't begin to imagine what you've been through. You never told us anything, and then of course your poor mother…"

"I know, I know." I put my arm around her frail body.

"There, there dear, I'm sorry, let's not be sad while you are home – your mother would not want that." She patted my hand vigorously. "Tell me about London, even the dull things eh?"

"All right Gran - there is something I want to tell you. You see I have met someone. He's called William, William Pearson."

"Ah Cherie! I wondered why you had taken off your ring," she gasped, a broad smile returning to her care worn face.

"No pulling the wool over your eyes Gran," I laughed.

"Well how long have you been seeing him?" she asked gleefully. "Truth to tell, Joyce did mention something when she came in the summer."

"That doesn't surprise me." We both smiled. "So you've known for six months and not said anything?"

"Well sort of dear - but why did you not tell us?"

"I had to be certain I suppose."

"So why now?"

Taking a breath I said, "He's asked me to marry him."

"Ah!" Gran took a handkerchief from her apron pocket and delicately dabbed her eyes.

"Oh Cherie," she cried, "this is the best news ever – your father will be so happy, and your Grandfather I don't think I can buy that new hat; we're going to need all the coupons - you did say yes, I hope?"

"Sort of," I laughed.

"What do you mean sort of?"

"Well yes, I have accepted, but obviously no date has been set…"

"Oh! Your mother would be so pleased."

I smiled at the thought of mother immediately swinging into action with plans and arrangements.

"So when do we meet him?"

"He's coming this evening. I hoped none of you would mind."

Her eyes widened. "Mind?" she gasped, "I can't tell you how happy I am for you - it has been too long…."

"I have told him about Peter," I said. "In as much as we were married and he was killed in action, that's all, so please don't…"

"There is nothing else to tell him dear- is there?" She kissed my cheek affectionately.

"No," I said closing my eyes to stop the tears. "Not a thing."

The train from London pulled slowly into the station and squealed to a halt in a cloud of steam. As the carriage doors opened and a handful of passengers alighted, I saw William emerging from a carriage at the rear, and ran towards him.

"Hello you," he said gathering me up in his arms. "How have the family taken the news?"

"Just as I expected," I laughed, "Gran's overjoyed that she will have a new outfit, and Daddy - well, Daddy is Daddy."

"How do I interpret that? Not disowning you?"

"He couldn't be happier," I linked arms with him as we walked out of the station. "None of them could. Daddy's lent me his car, they can't wait to meet you."

"I didn't know you could drive." William got into the passenger seat and closed the door.

"There's a lot you don't know about me," I laughed, starting the engine.

As I opened the front door I could hear my grandmother, obviously in a state of nervous euphoria giving orders to her husband and son-in-law. I gave Williams's hand a reassuring squeeze.

"I'm fine," he whispered. "It's you I'm worried about."
I kissed him briefly on the cheek, took a deep breath and entered the parlour.

"Daddy, Gran, Gramps I would like to introduce William."
William stepped from behind me and beamed a perfect smile.

"Very nice to meet you all," he said affably, shaking hands with each one of them.

"Will you have something to eat?" Gran fussed. "I'm sure you must be very hungry."

"They do have food in London Gran," I said fondly.
William smiled "Thank you Madame Arneau, I am a little peckish."
Daddy roared with laughter. "Said the right thing there young man. We haven't eaten all day, under strict orders."

"Yes lead the way George," said Gramps, guiding my father through into the dining room. "I could eat a house."

"Horse old man, horse," corrected Daddy.

"You eat what you want George," Gramps laughed "And I will eat what I like!!"

It was after the meal that the third degree began in earnest. Surprisingly, it was Daddy who started it.

"So how did you two meet?" he asked after cleaning the last morsel of roast beef from his plate.

"William saved my life."

"I think you exaggerate dear," said William, gently squeezing my hand across the table. "It was a case of right place at the right time, nothing more."

"Well, all I know is, that if you hadn't dragged me into that shop - he is really too modest. I had just got off the bus in Oxford Street when we heard a doodlebug. The next thing I knew I was being dragged into a shop and thrown under the counter, then – BANG. When I came out the place was a pile of rubble - that's when we met - William and I under the counter. The pavement outside where I had been standing was gone. And so would I have been. It was only later we found out we both worked at the War Office, How's that for a coincidence?"

"Well I think that deserves a toast." Daddy said opening another bottle of wine and filing everyone's glass. "Here's to William," he said standing up, "for coming gallantly to the rescue of my beautiful daughter - and to their forthcoming wedding."

"To William," chanted the assembled company, raising their glasses. "And to their wedding!"

"When is your wedding by the way?" said Daddy, which set everyone off laughing.

"When we can all manage it," I smiled. William took a small, black velvet box from his pocket and handed it to me.

"This is for you."

I lifted the lid. Inside was a beautiful solitaire diamond ring. Removing it, William placed it on my finger.

"Now Annabelle," he said softly, "I'll ask again - will you marry me?"

I looked at the ring then at William.

"Yes," I said. "I will."

The next morning I wanted to show off my finance to the whole of Kingsford. The first port of call was my old place of work.

"Hello Miss Dove – Vera," I called, peering around the half open office door. "Can we come in?"

"My goodness!" started Miss Dove, dropping the morning post. "You made me jump – hello stranger."

I immediately pushed my left hand forward and wiggled the engagement ring. "I would like to introduce you to William. Vera, my fiancé William Pearson."

Miss Dove shook William's proffered hand.

"How do you do?" she said brightly, then turned her attention to me. "What a gorgeous ring Annie, bet that cost a pretty packet."

"Honestly Vera!" I exclaimed, "You're as bad as Joyce, behave."

"Sorry – I'll bet its 24-carat though," she laughed, "My Arthur could only afford a 9-carat, but he's promised me a better one…" Vera tailed off as the door to the inner office opened. Michael, leaning heavily on his walking stick was stood looking out at us. For a second we stared at each other, as if, recalling some long forgotten secret.

"Hello Annabelle," he said quietly. "Joyce said you were back."

"Michael…" I faltered. "This is William - my fiancée."
I caught the split second of shock on William's face as he took in Michael's face, before he beamed and stepped forward.

"Hello Michael," he said warmly, "jolly good to meet you."

"Congratulations," said Michael as they shook hands. "I hope you'll both be very happy."

"Thank you Michael - I've heard a lot about you."
Michael glanced at me. "Hope it was all good; so when's the wedding?"

"Sometime next year we thought," William replied.

"And what about you and Joyce?" I ventured.
Michael looked awkward. "I don't know really. I… I've not asked her."

"Well it's about time you did," I said gamely, "before someone else does!"

"That's what I keep telling him," chipped in Vera Dove. Michael shot her a look of displeasure. Undeterred she went on, "I think perhaps he's waiting for someone special, don't you?"

"Isn't Joyce special?" I said, then leant forward and kissed Michael's cheek. "Be happy for me," I whispered.

From within the remnants of his features, Michael summoned a smile and gripped my hand. "How could I be anything else Annie?" Then turning to Vera Dove he said, "If you wouldn't mind holding the fort Miss Dove."

"As ever sir," she smiled.

"No to hell with it – come with us. The Horse and Groom's beckoning, and I insist the drinks are on me."

The bell jangled as we entered, the old, familiar smell of hops and tobacco bringing back a profusion of memories.

"You'll find nothing changed here Annie," said Michael.

"I'm glad of that," I said. "Hello Cornelius." I waved to the gravedigger, sat in his usual place across the bar. He nodded in reply. With a swoon I recalled the night I had seen him, rain sodden and distraught, bent over my mother's body.

"Are you all right darling?" William was holding my arm.

"What, sorry – oh yes…"

"I was just saying to Michael, everyone has made me so welcome in the village."

"That's what we do in Kingsford, we're very welcoming sort of folk," said Michael. "Peter always used to say - oh heck, sorry Annie I…."

"William knows all about Peter," I said. "We don't have secrets, do we darling?"
William shook his head. "Why should we?" Not a good way to start married life is it?"

"Now Michael," I said, "at the risk of harping on, what about you and Joyce? I know what she feels about you. I think she's probably waiting for you to make the next move."

"Got us all worked out have you Annie?" said Michael. "I like her certainly, but hell I only see her when she's on leave. And why can't a chap see a girl without everyone trying to march them down the aisle?"

"Joyce won't be in London forever. She's only waiting for her transfer papers, then she's coming home."

"Maybe I will pop the question, but in my own time. Who knows what will be. I've given up trying to predict the future. And please don't say faint heart never won fair lady!" Michael raised his glass. "For now – here's to the good times – and to you two."

"Yes Michael," I touched my glass on his. "To the good times."

CHAPTER THIRTY-EIGHT

"So did Joyce marry Michael, Nan?" asked Sally.

Thinking of Joyce, and how overjoyed at Michael's proposal she had been, I smiled.

"Oh yes dear, a few months after Michael asked her – before we did in fact. She couldn't wait. He'd got a job in London by then, really he'd always wanted to get out of Kingsford and with Joyce behind him he believed anything was possible.

They moved to Kent soon after, and we didn't see much of them. William and I got married in the November of 1945, and of course they came up for that. Joyce was heavily pregnant with their second child, and Thomas was still in nappies. What must she have been thinking? A month later she gave birth to Caroline, a sweet little thing with a shock of red hair, just like her mother. What a lovely family they were.

When Michael died Joyce was devastated. She went to live with Thomas in Norfolk. We stayed in touch for quite a while, but you know how life is. We still exchange cards at Christmas, and birthdays when I remember, and we have the odd gossip now and again on the telephone.

Funnily enough I rang her only yesterday, she's coming up tomorrow - first thing. We've not spoken in ages but I had something to talk to her about, something that she…Anyway it's lovely to hear from her. It's odd, but when we speak, the years dissolve and I feel as if we are the young girls we once were again, chatting about serious thing one minute, silly aimless nonsense the next, and so very earnest about all of it!"

"Where did you and Granddad live when you first got married – did you stay in Kingsford?"

"We moved to Weavers Green, a small village on the outskirts of Manchester. He'd inherited some money from his parents who had died before the war started, that's how he was able to set up the engineering business. He worked terribly hard developing it and I helped him with the bookkeeping."

"Didn't you miss your father – and your Gran and Gramps?"

"William had bought a car and we visited when we could. Gran and Gramps seemed to have really settled into English village life. There was never any mention of them returning to France. But all that was to change. It must have been about a year after we moved when I had a call from my grandmother. I hadn't been feeling myself for a couple of weeks, and when the phone rang at 7am, somehow I knew it could only be bad tidings… I rushed downstairs and picked up the receiver.

"Weavers Green 5822."

"Annabelle, Annabelle - is that you?" The old lady sounded very distressed.

"Gran - what's the matter, do you know what time it is? Is someone ill?"

"It's your silly Grandfather. He wants to go back to France, to Maison Vert. I've told him it's not safe but he insists on going."
I sat down on the hall chair, trying to grasp what she meant.

"Did you hear, Annabelle?" said Gran. "He wants to go back home."

"Sorry Gran – I've not been well for a few days myself - well look, if he wants to go back, perhaps he should."

I wished now I had stayed in bed and let the phone ring. I thought of asking to speak to Daddy for some advice while I was on, but realised Gran might feel ignored.

"I knew you would take his side," she said moodily, "why is every one against me in this matter?"

"I'm not against you Gran," I said, I just think maybe it is right that he, you, both should go back. Anyway why is it so urgent that you call me at this hour?" I immediately regretted saying this – Gran was clearly upset.

"We have been sent a letter from Madame Dufarge. She says Maison Vert is derelict and that St Jacques lies in ruins. I fear the worst. Oh Annie, please come and talk some sense into him. Did you say you weren't well dear?"

I realised I would have no peace until the issue – whatever it was - had been sorted out.

"Oh its nothing much," I said. "Listen I'll catch the 10 o'clock train and see you in an hour or so. Could Daddy meet me at the station?"

The moment I entered the house Gramps thrust an envelope into my hand.

"Read it," he said rather hysterically. "Our lovely home has gone, destroyed by those damn Germans. What are we to do?"
I unfolded the letter and read. It was a long and rather confused account from Madame Dufarge. One sentence however jumped out at me: "…Maison Vert burned to the ground…."

"Look, if I can't talk him out of going," Gran said, overriding her husband's anguish, "maybe you and William could come with us - for how do you say - moral support."

Perspiration was rising on my forehead; I needed air, couldn't breath. For it was a strong possibility that unbeknown to my family, I was the cause of their distress.

"I'll ask William," I said, trying to keep my voice steady, "but he's so busy - with work."

"It's time you both had a rest," said Daddy, who until now had been sitting in the chair looking thoughtful. "You've been married 12 months and not had a break. You could call it a late honeymoon."

"Oh Daddy please - don't go on so," I said crossly, "I've told you, I'll have to ask William. He's trying to get the business off the ground. Most of the money his parents left him has gone into the house and setting up the firm."

"Why you had to go and live away in Rovers Green…"

"Weavers Green, Gran…"

"…I'll never know. Why can't William get a job and work for someone else?"

"Because he's a qualified engineer and wants to set up on his own, and why should he…."

I felt my legs giving way, waves of nausea rising up, then blackness.

"Annie, Annie." A voice was calling to me from far away. "That's it dear, that's it"

I was sitting in the armchair and Daddy was holding a bottle of something under my nose. I coughed as a pungent odour hit the back of my throat. "What happened," I asked.

"You fainted, that's all," said Daddy. "Your Gran says you told her you've not been well - what's the problem?"

"It's nothing really - just a sort of sick feeling – it comes and goes."

"All this nonsense about France that's upset her," Gran said glowering at her husband.

"You're the one talking nonsense…"

"Oh stop it both of you," I said getting up unsteadily from the chair.

"Annie," said Daddy, "why don't you go and rest in your old room." He smiled at me. "Then we'll have a chat later. And no more raised voices, any of you."

At the door I turned to them and said, "If Gramps want to go back to France I think he should and so should you Gran."

Gramps smiled at me. "Thank you my child, and, will you come with us?"

"Yes will you Annie?" echoed Gran.

CHAPTER THIRTY-NINE

We reached St Jacques just as the church clock chimed noon. The last stroke resonated in the warm summer air and then was gone, gathered up in the general midday hubbub of the village street.

Daddy paid the taxi driver and gathered our suitcases on the uneven pavement. The village looked very different from my last visit. One side of the road was as I had always remembered it - the dress shop, the boulangerie, and Mademoiselle Barr's shop at the far end. The other side was utterly derelict, the shops and houses that once stood there now either in ruins, or completely obliterated. Together we stared in silence at this altered landscape.

"Simone, Michele..." called a voice from behind us. "At last you are here."

Running from the boulangerie came Madame Dufarge; her right arm waving vigorously while her left held firmly onto a wicker basket laden with bread and groceries.

"Bonjour, Bonjour," she wheezed breathlessly, "It is so good to see you all again."

"Madeleine!" Gran exclaimed, as the two friends greeted each other. "Oh it seems such a long time. How are you?"

"We survive, we survive," said Madame Dufarge. "You must come now to my house, your rooms are ready."

"But what of Maison Vert," my grandfather asked anxiously, "have you been up there?

Madame Dufarge paused for a moment. "I have Michel. It is as I wrote to you. There is nothing left – nothing but charred wood. I am sorry."

The look on Gramps face was painful to behold.

"Our home, gone," he sighed, "I've spent my whole life working on that farm, and you say it's gone." The old lady nodded.

Daddy put his arm around the old man's shaking shoulders, and together we followed Madame Dufarge to her home.

"George you can put your suitcases in the salon here," she said, indicating to Daddy a door on her left. "Then all come with me to the kitchen."

A dog barked as we entered the kitchen.

"Does he bite Madam?" asked Daddy, who had had some encounters with dogs on his doctor's rounds over the years.

"Only if you're German," smiled the old lady wryly. "Like his owner, Gaston has a long memory – and sharp teeth. See for yourself."

"Is it really Gaston?" said Daddy, "well I'll be…"

Picking up a ham bone Madame Dufarge tossed it to the animal. The dog caught it deftly in his mouth and began stripping the meat. Then, as Gramps came into the kitchen, he dropped the bone and went bounding in a state of pure excitement at the old man.

"Gaston, oh Gaston boy!" he cried joyfully as the creature licked his master's face. "Oh Madeleine, what can I say - thank you a thousand times for saving him!"

"I was pleased to have him here Michel. When we realised you weren't coming back we sold the animals and closed up the farm for your return, I kept Gaston. He has looked after me, haven't you Gaston darling!" She patted the dog affectionately.

Putting her basket on the kitchen table she went to the dresser and took out a small brown envelope.

"Here," she said offering it to my grandfather. "I have the money for you."

Gramps took the old woman in his arms and hugged her

"Thank you Madeleine," he exclaimed, "and thank you again for saving Gaston. You are a true friend."

"Yes dear, we cannot ever repay you," said Gran, also embracing her.

"Ah - I am just glad you are both well and back in St Jacques. It has been terrible here I won't pretend - and poor Mademoiselle Barr - she was only helping…." Madame Dufarge began to cry.

Gran pulled one of the chairs from the kitchen table and guided her friend towards it.

"Sit down dear," she said, "and you tell us what happened."

The old lady pulled a handkerchief from her apron pocket and wiped her eyes. "It has been dreadful here; you cannot imagine. The Germans took most of the young men; if they did not shoot them they took them away. Loaded them into trucks and drove them out to God knows where. Even now, with the war over almost two years we still have no news of them."

"Is Mademoiselle Barr still here?" I asked hoping against all hope she may have survived.

At this Madame Dufarge's eyes bored into mine. "She is dead child, killed by the Germans." After staring at me for a moment she rallied herself. "Enough of this talk for now," she said. "If you would like to get settled into your rooms I will prepare a meal for us all. Shall we say in about one hour...?"

"More wine George?" Madeleine Dufarge refilled Daddy's glass. "The Germans didn't get this thank goodness – mark you, we had it well hidden."

"What happened to the village – all those houses flattened?" my grandfather asked, "I didn't think the British bombers got this far inland. The newspapers said they stopped at Dieppe."

"There are lots of things the newspapers kept from you all," she laughed bitterly. "The British bombed Dieppe, and the surrounding areas just before D-Day, that is a fact."

"That would explain why the small hamlets we drove through from Dieppe seemed to be deserted," mused Daddy.

"But what of Maison Vert?" said Gramps. "Did that go the same way?"

"Well now, Michel." Madame Dufarge drained her wine glass. "I will tell you what happened to your farm, and why. It was 12th February 1942 - life here had not been so bad for us until that night. It was the early hours of the morning; I remember the noise of the German trucks rattling down the street. The troops, their jackboots thundering on the cobbles as they ran from shop to shop, house to house, searching everywhere."

"Ah - what were they looking for?" Gran asked.

"Who, my dear, who; they turned this house upside down. I tried to stop them but they hit me and I fell to the floor. Gaston took a bite out of one of them. They were going to shoot him but I stopped them – don't ask me how."

Daddy made some sort of light-hearted remark about compassion, but Madame Dufarge glared.

"Compassion, George; compassion? They showed those young men no compassion when they threw them into the trucks and drove them away. And the men and women here who tried to resist, rose up against the oppression, do you know what they did to them? They strung them up on meat hooks in the butcher's shop and made the whole village go and see their lifeless pitiful bodies hanging there."

It was several long seconds before Madame Dufarge broke the heavy silence that followed. "They were searching for a British Agent. She was on the run having apparently killed a German soldier."

"She?" Daddy exclaimed. "A female agent?"

My hand flew to my mouth to stifle a cough. Daddy turned to look at me.

"Are you alright Annabelle?" he asked.

I nodded. " Just a little sick."

"No wonder," Gramps said, handing me a glass of water, "Madeleine did you have to tell us this?"

"The war here was not all dances and Americans. It was cruel, terrible."

"Using women for espionage, well I never," Daddy said shaking his head. "We had Mata Hari in the first war of course, but…did they find her?"

"No. They came back later in the day and searched everywhere again, but she had gone. They said one of us had helped her."

"And did anyone own up to that?" Gramps asked.

A sardonic, almost hostile smile creased Madame Dufarge's thin lips.

"Do you think we would be so stupid?" she said. "We lived through hell here, not knowing who to trust, or whether a knock at the door was a friend or the Germans come to take you. Oh, even in our small village we had – collaborators. But we had our revenge too."

Gramps shifted uncomfortably on his chair. "Madeleine forgive me, I didn't realise…"

"No one in England realised," she snapped.

An awkward silence fell, and taking a moment to compose herself she continued. "So, they came back. They told me that this agent had shot the soldier in your farm house, Maison Vert."

"Our home!" Gran exclaimed.

"Yes, that is why they burned it down. They also took several of our friends and shot them, in the street in front of the whole village, stood them against the wall of the church and opened fire. Mademoiselle Barr was the last. They said they had information she had helped the girl escape, so they beat her before they shot her. I wish they *had* found the agent. I would have gladly watched her being shot to have saved my friend."

I gripped the edge of the table, hoping no one had noticed the beads of sweat on my face, the sickly feeling growing more intense. The voices around me fused into an incoherent mumble as the blackness came on again. Swaying first one way then the other, I fell limply from the chair and hit the floor with a crash.

The next morning I waited until Madame Dufarge, Daddy, Gran and Gramps had left the house to visit what was left of Maison Vert, before I got up. I didn't want to see anyone, or to have to explain why I had fainted last night, or answer any questions about what they thought might be the matter with me. However as I opened the kitchen door I was greeted with, "Hello sleepy head, want some breakfast?"

The thought of food made me retch and I declined the offer. As I sat down at the table I could feel Daddy watching me.

"Why didn't you go with them to Maison Vert?" I asked.

"I didn't want to. But I do want to talk to you."

"What about?"

"About your – sickness," he replied "I think you should see the doctor while we're here – not me, someone else. I've arranged for you to visit him this afternoon."

"Daddy, you shouldn't have done that," I said irritably, "I'm fine."

"No you're not," he insisted. "In fact I know what's wrong with you, but I want a second opinion. You're going to see the local doctor and that is final."

I was about to protest further but thought better of it. It wasn't often that my father was cross. Perhaps it would be best to get some treatment for whatever was ailing me.

I dressed and returned to the front parlour. Daddy was sitting by the fire reading, but put the book down when I mentioned I was going to take a long walk.

"I'll come with you," he said, "I could do with…"

"No Dad!" I interrupted rather harshly. "I'd prefer to go on my own."

My father opened his mouth to reply, then returned his gaze to his book.

I lifted the latch of the cemetery gate and surveyed the rows of graves. I found Mademoiselle Barr's easily enough. I knelt down and laid the single red rose against the headstone. Mademoiselle Barr, the woman who had helped me to safety had then given her life to save mine.

Tears of remorse fell, I felt someone touch my shoulder. I turned and saw my father stood beside me.

"Daddy…!"

"I had a feeling you'd be here." He lifted me to my feet, took a handkerchief from his pocket and wiped my eyes. "Thousands died you know – millions the world over."

Yes but she…" I began.

"You knew her of course. And she was a heroine, no doubt about that. She'll be pleased to know you came up here – to know you cared. Your mother would be proud of your gesture too."

"But Daddy you don't understand – I feel so guilty about her…"

"We're all guilty Annie – we survived," said my father, as taking my arm he led me out of the cemetery.

William was waiting for me on the platform as the train pulled in to Weavers Green. It was with a wonderful feeling of contentment that I received and responded to his kisses.

"I've missed you," he said fondly. "How was la belle France?"

"Sad – so very, very sad," I replied, burying my head in his shoulder.

"They went through it over there – your grandparents must have had very mixed feelings going back, from what you told me."

"Right enough," I said. "I've missed you too you know – terribly so."

I lifted my head and gazed up at his soft eyes, eyes like molten brown sugar, or was it honey - no, I thought, there was more, something stronger than mere sweetness about him. The way he looked at me still ignited a flame deep inside me, but with it was always tenderness – kindness – that, I had never seen or felt with Peter.

In time I would forget the pain of Peter, he was already moving, making his home in some other, permanent but removed place in my heart. But what I wondered, would my new husband make of the news I was about to give him?

"William…" I said, as we got in the car.

"Hmm?"

"I do love you so."

"Oh darling," he breathed, leaning over to kiss me, "and I love you."

"There's something else – I have to tell you…"

William paused with the ignition key in his hand.

"My sweet – whatever is it?"

Resting my head back on his shoulder I said, "I'm going to have a baby."

CHAPTER FORTY

The sound of a voice returned my mind to the present, and to present company. It was my daughter, telling me yet again how incredible my story was, and asking why I had never told it before.

"Didn't seem to matter," I sighed. "Not till now, you see I have to tell you everything before…" I stopped and turned to face them. "We were happy you know, your father and I. And I did love him, very much, but – "

"You should have told us before," repeated Laura, this time with what, for her, passed as empathy, "because I'm seeing you in a different light now."

I smiled, as if I cared what she thought of me - or any of them. I was too old to worry about making an impression, other people's opinions - all that nonsense. It was one benefit of age, the loss of vanity. Thank god for small mercies.

Nicholas knelt by my chair and took my hand in his

"Maria tells me you've been having the bad thoughts, as she puts it, again…should we let the doctor know?"

"Don't you dare!" I replied fiercely. "And I'll be having words with *her*."

"But Mum," Nicholas pleaded, "If you're unwell…"

"Oh do stop fussing. I'm as right as I'll ever be. I'm an old woman with little time and many memories."

"I told you Nick - the first signs of dementia." Laura spoke in a voice intended to be too low for me to hear. She smiled over-broadly as she poured the tea into the cups, to give the impression she was talking about something quite different.

"And as for these tall stories about the war, well do you believe a word of it? She's not been right since father…"

And on it went, so much to say that beautiful daughter of mine.

"I *am* here dear." I said loudly, "you can include me in the conversation."

"For goodness sake mummy, "Sally broke in, "Nan is as sane as you or I, and we're having a wonderful day, please don't spoil it."

I smiled at my granddaughter, my ally and my champion.

"Yes Sally dear, today has been one of the best days I've had in a long while."

I watched my two children as they talked busily amongst themselves. I thought: how lucky they had been really. Laura especially had it all, a doting husband, a fine house, fast cars, and plenty of money to indulge her very expensive tastes. How would she take it? She was having trouble believing me already, and she had really heard nothing yet. But when I showed her the proof, ah… And Nicholas, how like William, but without secrets of course…"Well my dears, are you ready for the next installment?"

Prompted by a glare from Sally and a diplomatic cough from Nicholas Laura said brightly, "That would be lovely Mum," at the same time glancing discreetly at her watch.

Composing myself, I prepared to tell the final part of the story; the part that would explode their self satisfied little worlds like a lighted match thrown into an armoury. They didn't want to listen to my ramblings, but I had to tell this despicable truth.

"Like all mothers I treasured the memories of my children's early years, and would often take out the old photos and gaze fondly at the little bundles of joy that had brought us such happiness. 'You sentimental old thing,' William would laugh whenever he found me in the bedroom smiling over the family album, gentle tears of nostalgia in my eyes.

One afternoon, when William was out, I had taken myself off upstairs - ostensibly to clean, but really with the intention of looking through the album - only to find it was not in its usual place in my dresser. I looked in the other compartments but could see it nowhere. Then I noticed the drawer at the bottom of William's wardrobe was slightly protruding. I smiled. I knew my husband sometimes looked surreptitiously at the album himself.

Having gone to bed early the night before, had he I wondered been quietly perusing it, and on hearing my approach hid it hastily in the nearest place? I opened the deep drawer of the wardrobe and began rummaging. For an engineer, William was surprisingly disorganised with his private possessions, and kept an impenetrable mountain of old letters, bills, receipts and yellowing documents, personal paraphernalia, that seemed to have lain untouched for years.

Riffling through the haystack of paper, sure enough I found the album. As I dragged it out, another bulky object rose to the surface. It was a plain oak box, which I could not recall having seen before. Lifting the lid I found inside a large envelope, crammed full of papers and smaller envelopes. The little envelopes looked as though they had once been stuck down, the seals now broken with age. Curious, I opened one of them. There were faded photos, some of which William had shown me years before – members of his family and old school friends.

I was about to replace everything when something made me pause. In among the smiling relatives and old school portraits was another kind of picture. It was a figure in uniform, but not that of any British regiment. It was the uniform of the German SS. My head began spinning.

The dark place in my mind I had kept locked for forty years was opening. Suddenly I was back in the room in Avenue Foch, the bright light scorching my eyes, the stench of sweat, the fist thumping the desk, and the jarring, smashing sensation as something hit my face again and again and again. Then came the shot that would end my life. Only it didn't. It was to be the next one that killed me, or as good as…

But why on earth did William possess a photograph of an SS officer? In a storm of emotion I flung the envelope onto the floor. As it landed something rolled out. It was a ring. Bending down to pick it, I felt as if I would faint. The ring was engraved with a black panther's head. I looked again at the photograph – there did appear to be a ring of some kind on the finger.

There must be hundreds of them, I thought, fighting to quell the panic now gripping my heart. If William had this photograph, why might he not also have this SS ring? After all many men kept wartime trophies – perhaps he had been given the items by some military friend who had been in Germany at the end of the war. There was something about the photograph itself though that seemed strange to me.

I reached into the bedside cabinet for my reading glasses and peered intently at the faded image. Then as I scrutinised the face, my hand flew to my throat. I let out a strangled cry of terror. There was no doubt about it - the face staring out at me was that of my husband William.

Two hours later I was still in the bedroom. I had moved only from the bed to the dressing table, where I now sat staring blankly into the mirror. Though in shock, I was also aware of being so, and trying, in the stillness and silence of the house, to make some kind of sense of my discovery. There could be a rational explanation, I kept saying to myself. Everything was where I had left it, the polish and duster I had brought from the kitchen still on the floor, the vacuum cleaner in the doorway to the landing and the photos still laying on the bed.

A noise from outside made me sit up. William's car had just pulled onto the driveway. Still I did not move

"Darling?" called my husband from the living room. Galvanised by the voice I sprang up and tried to cram the photos and envelopes back in the box, but too hastily, the lid refusing to shut. I could hear William on the stairs now. Leaving the box and half its contents scattered on the bed, I ran onto the landing and closed the bedroom door behind me.

"Hello dear?" William paused on the top step. "You startled me springing from nowhere like that, what's the matter. Goodness you look so pale – is something the matter?"

"No, no, everything's fine" I said in a strange querulous voice that seemed to come from somewhere outside of me. "Bit of a headache that's all."

"Then come and lie down," he said moving towards the bedroom door. "Would you like the radio on?"

"NO" I shouted. William stopped as I barred his way. "I - I've got your present in there - and I don't want you to see it yet."
He smiled but there was a look of puzzlement in his eyes.

"Oh, well in that case - are you sure you're all right Annie" he asked "I've never seen so serious about a present – I must be in for an awfully big surprise!"
I smiled weakly. I could feel the sweat running down my face, "Just a headache."
William stared at me for a second then said, "Then I'll go down and pour us a drink. Your usual?"
I nodded, "I'll come down and join you in a minute."

When he had gone I went back into the bedroom and closed the door behind me. I put everything back in the box and replaced it in the draw. I then sat at the dressing table and stared at my reflection. In the space of a few minutes my perfect world had exploded and lay in ruins.

My life with William had been nothing but an illusion. The man I had loved, the father of my children was a monster. It was too much to comprehend, the agony of such knowledge simply too great to bear. Perhaps I should kill myself now and have done with it.

I opened the bottom draw of the dressing table and from beneath my underclothes took out a wallet. It contained a faded photograph of Peter, my first wedding ring and a picture of me taken just before the war. I ran my fingers tenderly over Peter's face then caught sight of my reflection in the mirror again. The features staring out made me start with fear; it was the face of a haunted person, a countenance filled with remorse and hatred.

The comforting realm of sleep was for me that night somewhere a million miles away. Nothing would silence the deafening cataract of thoughts that roared through my head, clamouring, as it seemed, to be silenced by whatever means I might summon.

Some dreadful act was called for, but where could I find the courage or resolution to perform it? If there was a hell then surely I had been plunged into it. I stood by the bedroom window, and saw again my reflection in the dressing table mirror. I appeared almost wraith like now in the moon's eerie light and shivered at the apparition Perhaps I was dead already, and for some past sin – mine or someone else's - was destined now to walk in purgatory – until someone was made to atone. I knew what that meant.

That evening I had played my part well, laughing with William, holding his hand and kissing him as he gave me a beautiful diamond bracelet. He didn't suspect a thing, but inside a fire was raging in my heart, consuming me in its flames.

At moments the whole situation seemed almost absurd, certainly too far-fetched for any one else to believe. Yet there it was, this Nazi commandant who had given the order to kill Peter, had made no attempt to save him was here, sleeping in my bed, my beloved, abhorrent husband. I looked out across the road. Everything was so normal; ours and the neighbours' cars in their customary spaces, the lawns all neatly mown, nothing out of place.

My mind was a turbulent mixture of confusion and dark thoughts bred even darker ideas. I should question William, confront him with this obscenity – ask him to explain it away, cleanse and expunge it from our life.   But what answer could he give, other than one that would tear me apart, confirm the evil – give it a voice and a shape and a reality? How could I ever understand let alone forgive such a deceit? It was impossible.

Turning from the window, I leaned over William and listened to his gentle rhythmic breathing. His unexpected movement startled me and I quickly moved back into the shadows. As I did so, brushing against the bedside table I sent a small glass medicine bottle tumbling onto the carpet; the tablets – William's pills – rattled inside.   William stirred again. I picked up the bottle, my fingers closed around it. A chill breeze entered the room from the window and I moved quietly to close it.

Sitting down at the dressing table I watched my husband in the mirror, staring at him, wishing pathetically it were all a dream and that I would wake up soon. Then, he stirred, and this time sat up. He switched on the light. "Darling, what's the matter? Why are you sitting there? Its 2 am."

In the mirror my eyes fixed his. I felt sick. Now I had to do it, I had to speak.

"William"

"Yes - what is it?"

"Do you remember when you first saw me?"

I saw him flinch; it must have been the tone of my voice that caused his discomfort. "Uh - of course I do my love. Is this something to do with our anniversary?"

"Then tell me - where did you first see me?"

He stared back at me in the dressing table mirror.

"Surely you haven't forgotten - in that shop, in London. Look if you can't sleep…."

I slowly turned around to face him. He had lied again and I was no longer incredulous. Now I hated him.

"I mean the *very first* time you saw me. Surely you remember…Avenue Foch?"

My voice sounded almost normal, as if I was discussing a dinner engagement that had slipped my mind. Now it was his expression that changed. The face I had looked at almost every day for so many years had suddenly contorted into something unknown. With a ghastly sickly look, he threw aside the bedclothes and stood up.

"No, No," he shouted throwing off the bedclothes, "You don't understand…"

"I understand only too well." I said, and with shaking hand took out the photograph of Peter. William rushed towards me,

"Annie please…you don't …I… you're making a terrible mistake."

"To late Herr Commandant – I know who you are."

"Annabelle, please… It wasn't like that…" he grabbed my arms.

"Let me go." I pushed him away. "You killed him, Peter, it was you gave the order to shoot him. I hate you"
William didn't reply but instead gripped his chest, as a different kind of pain creased his features.

"My tablets" he gasped and motioned to the bedside table.

"Looking for these." I held out my hand showing him the bottle of heart tablets I had knocked off the table. He nodded, unable to draw breath. As he reached for the bottle I threw it across the room.

For a second he looked at me and tried to say something, then, with another short gasp, crumpled and fell motionless at my feet.

CHAPTER FORTY-ONE

The stunned looks and the silence said enough. They didn't believe me. Nicholas, Laura and Sally stared at me with utter incomprehension. Sally's face bore a sad distressed look that suggested even she thought I had finally succumbed to madness. As I began to talk again, Laura spoke up.

"Shut up Mum!" she said violently, putting her hand to her face and shaking her head. "Please – stop this, this – horrible, warped nonsense – this fantasy. Do you take pleasure in upsetting us – is that what it is? If you want to make up stories, for god's sake just write them down or something, but spare us this – cruelty!"
I felt too tired to answer her, let alone argue.

"See Nick," Laura went on, "I told you she was losing it. I just hope poor Dad, wherever he is, isn't looking down and hearing this – this filth!"
Nicholas looked uncomfortable and dragged is hands through his hair.

"Mother," he said a little shakily, "Father died of a heart attack, we all know that."
I begin to speak again, but Laura tells me to shut up, she's in such a rage, just as I thought she would be. I don't want to argue, I'm too tired for that.

"Shut up Mother," she yells, "Just shut up. Daddy would never do anything like that. How dare you speak of him in that way."
Nicholas bewildered by the revelation spoke quietly.

"It's all too fantastic Mother. Dad did die of a heart attack."
I nodded, "Yes he did, but I could have saved him, given him his tablets"

"You're actually saying you're partly responsible for his death? Said Nicholas

"More than that – you could say I murdered him."

"Oh, please!" said Laura, grinding her teeth.

"Here," I lifted the box from the table beside me and offered it to Laura. "It contains all the proof you need."
Seeing it she recoiled slightly, as if it might contain a venomous snake, then defiantly she said. "Open it then. Open it and show us your proof."

Turning the key I felt my heart shiver. Outright disbelief - this was somehow not how I had expected it to be. But then, what had I expected?

Before I could lift the lid Laura has reached over, grabbed the box from my hands and emptied the contents onto the table. She threw the box hard against the wall, the impact splitting it apart. Her face clouded with emotion, she began with trembling fingers to sift through the heap of papers and photographs, scattering some of them onto the floor as her search became more frantic. Finally she stopped. She held up the photograph, the man in the SS commandant's uniform, and studied the face closely. She turned to look at me, then, gasping for air looked away, dropping the photo.

Nicholas picked it up, put on his glasses and bent over the image before holding it at arm's length as if to gain some other perspective. Lowering his eyes he gave a sort of low moan as if winded.

Sally snatched the photograph from his hand and examined it. Then in silence, she too let it fall to the floor again. "Granddad...?" she said at last, her voice like that of a small questioning, incredulous child. I stretched my hand towards her. She turned her back and ran to the window as if I had just struck her.

"I never meant to hurt you," I said, "any of you. But – you had to know."

"Please don't say another word Mother," Laura then snapped. "Not another damn word."

"Why - didn't you tell us sooner?" Nicholas asked, his voice hollow, his brow furrowed in concentrated bewilderment. "I mean - how are we supposed to feel about this now?"

"The fact is I cannot help how you feel. Your shock was inevitable. I have borne the hatred, and the guilt for all these years. Perhaps you are right – I should have told you before. For your sakes and mine, I wanted you – before its too late - to know the truth about your father."

Sally turned suddenly from the window now. "Ok, he was really a German officer," she said passionately. "Lots of English people married Germans after the war. Oh but you...oh Gran. !" She turned away again and began crying.

"Sally – there's something else you don't know, you see..."

"If it was true, why didn't he tell her when they first met?" interrupted Laura.

"Don't be daft Mum, the war was still on," blurted Sally through her tears.

"Well then he can't have been a German – they met in Oxford Street for gods sake!" Laura replied as if this settled the matter.

"Maybe he was some kind of double agent," said Nicholas thoughtfully. "Mum would have had to turn him in if she knew - or become a traitor by not doing so. He'd have been shot, perhaps Mum too."

"But Gran – why couldn't you forgive him? The war was all over and done with – he obviously never told you because he loved you, and he wanted you - and you, you let him die...!"

"He was not just any German officer my dear," I said, summoning every ounce of strength to be heard over Sally's crying. "William – your grandfather - was the SS commandant who gave the order to kill my first husband, and my first love, Peter. Knowing that, I could not let him live. And for masquerading all those years – in my home, my bed, fathering my children and pretending he loved me! I can never forgive him, and I hope he is in hell. So I am sorry for not seeming to care about *your* feelings. Believe me I do. You will have plenty of time to reflect on the implications of what I have revealed to you - how *do* you both feel about having Nazi blood running through your veins?"

"Nazi blood!" Laura exploded. "Don't be so ridiculous Mother. For all we know you could be the Nazi. You've got lots of secrets as we've just found out. I don't believe a word of what you've said, the whole thing's crazy."

"But the photo..." began Nicholas.

"A put up job," barked Laura. "He probably wore that uniform for a bet and someone had a camera – Daddy loved us, he was a good man and nothing you can say will ever make me think any different of him."

I shook my head. "It was all a lie from beginning to end. He created and maintained the pretence from start to - till I, finished it. You see I knew, because of the ring."

"What ring?" demanded Laura.

"It's there on the table, it was in the box," I said. "I'd seen it before on a commandant's finger, in the interrogation room at Avenue Foch."

"Mother there were probably hundreds of those rings!"

"I remembered certain distinctive flaws, marks in the surface – burned into my memory…"

"Utter nonsense…!" fumed Laura.

"But Mother," Nicholas asked sombrely, "why on earth did he marry you?"

"Because," Sally cried from across the room, "he loved her. Any fool could see that!" There was a lull, all three of them looking away, their minds working. After a moment Sally walked over to the broken box that was lying against the wall where her mother had thrown it. Mechanically she picked it up and brought it back to the table.

As she set it down she paused and looked more closely at the box, examining the place where it had split open. "Gran," she said, "have you seen this?"

"What is it Sally dear?"

"Take a look." Sally passed me the splintered box. Where the canvas lining at the bottom had been partly torn, there was a small white tab sticking out beneath it. I gave the tab a gentle tug, whereupon the whole of the lining came away. Revealed was a yellowing envelope. It bore a single word: 'Annabelle' I stared at the handwriting; it was William's. Shaking now, I opened the envelope. Inside was a letter of several pages, also written in William's unmistakable hand, and addressed to me. With trembling heart, I began to read.

CHAPTER FORTY-TWO

June 25th 1984

My Dearest Annabelle

What follows will come as a surprise to you – a terrible shock more like, but there are things about me you have a right to know, and it is my duty to tell you them.
So many times I have tried to explain but never found the courage, maybe because I knew you would go, leave me, and I couldn't bear that. This dreadful secret, I have carried with me all our married life - hoping, praying that you would never find it out while I was still alive. But now, if you are reading this, I am dead. A coward you might call me, and worse, and I wouldn't blame you. You'll probably hate me, that I can understand, but Annie, I have to tell you what really happened all those years ago and maybe, just maybe, you will forgive me.

My real name is Wilhelm Von Krieg. I was born in Munich in 1913, my father German but my mother, bless her heart, was English. They met while Mother was teaching English at my father's school - he was the head. They married after knowing each other only for a year and soon after, my brother Hermann came along, and I was born, a year later.
At the start of the First World War in 1914 my mother, choosing not to be interned in a concentration camp, returned to England taking my brother and I with her, while Father stayed in Munich. We went to live with my grandparents in Norfolk, and there I spent my very early years.
In 1919 my mother, against her family's wishes, returned with us to Munich, to my father. One day in 1923 mother disappeared, Father told us she had gone away, left us; we tried to find out where but he wouldn't tell us any more. He had joined the National Socialists, and believed in the ideals that Herr Hitler and his henchmen preached.
I was forced to join the Hitler youth, after which I joined the army and eventually became an officer in the SS. But in my heart I was never a Nazi, I did not believe in the 3rd Reich, or 'The greater good'.

I despised what Germany had become, what Hitler and his barbarous murderers had turned my country into. When my brother Hermann was later killed at the Russian front, I despised them even more. From early on my mother had taught me to be true to myself. Knowing I had to do what I believed in, I offered my services to British Intelligence. I became, what is known as a double agent.

The information I passed on was useful, but of course I had always to be careful – I could trust no one, not even my closest friends in the army – some of whom, patriotic Germans may well have been sympathetic to what I was doing. Often I was tempted, over a few steins of beer to share my secret, even try to enlist one or two of my colleagues, but the risk was always too great – just as was the risk of losing you, later on.

Wherever I was stationed, I would make myself known to the resistance, to help them in any way I could, and I did the same when I was sent to Paris in September 1941 to replace Captain Muller as the commandant of the Gestapo HQ.

The day you were brought in, I had been told a British woman spy had been captured. But I was not expecting one as beautiful as you. When I looked down from the window and saw those guards dragging you inside, I knew from that very moment I was in love with you, and somehow I had to save you.

I introduced myself to the Paris cell and was sent to meet with a certain Madame Dupont. As soon as I saw her I knew she was living under an assumed name. You see I already knew her as a Mrs Von Krieg - .she was my mother. She however did not recognise me – at first. I felt torn apart, wanting one minute to confront her, condemn her for abandoning Herman and I, the next filled with tears and wishing to throw myself at her feet. Then, sitting in a café afterwards, I thought of you again. I had fallen absolutely in love with an unknown woman, and then within a few hours, stumbled across the first person I had loved, my mother – who had in her power the means to free you, and perhaps bring you to me.I felt these two astonishing events could not be mere coincidence – call it fate, pre-ordination, the ultimate gift of love from a mother to her son, but I became convinced that some hidden hand of destiny was at work, if not that of British Intelligence!

When I went back and told Madame Dupont I was her son, she was overcome – wrapping her arms around me in equal measures of guilt and joy; she was also filled with despair at the situation we were both in. But sure enough, she helped me to arrange your escape.

After that though I lost contact, and could not find out what had happened to you. I was sent to Prague, and in May 1942. Reinhardt Heinrich was assassinated. I played a minor part in helping the Czech resistance, but unfortunately I was found out and only escaped back to England by the skin of my teeth.

I came to Britain for debriefing, and there met for the first time my controller. I was surprised to find she was a young woman, high up in British Intelligence, though her position was treated as extremely hush-hush and its probably best for all concerned not to disclose her identity even now.

Anyway she knew Madame Dupont and organised much of what went on in France She helped me re-adjust to life here. My job now became one of sending false information to the Germans and locating enemy agents at large in Britain. I also had my SS tattoo removed as soon as possible; you may remember every SS man had his blood type written just under the left armpit. The only way to get rid of the thing was with acid, which burned out the ink but left a scar. I remember your curiosity the first time you saw it, and I told you it was from an operation. You never mentioned it again, and I always wondered if you thought there might be more to it.

I also discovered that my controller knew about you, and when I asked was thrilled to learn that not only had you made it home, but you too were at the War Office in London – we were working in the very same building! I asked my controller if she could somehow introduce us. She said this was awkward, but did tell me which department you were in.

I made it my business to watch out for you, find out if it was really you – so far it seemed too good to be true, but the sense of destiny I had felt about us in Paris was still with me. A week or so later I was overjoyed to spot you on the stairs, but never quite got up the courage to speak.

Then one day I followed you home, and watched you entering the flat above the shop in Kensington. The following day was Saturday, and I returned very early and waited across the road for you to come out – I suppose I wanted to see if anyone else was in the picture – a boyfriend or fiancé perhaps. Anyway you came out alone and got on a bus, so I followed in a taxi. As you got off the bus the V1 came down – yes it was that day. After that the ice was broken I suppose, so a couple of weeks later, I approached you in the canteen. The rest is what you know. When we were finally married I was just so happy.

After the war, I was given money to start my own business, and, with your help of course, our future and that of the children was made secure.

The ring oddly, was a present from my mother. I loved her you know, and I did get her out of France. She died a few years after the war. I was sorry you and she never met again, but we agreed that that would mean giving you the whole story, which we could not risk. I often sent her pictures of the children, her grandchildren, and she would always ask after you

As for my identity papers and the photo, why did I keep them? I don't have a proper answer – perhaps I always knew I would one day tell you all this.

All of this will be painful for you, and I know that you will probably hate me for a while, but not I hope forever. Hurting you was always the last thing I wanting to do, but I pray that is not to be case, when you have time to think over these revelations. My dearest sweetest Annie, you had to know the truth. Forgive me.

William

I folded William's letter and placed it carefully on the table. I looked at Laura, then Nicholas. I could not yet bring myself to look at Sally.

"I appear to have - made a mistake." I said quietly

"Mistake?" spluttered Laura, "I'll say!"

"Laura, don't." said Nicholas in a conciliatory tone.

"Don't, he says! Don't what? She's the one who played judge and jury on poor Dad, and she must face up to it."

"Laura, I'm sure she'll have plenty of time to do that for herself without you turning the knife in the wound – I mean lord knows this is hard enough for us to take in, can you imagine what Mum's feeling? God the whole thing's a nightmare!"

"You can say that again."

"Children," I said, "I think it would be best if you were to leave me now."

"Mum," protested Nicholas, "we can't leave you like this, not after..."

"This letter has come as a great shock of course. I expected today that you would be the ones left reeling – instead I seem to have brought the heavens crashing down about my own head too."

"Of course," said Nicholas. "Oh Mum I'm so sorry, but you mustn't blame yourself for all this you know..."

"Mustn't she?" interrupted Laura curtly. "I don't see who else is responsible, if she hadn't gone jumping to conclusions and I repeat, playing judge and jury on Dad – and executioner..."

"She did not play executioner!" Nicholas, rising suddenly to his feet bellowed out the words. Laura shrank back in alarm for a second then retorted, "Of course she did – she told us herself."

"Laura – I swear if you say another word I'll..." At this point he lifted the chair he had been sitting on and gripped it hard, his normally placid features distorted with rage.

"You'll what?" jeered Laura, "throw a tantrum, or tell Mummy, like you used to when we were kids? I'd be careful if I were you, now you know what's she's capable of."

"And she might not be the only one!" snarled Nicholas through gritted teeth.

"Oh spare us," drawled Laura, "we've had enough drama for one day. You were always a nasty violent little boy underneath that goody-goody act!"

"And you were always a spoilt, spiteful little cow!"

"Stop it!" Stop it both of you!"

Laura and Nicholas halted in mid-breath and turned to look at Sally, who sat with tears streaming down her face. Nicholas, shamefaced and bewildered, lowered the chair and sat back in it, wiping his face with his handkerchief.

"I'm sorry, he muttered, "sorry. It's all been a bit...much that's all."

Laura began tapping her foot and looking around in an agitated, impatient manner.

"Sally dear," I said. "I'm so very sorry - all of you."

"I'm sorry Gran," moaned Sally through her tears.

"Whatever have you to be sorry for?"

"If I hadn't shown you that letter…"

"But you did dear – and you were right to. Like Pandora with her insatiable curiosity I was first to open the box – and the world turned to darkness. If anyone is to blame it is I. But thanks to you I now know that William really did love me, and that he was an honourable man after all."

"Perhaps Dad's to blame partly," said Nicholas, his voice a little cracked still with emotion. "I don't mean him personally," he added quickly. "I mean he was caught up by the war – as you all were then – it drove everyone to do things they wouldn't otherwise have done."

"Good, so the war was to blame," said Laura briskly. "Can we all go home now? I think Mum needs some time alone."

"Laura I really don't think…" began Nicholas.

I raised my hand. "For once – your sister is right," I said. Laura gave a brief smirk and reached for her bag.

"But are you sure you're going to be all right?" Nicholas said, coming over and placing his hand on my arm.

"You forget – I was in SOE my son. We were trained to expect the unexpected."

"But this…"

"I shall consider it a challenge. Working out the puzzle. I always finish the crossword too quickly these days, this one will keep me going till – well, for a good while."

"But Gran," said Sally, now taking my other arm, "surely the puzzle is solved now, its over. You know you mustn't blame yourself about Granddad – he would have died anyway, he had the heart thing didn't he? He would have understood, he said in his letter you'd be upset, and he died knowing you'd find the letter eventually."

"Yes – I suppose so."

"And now you know the whole story – we all do."

"Does one ever know the whole story? I wonder."

"Bye Mum – I'll phone you. Try not to brood on all this," said Nicholas, kissing my cheek.

"Nor you dear."

"I'll be having a stiff drink tonight!"

"Goodbye mother," said Laura, placing her lips on my forehead. "And do talk to the doctor if you feel queasy. Come on Sally, don't be all night saying goodbye - let's at least try to beat the rush hour."

After they had gone I examined the box; it lay broken, on the table - it had certainly become my nemesis. Now it was broken, all its secrets revealed, like Pandora's box – all that was left inside was hope. But my hope was fading; perhaps the shock had yet to hit me. What a fool I had been, thinking I was going to set the record straight, deliver the bombshell then play the great wise lady – oh how the gods play with us for their sport! I got undressed and into bed. What a lot I have to tell Joyce tomorrow. Poor William, he would have understood. He loved me and I him all along. If Sally hadn't found that letter I'd never have known. God bless you William.

I closed my eyes; then just as quickly opened them again. There was still the question of Peter, returned from the dead not once but twice. I had loved Peter. I still did, didn't I? Should I tell him all this, was this somehow, why he had mysteriously come back, so that together we could complete the puzzle? Whatever would Joyce say about it all?

Picturing the look on her face on hearing so many dramatic revelations – appropriately indignant and horrified, yet beneath her indignation an undeniable, girlish sense of glee about it all - almost made me feel better about the whole business. Somehow Joyce – gossipy, chattering Joyce, yet ever loyal - had always made everything seem less important, less of a worry. 'Remember Annie.' she would say, 'a problem shared is a problem halved.' What a daft saying!

Outside an owl hooted. I drifted off to sleep and dreamt I was on holiday with Mummy and Daddy, and Gran and Gramps at Maison Vert, a long time ago before the war.

CHAPTER FORTY-TWO

Just as the anniversary clock chimed ten, Joyce came breezing into my room. She was full of all the light hearted, carefree vitality that I had always so warmed to, right from when we were girls. Placing an armful of flowers on the table she leaned over and kissed me.

"What a week I've had Annie dear, our church volunteer was off sick and we like to keep the place open, but people wander in and take things if there's not someone standing guard."

Puffing a little she began rearranging my cards on the shelf.

"You'd be surprised how many of our floral displays from the side altar find themselves on a grave in the churchyard. The vicar caught a woman in the act one day – had the cheek to say she was recycling!"

"Thank goodness for that," I said with some relief, "I was worried there was something the matter, something you weren't telling me."

"Like what?"

"That you were ill or something."

Joyce laughed. "I'm as fit as a fiddle Annie, and everyone else is fine before you start worrying again."

Joyce never changed. She was fiddling with the net curtains now. She could never visit without doing things for me, whether they needed doing or not, and I loved her for it. It was always so good to see her.

She was undeniably 'wonderful for her age' as people said, though only a year younger than me, and elegantly dressed as ever. And yet, today, beneath the usual brisk, hearty manner, the cheerfulness, something didn't seem quite right. Something was bothering her.

"The flowers are lovely dear thank you,' I said. 'Better than the half dead ones my daughter usually brings – there's her bunch on the shelf. I think she gets them reduced, or probably from your churchyard. I shouldn't say that should I!"

"Why not!" chuckled Joyce, "honesty Annie, honesty – I'm a great believer in it."

"Laura probably thinks the flowers are appropriate for me," I said.

"How do you mean?"

"Half dead," I laughed

"Annie, stop it."

"You're the one who believes in honesty dear."

"Yes, and it's my honest opinion you'll outlive the whole lot of them. But enough of this" She sat herself down and gazed at me with an anxious, pensive expression. I could see that we were about to come to the point, the real reason for her visit.

"Annie, forgive me asking again, but are you sure it's him?"
Before I could answer Maria brought a tray of tea and biscuits. When she had left us alone again I said, "Yes Joyce, I've spoken to him. It really is him."
Joyce drew in her breath. "I can hardly believe that he was in this room - after all these years."

"Imagine how I felt, and I was face to face with him. It's funny I was thinking last night about when I spotted him that day in Paris, I got such a shock. All along I had thought he was dead, and there he was large as life dressed as an old man. And now it's like it's happened all over again, he's returned from the dead again, except that this time he really is old. Soon we'll both be dead. I should have asked him straight out yesterday, when he was here in this room, asked how he could possibly have escaped from the Gestapo, have cheated death like that but I was in shock at seeing him again. Now if he doesn't come back I'll never find out."

Joyce, about to take a sip of tea stopped, the cup suspended in mid-air. "But I thought he was coming back, this afternoon you said?"
I nodded. "So he said."

"What I want to know is how he got here? How did he know where to find you? He couldn't have turning up out of the blue like that without doing some digging around."

"Perhaps he paid an investigation agency. Like I said, he had a very expensive car, and a chauffeur."

"Done very well for himself then it seems," Joyce mused rising from the chair. "I think those flowers had better go in water Annie."
I watched her busily arrange the blooms in the tall vase she had taken from the windowsill. Again I felt something on edge about her.

"I recognised him as soon as he emerged from the vehicle," I continued. "Unmistakable, and when he came to my room - spoke to me – there was no doubt it was him."

"I wish you'd never met him to be honest Annie." Joyce's back was turned as she said this. "But thank God you met William later, you were happy with him?" She faced me again now.

For a moment I remained silent, thinking. Joyce didn't know about the letter, or who William really was. I decided it was best she remained in ignorance.

"Of course," I replied, "He was a good man. After all he did save my life."

Joyce smiled, "It's a good thing he was in the shop that day when the bomb dropped – in more ways than one."

I nodded. "And there you were," I jested, "matchmaking in the canteen from the minute you met him."

"Yes!" she laughed, "I must say he looked a lot better then than when we got him out of Prague."

In the midst of her chatter I suddenly felt something like a thunderbolt hit me. I stared at her in amazement.

"Joyce" I said quietly, "How did you know William had been in Prague?"

"You told me, years ago, let's have another cuppa." Avoiding my eyes she began to pour.

I shook my head. "I didn't find out until yesterday that William had been in Prague. So I ask you again; how did you know?"

I continued staring at her. She put the teapot down and sat very still now, her face expressionless, her eyes strangely void, somehow disconnected as if a switch deep within her had been suddenly thrown. Then I remembered something else William had said in his letter. He had met his controller, 'who I was surprised to find was a young woman... probably best for all concerned if her identity remains confidential even now...' I said, "Joyce - who was my controller?"

"Controller - what on earth do you mean? How would I know? I only typed letters and did the filing, the same as you when you came back from France Annie. We couldn't speak about our work you knew that. Don't you remember?" She gave a foolish kind of half-laugh.

"Oh but come on, Joyce, you must have had some idea - a whispered name here and there, a shadowy figure disappearing up the stairs - I don't think you and I of all people need worry about the Official Secrets Act any more."

"No, no of course not – but I didn't know who the real bigwigs were…"

"Joyce let's stop pretending," I said. "It was *you*."

"Me? - What – what on earth are you talking about – I was - don't be daft…I wouldn't have been old enough for a position like that…"

"You were exceptionally bright Joyce, always. You appeared a silly girl, but you were always top of the class at school. Now I remember there was talk of a scholarship, a place at Oxford, even a good job at the bank. Then the war started, and the service snapped up clever girls like you, young people with sharp, agile minds. Some went to Bletchley, some to SOE control, as you did. There you would have had people at the top making use of that fine, clever mind of yours." Joyce was silent, her eyes cast down.

I went on: "So, there we have it then. I believe you were William's controller, and also mine. And you must therefore have known all along that Peter had survived - right from the beginning, when I was eaten up with grief." Still Joyce stared at the carpet.

When she began speaking her voice had lost all its singsong quality. It was expressionless, like a recorded message. "Not at first," she said mechanically. She looked up now and stretched out a hand towards me in a gesture of appeal. "Nothing was certain, I swear."

"But you found out?"

"Later, yes"

"And you still let me believe he was dead."

"There was a reason Annie, believe me there was a reason…."

"I'd like to hear it!"

"I'm not sure that you would actually."

"Oh wouldn't I actually – well I'll be the judge of that!"

"Annie don't get upset – I mean don't get angry – not till you've heard me out. I may have deceived you at the War Office – but there was nothing I could do about that, we were all compelled, it was my job don't you see?"

"I see someone I thought was my best friend."

"Oh god Annie this is so hard."

"Hard? How do you think it is for me?"

"I know, I know, that's why it was always impossible to tell you."

"You're not the only one who had secrets," I said.

"What do you mean Annie?"

I passed her William's letter. She unfolded it, looked at me intently for a moment then read it. "Oh! Good lord!"

"You obviously already knew everything contained in that letter didn't you?" Joyce cast her eyes down again.

"Yes. Look, Annie, I know this is hard to understand, but the fact is, my job and our friendship – well they were two completely separate things, the things I had to do – they were nothing to do with us, you and me."

I shook my head. "How can that be true? Did the notion of trust, of honesty, mean nothing to you?" I paused. "All right, perhaps in your position I would have had to do the same. Unfortunately though, there's one aspect of your story that is much harder for me to understand – or forgive."

"What?"

"That it was you that sent me to France – you didn't just ask the Department to try and find me a job to stop me moping – you deliberately had me sent out there, to what was assumed would be my death."

"Annie," said Joyce desperately, "you were dying anyway – dying of grief for Peter – God knows anyone could see it. The job gave you a reason to live, to survive - to go on."

"Very convenient, so you sent me to a war zone for my health! God Joyce that's hilarious, you always did like a joke..."

"Annie there was more to it than that..."

"Oh I'm sure there was Joyce, I'm sure there was, there's always more to everything – nothing will surprise me now – so what was I really sent out there for – to be Eva Braun's double – a mistress for the Fuhrer perhaps, find out his secrets and post them off in an airmail letter once a week to Colonel Heath? Till of course Adolf rumbled me and I got strung up on a butcher's pole! Still, job done eh Joyce, job done, all in a good cause and a pat on the back from the department and a decoration for you..."

"Annie, please!" Joyce was breathing hard. "Please listen to me. Did you ever hear of a German SS officer called Gruber?"

"Gruber - oh yes, I heard of him, he was there in that hell hole in Avenue Foch, he held the gun to my head and would have killed me if William hadn't intervened."

Joyce's face was grim. "Let me tell you about Gruber Annie, and the real reason I'm here."

Joyce began in a slow, deliberating voice to tell me whatever it was she now had to tell me about Kurt Gruber. I listened attentively to her, as if to a radio play or to the mesmerising narration of some entertaining if implausible piece of fiction.

"Gruber's arrival in Paris in September 1941 was of special interest to Madame Dupont, and to us at British Intelligence. He was an idealistic young man and we had been keeping tabs on him for a long time. Then suddenly we lost contact - he simply disappeared, and no one had any idea where to look. Since 1938 he had been running an espionage network in England bringing agents across the channel and installing them in various safe houses around the country. One was with Colonel Travers in Kingsford…"

"So the rumours were true," I interjected, "about Travers being a Nazi sympathiser. Of course, Peter must have met some of them at that party the colonel held, the night Michael and I saw him, he must have known what was going on - and he must have known about Gruber."

Joyce nodded. "Yes. In September 1940 Gruber crossed back to France and infiltrated the resistance cell in Lyon. He stayed with them almost a year, his information proved extremely useful to the Germans. We found out purely by chance he was there and active, and contacted the Lyon cell. We wanted him caught now and sent back to us, but he somehow escaped only to re-appear in Paris a year later. He had now gone back with the Gestapo; we couldn't touch him."

"So that's why Peter was dressed as the old man when I found him - he was trying to locate Gruber."

Joyce did not look at me, but went on. "The destruction of the train was his downfall as he had been responsible for its safety. Overnight he fell out of favour with German High Command, and knew he was facing a firing squad before long. He had to get away. He knew Paul from the Lyon cell and with his help, and that of Madame Dupont a road ambush was staged."

"She and Paul were collaborators?" I said in amazement.

"They convinced Gruber they were. It was arranged they would take him to a safe house, and there our agents would apprehend him and bring him in. But he never arrived at the safe house; once again he had simply disappeared."

"Quite the Scarlet Pimpernel"

"Quite. It was April 1942 before we finally caught up with him. A keen eyed young soldier spotted an error in the documents of a young man leaving London and arrested him. At last we had Gruber."

"Was he interrogated?"

"Naturally, that was why we wanted him alive. He was a tough nut to crack but they wore him down eventually. He told us everything. After the ambush he had got suspicious of Paul and given him the slip. He made his way to the coast and got away in a small fishing boat, landed at Felixstowe. He went first to Guildford, but found the safe house there was no longer so, and travelled on to Kingsford, hoping to seek refuge with Colonel Travers."

"To Kingsford - my god"

"But the colonel was afraid, the military wanted his house for the duration, and he wanted shot of the German spy ring. When Gruber arrived he ordered him to leave and take the other two agents holed up in the barn with him. Gruber wasn't having that; it was he who killed the colonel and his wife and set the house on fire. He and the other two agents hid in the woods till nightfall. At about 9.30 they left for the village hoping to catch the late train but that night the train had left early."

"Joyce,' I gasped, "was it Gruber that killed my mother in the alley that night - is that why you're telling me about this man? Is this what he has to do with me?"

Joyce nodded and looked away.

I sighed. "So what were you hoping – that putting a name to her murderer might give me 'closure' – is that what they call it nowadays?"

Joyce opened her handbag, took out an envelope and handed it to me. "Yes Annie, Gruber killed your mother. But I'm afraid there's more. What's in there…is…far more than…" She stopped short and looked away. Slowly I opened the envelope.

CHAPTER FORTY-SIX

Inside was some sort of identity card. Putting on my glasses I peered closely at it. The card bore a swastika, and in large letters 'SS'. I felt a little spasm of fear, the conditioned reflex intact.

"Why have you brought me this?" I asked. Joyce was watching me closely. "You really think I want a reminder, a souvenir…"

"Annie -" Joyce reached towards the table and handed me my magnifying glass. Bemused I opened the card and looked again.

I saw the word 'Gruber' and a faded headshot photo with the mark of an official stamp. Peering intently at the faded photo I uttered a sort of strangled cry.

The face that looked up at me was one I knew so well; I'd seen it only yesterday in another image, an old photograph that I'd always kept hidden beneath the brown envelope in the box. It was the face of the man who I had fallen in love with in the shade of the ruined abbey in the green fields of France so many years ago. It was Peter Barker – my first husband.

Tears rolled down my cheek, the magnifying glass clattered to the floor and I lolled back in the armchair. Joyce sprang up in alarm.

"Annie, oh dear, are you all right, I'm so sorry, I should never have done this – shall I call the nurse?"

I coughed and waved a hand at her.

"No," I spluttered, "I'm all right…I…one of those pills, on the dresser, some water…"

Joyce brought the pills and water and I swallowed them down.

"I realise what a shock this must be for you Annie."

She knelt at my side, took my hand and waited till my breathing was steadier then began to speak. Joyce her face ashen said quietly. "He handed this card to Paul so he could convince the Germans their man had been killed. British Intelligence wanted to keep it that way, the Germans thinking Gruber was dead.

In fact he was captured in London in '43 and has been in prison ever since his arrest. He had successfully infiltrated British Intelligence, and as I don't need to tell you Annie, fooled everyone. He was the perfect spy. He knew everything about us, and thus was extremely dangerous to our security."

With a calm that surprised me I considered everything Joyce had just said. I took another sip of water.

"So tell me, how did you finally find out, that Gruber and Peter were one and the same man?"

"As so often the case it was pure chance. A neighbour of his so-called aunt and uncle in Surrey had reported odd comings and goings at their home, suspicious looking young men seen visiting in the dead of night. After some investigation a raid on the house found a young man in the attic with a radio and other equipment. All three were arrested, and confessed to being Nazi sympathisers and aiding Peter's espionage activities. They revealed his true identity as Gruber."

"But by this time presumably Peter - Gruber - was safely back in occupied France?"

"Precisely" Joyce continued, "We were at a loss how to capture him, until someone suggested you. If there was the slightest chance you might find him we had to take it"

"So you did know what was happening to me in France. You knew I'd been captured!"

Joyce sighed heavily. "Yes Annie. But you got through it, I knew you'd survive."

"How could you? You had no idea what it was like, and no one knows what they can endure until it happens to them."

"That's true, but I saw the ones who came back, I helped in their debriefing. Shattered, nervous wrecks and they thought they were the lucky ones."

I sat back and closed my eyes. "So why is he here? Why now?"

Joyce stamped her foot angrily.

"Oh damn it Annie," she snapped, "why can't they just leave us alone?"

"Joyce," I said slowly, "tell me what is going on."

She sighed, a long deep heavy sigh.

"Over the years Peter has given us a lot of information but Intelligence believes he still knows far more. He's never revealed who got him into the military so easily, who the real traitor was. We have our suspicions, always had, but no proof. We suspected members of parliament or someone high up in the military but we want to know for sure. Whoever it was, they were always one step ahead of us. They may still be alive and if so they must be dealt with. We encouraged Peter – Gruber - to come and see you."

I shook my head in disbelief. "Why on earth would he want to see me after all these years? I certainly don't want to see him."

"He's not got long to live Annie, we've told him a matter of weeks but actually it's longer than that, a few months, maybe a year. We told him that he and you had unfinished business. He's very wary of us all even after all these years but you are the one person he trusts. You are the only one who could get the name for us Annie. He's here for a week, possibly two if you need the time."

"If I need the time - that's very funny Joyce. You people are incredible, after all these years you're still controlling me, still deciding what is right without my knowledge, still persuading me to do your dirty work. What a fool I've been…"

"I didn't want to do this Annie, God knows I didn't but they need to close the file, put an end to it."

"Tell me Joyce, did you order William to make advances to me to see if I knew anything."

"He did love you Annie."

I closed my eyes with a shiver of disgust at the remark. Turning towards the window I saw our reflections in the glass.

"I'll get you the name," I said, "take it back to the faceless ones with my blessing, and then our friendship dies. It's time you were gone Joyce. Now, leave me alone."

"Annie…"

"Go. Please Joyce, just go."

Joyce rose and crossed to the door, hesitated a few seconds then went out. As the door closed, I tried to cry but no tears would come.

CHAPTER FORTY-SEVEN

Joyce's revelations have left me numb, void of all emotions; my true and trusted friend was devious as the rest. Now I know why Peter is here; how foolish of me to think he cared. A fine line between love and hate they say and I've just crossed it. God I hate him.

And all this nonsense about a name – what if I do get it, what then – who do I give it to? For goodness sake it's been sixty years. Why would any one care about that now?

I did love Peter, maybe still do. But did he ever feel the same or was I just a means to an end? With what I know now I think the latter. He's coming back soon to tell me 'everything' - I'll listen, it's all lies - every word. Even William was ordered to love me. My life has been a sham and I'm the unwitting stranger in it - manipulated, controlled by everyone for their own ends, what a silly trusting little fool I've been.

I should have married Michael, safe kind Michael. I'd have been a solicitor's wife, with nice children, a happy family, how good it would have been. He never trusted Peter, good as told me so but I didn't listen. And mother - too perfect she called him, she knew, tried to tell me, but loved me too much to break my heart. The torment I must have put my parents through. How dare Peter involve them in his web of deception – Mother's death is unforgivable. Daddy was so sad when she died in such tragic circumstances; never got over it - just faded away.

This paperknife belonged to my father; he used it many times, as I have done. It's opened many letters, both good and bad news. It cut open the envelope that told me Peter was missing. I'd never admired its beauty until now. The ornately decorated handle carved in ivory and the cold, sharp silver blade glistens in the light. Yes – the blade's quite sharp - it will come in useful for what I have in mind.

As I hold it in my hand a deep, despairing sense of sadness overwhelms me. Why did I have to meet him? Why did I fall in love? Thank God I didn't tell my family. At least they will be spared the humiliation of all of this. Oh God is anyone real?

I'm going to ask him to stroll with me by the river. He can push the wheelchair along the path, he will talk - I will listen. We'll stop at the waters edge, it's a peaceful spot, but it will hold no comfort for me today - not today. Then *he* will listen. I have few words but my actions will speak volumes. I care not of the consequences; nothing matters now…no, nothing matters now…And here he is, knocking at my door…

EPILOGUE

The young man turned from the window as the door opened.

"Good morning sir," he said, quickly pulling out the chair for the older gentleman who had just entered. They both sat at the desk on which a newspaper lay open.

"Shall I read it out to you sir?"
The elderly man nodded. Clearing his throat the young man began to read:

Death of a Spy
by
Archie Lomax

Today I have to report on a very strange and mysterious event. Mrs Annabelle Pearson 80 years of age and resident of the Heartland nursing home was found dead in the arms of a man of similar age. Her wheelchair was found on the riverbank and their bodies, locked in each other's arms were discovered in the river Heath, at a point where the grounds of the nursing home back on to the river.

A post mortem report established that she had drowned. The man with her however, who was not resident at the home, had died from a single stab wound to the heart. A large antique paperknife was recovered from the scene. It has been identified as the property of Mrs Pearson.

On interviewing Mrs Pearson's grieving relatives it emerged she had a secret and adventurous past. Married just prior to World War Two, her husband died soon after while on active service in Europe. Speaking fluent French she enlisted as a field agent in the Special Operations Executive, or SOE, the undercover unit formed by Churchill, and was dropped into occupied France where she served between 1941 and 1942.
After being captured and interrogated by the Gestapo, aided by the resistance she eventually escaped back to Britain.

On returning she saw out the remainder of the conflict at the War Office in London. Having escaped the Gestapo she came close to death one day on the streets of the capital when a bomb exploded in a doorway she had been sheltering in only minutes before. She was rescued from the rubble by the man who later became her second husband; William Pearson. After his death in 1985, Annabelle Pearson remained a widow.

The mystery now focuses on the man who died with her, who has so far not been identified, despite appeals in the media. The only information so far is from a nurse at Heathland Nursing home, Maria Jones.

"He turned up a few days ago out of the blue to visit Annabelle," said Mrs Jones. "All she told us was that he was an old friend, but played her cards close to her chest about it. I believe she had a few secrets. I was so shocked and upset about what happened, but at least they say it was a quick end for her."

There were no witnesses to the incident.

The older man took the paper and peered at the picture of Annabelle

"Did she get the name?" he asked.

The young man shook his head. "No sir, no name."

His superior, taking the dog-eared file from the drawer, opened it and glanced briefly at the photograph of the young woman inside. He gave a wry, relieved smile; then took a pen and across the front cover of the file wrote in large letters:

CASE CLOSED

Printed in Poland
by Amazon Fulfillment
Poland Sp. z o.o., Wrocław

63197469R00145